Jessica's Vineyard

A NOVEL

for Mary

with all best wishes

David

DAVID H MARTIN

JESSICA'S VINEYARD

David H Martin has asserted his right under the Copyright, Designs and Patents Act 1988 to be identified as the author of this work.

This is a work of fiction. Names, characters, places and incidents either are the product of the author's imagination or are used fictitiously. Any resemblance to actual persons, living or dead, events or locales is entirely coincidental.

Copyright © 2024 David H Martin
All rights reserved.

ISBN: 9798320348995

JESSICA'S VINEYARD

For my friends in the Malvern U3A Wine Tasting Group.

JESSICA'S VINEYARD

Contents

CHAPTER 1	7
CHAPTER 2	25
CHAPTER 3	40
CHAPTER 4	57
CHAPTER 5	67
CHAPTER 6	78
CHAPTER 7	98
CHAPTER 8	110
CHAPTER 9	127
CHAPTER 10	150
CHAPTER 11	162
CHAPTER 12	173
CHAPTER 13	191
CHAPTER 14	216
CHAPTER 15	227
CHAPTER 16	242
CHAPTER 17	260
CHAPTER 18	277
CHAPTER 19	294
CHAPTER 20	309

JESSICA'S VINEYARD

CHAPTER 21	325
CHAPTER 22	339
CHAPTER 23	352

| Books by the same author | 395 |

CHAPTER 1

I knew it was exactly what I wanted the moment I saw it: a beautiful and remote hillside planted with vines.

The spring sunshine bathed the sloping vineyard in a somnolent haze. Serried ranks of wooden posts strode up the hillside to the distant trees at the summit. They seemed to say, we have climbed this hillside, why don't you?

This surely was where I could lose myself. This is where I could begin a new life. This is where I could leave the angst and the anger of the past behind and start again.

The sturdy trees standing sentinel over the gateway to the vineyard whisper their agreement. This is for you, they say. Pass through this gateway and enter into your inheritance. We have been waiting for you. This is yours.

But, of course, it wasn't mine. I didn't own a square inch of it.

However, I had my alimony and the property was for sale, and so, why shouldn't it be mine?

JESSICA'S VINEYARD

The sun glinted on the taut wires stretched between each post: post to post, bound together through the unfolding seasons of the year. In winter, to let the cruel wind play its soulful music over the frozen earth beneath; in spring, to hum with unrestrained joy at the first signs of new life; in summer, to expand with voluptuousness under the warm embrace of the sun; and in autumn, to heave under the weight of fruit-laden trusses. The wires are a string orchestra awaiting a conductor to coax music from them: music to fill the valley with shouts of laughter and joy.

Beneath the sentient poles and the taut wires rest the gnarled rootstocks, awaiting the annual resurrection of all green and living things.

The sale particulars say the property consists of five acres devoted to viniculture. They claim that the site has been used for the cultivation of vines since the twelfth century when Cistercian monks inhabited Dore Abbey.

The vineyard's south-facing aspect certainly captures the expansive warmth of the sun even on a day such as this in early spring. It is an ideal location to cultivate grapes.

The property lies in a fold of the foothills of the Black Mountains. It is remote.

I want somewhere remote.

JESSICA'S VINEYARD

For five years I have wrestled with a job that sucked the life out of me. My work was like a ball and chain dragging me deeper and deeper below the waterline and drowning me. I need oxygen. I need to cast off my so-called promising career and escape.

Women have to work so much harder than men to make good. Men are willing to overlook their male colleagues' mistakes, but no such allowance is made for women. I had to prove myself over and over again in order to be regarded as an equal.

At first, I was all for the challenge. I was as good as any man. I would prove I was strong-willed, focussed, and even ruthless when it came to clinching a deal; but the constant battle to prove myself has eaten into my soul. Life is slipping by and what have I achieved? Do I want to spend the remainder of my life battling with men in order to prove a point?

I might have found fulfilment in motherhood, but that was not to be. Some women are destined to be mothers and others are not. I was one that was not. Children would certainly have given me a new focus in life. I could have nurtured and showered love on children rather than project a false cheerfulness and confidence to my work colleagues. Children would undoubtedly have changed my perspective on life. There would have been others to cherish and nurture. I might have achieved something good and

JESSICA'S VINEYARD

satisfying. I might have discovered a genuine
maternal vocation; but, alas, that was not to be.
At least vines are fruitful. The old and twisted
rootstocks may look gnarled and barren but, come
the summer, they will shoot forth tendrils and clothe
their nakedness with verdant growth.

Creation stirs and the promise of new life beckons.
Vine blossom may be small and insignificant, but that
is of no consequence to the insects that skim from
plant to plant trailing fecundity in their wake. Nature
is alive. This blossom will become grapes that will
ripen and yield a wondrous harvest.

My vines will produce fruitful offspring even if my
body cannot. I will be nature's midwife, tending each
cluster of grapes, shielding them from harm,
nurturing them with maternal care, encouraging them
on their journey to maturity. I will be the mother of
the vineyard.

My secateurs will snip the umbilical cords and free
each bunch of succulent grapes from its parent. I
will usher new creation into the world with happiness
and smiles in its wake. Rather than being a barren
and unproductive woman I will be the archetypal
midwife, praised and lauded whenever a glass of my
wine is raised in celebration.

Could this sleeping vineyard, deep in rural
Herefordshire, fulfil the innate desire I have for
wholeness and fulfilment?

JESSICA'S VINEYARD

The rows of posts and wires stretch as far as I can see. It is a sizeable parcel of land. Can I manage it on my own? The doubts begin to creep in.

My confidence has been dented in the past. Alan said I was big on ideas but weak on implementation. That was his way of saying that men are more practical than women. He ensured he was never challenged. He always undertook the practical tasks around the home.

I may have been prevented from working with my hands, but there is no denying I could organise complex and demanding contractual business at work. I often did far better than my male colleagues. I am no slouch. If I can steer a project to a successful conclusion, what's to stop me using the same skills in viniculture?

The dormant rootstocks are silent. Their gnarled and twisted shapes stare at me in defiance. Master us if you can, they seem to say. We have served many masters but never a mistress. Can you make us fruitful? Can you succeed where others have failed?

'I can and I will,' I assert in a loud, resonate voice. My words echo around the fold in the land.

The trees hear me. The vines hear me. The sky hears me. All bear witness to my intent. They have heard my credo. There can be no doubting. I am resolved. I can and I will own this land. I will till it with my hands. I will harvest its fruit. I will press its grapes. I

JESSICA'S VINEYARD

will ferment its juice. I will create wine; my very own wine; wine from Jessica's Vineyard.

But first I have to secure the land.

The sale particulars say there is a stone farmhouse and associated outbuildings containing stainless steel storage vats and associated winemaking equipment. Leaving the vineyard dozing indolently in the afternoon sun, I drive along the narrow lane to the farm buildings. I am pleased to see they are fairly compact. Many properties I have viewed were simply a jumble of steel and asbestos agricultural sheds devoid of all beauty. I must have beauty. I cannot live in a rural slum. I want to wake up in the morning to behold the beauty of nature. I want order and enchantment in my life.

If I am to live in the country, I want the beauty of the countryside to open its arms and embrace me every new day. I want to throw open my bedroom window and hear the birds singing their morning hymn of praise. I want to look out over acres of unspoilt countryside, uncontaminated by the hand of man, as far as my eyes can see. Abbeydore Winery is exactly what I am looking for.

The farmhouse is extremely modest in size. It is old. It is built from locally quarried stone that has an unusual purple-grey colour. It looks so old it might have been built by the monks of Dore Abbey. The

JESSICA'S VINEYARD

roof is constructed of diminishing courses of stone tiles.

I can tell from the recessed windows that the walls are exceedingly thick. That should ensure the house remains cool in summer and retains heat during the winter. There is a porch protecting the stout front door. The door looks as if it is rarely used. A similar, much larger porch runs along the rear of the building and must, I surmise, open into the kitchen.

I have no keys to the property; but I am not averse to peering through the windows to gain an impression of the interior.

I espy a large inglenook fireplace at one end of the main room. The plastered walls are painted cream. The floor consists of dark stained boards, possibly oak. The room is devoid of all furniture.

I see myself sitting beside the fireplace. A blazing log fire is burning in the grate. The room is perfumed with the incense of wood smoke. The logs crackle and shuffle and the glowing embers fill the room with warmth. I have a book in one hand and a glass of mulled wine in the other. It is Jessica's wine, made with my own hands: weeks of unremitting labour encapsulated in a glass and relished at my leisure. This will be my snug. This is where I will relax and unwind after a hard day's work. This will be my very own special place where I can be alone with my thoughts and dreams.

JESSICA'S VINEYARD

The kitchen is a practical farmhouse kitchen. I see an Aga in the far corner. I assume the large Calor gas tank situated a short distance from the house supplies the Aga and the central heating system with fuel. I must ensure to keep the tank filled. I must also maintain a generous supply of logs for the winter months. Abbeydore could easily be cut off from the rest of the world during the winter. I must ensure I maintain a good supply of fuel.

The sale particulars say that the house has three good-sized bedrooms. One is enough for me. There will be no visitors.

When I left Alan, I wanted a clean break. I was determined to make a fresh start on my own. Being childless could have made us more dependent on each other and bonded us together, but it didn't. Alan compensated for the lack of a family by immersing himself in his work. We spent less and less time together. It was as if an invisible blanket had imperceptibly descended between us. We spoke to each other but it was only words. There was no soul-talk. I no longer knew what was in his mind. Perhaps he was unable to know what was in mine. We grew apart. Our marriage became a formality. The love we once shared evaporated. The future was uninviting. I suppose I could have let life rumble on, like a mountain stream following its inevitable downward course until it is finally subsumed in the ocean; but I

JESSICA'S VINEYARD

decided I needed to escape. And so, here I am, in deepest rural Herefordshire, about to purchase a vineyard.

I have always liked wine. The infinite variety of wine fascinates me. Every wine is different. Each wine is unique, just as each person is unique. There are smooth and mellow wines that are like liquid velvet in the mouth, radiating contentment and peace. There are piquant and playful wines encapsulating the carefree abandonment of childhood. There are dark, sophisticated wines, where each sip reveals a new layer of delight. There are young wines, sharp and acidic. There are old wines, seductive and beguiling. There are wines with the tang of grapefruit trapped in a bottle. There are wines that lead down Memory Lane to old fashioned grocery stores with coffee beans being ground and the aroma spilling onto the pavement outside. There are strong, muscular wines. There are delicate and fey wines.

The wine I make will express my personality. It will be my unique act of creation. I will fashion it with my hands. I will till the soil and prune the vines, crush the grapes and ferment the must, strain, store and bottle the wine to produce something that is unique. And I will do it myself. I will not have to justify my actions or decisions to others. I will not have to prove myself to others. All I have to do is produce wine that brings pleasure to others.

JESSICA'S VINEYARD

The adjoining buildings are constructed in exactly the same purple-grey stone as the farmhouse. The large barn doors are padlocked and, as there are no ground floor windows, I cannot see inside. The sale particulars say the barn contains four large storage vats for wine.
There is a single window high in the apex of the barn suggesting there must be a room of some sort at first floor level.
I read and re-read the sale particulars. I also meticulously study the accompanying financial statements. The property is being sold as a business concern, but the business accounts tell a gloomy tale. For the past five years Abbeydore Winery has failed to produce a sustainable income for its owners. No wonder it is up for sale.
In one sense, this works to my advantage. There should be little interest in purchasing a failing business.
But there must be a reason why the vineyard has proved unprofitable.
Is it because the vines are too old and fail to produce sufficient grape juice?
Is poor husbandry the reason for the poor yields?
Is the wine substandard?
Is it due to a failure of marketing?
I have assiduously scoured the internet to find bottles of Abbeydore Wine but without success.

JESSICA'S VINEYARD

Can I succeed where others have failed?
I wander around the deserted buildings. A silence clings to the old stone walls. They could tell so much. Locked into the walls are tears and laughter: the screams of a mother in childbirth; the chatter of children around the dining table; the anger of an enraged father; the tears of a jilted lover; the hopes of an apprentice striding out into the world in search of fame or fortune; the gentle snores of a slumbering household; the Christmas celebrations and the aroma of roast poultry wafting through the house; the scratch of a pen on paper; the click of knitting needles; the pain of poverty; the whispered conversations lest the children should hear; the sombre knell of death as a soul passes from this world to the next. So many memories enshrined in these walls. Will I add to their number?

*

I am extremely nervous. I have never before attended an auction.
I glance around the hall at the others sitting in the carefully arranged rows of chairs. They are nearly all men - or men accompanied by women. I presume the women are their wives. I see no other single women.
I am entering a lions' den.
I register my name and other particulars on entering the hall and am issued with a number on a large card.

JESSICA'S VINEYARD

There is a general hubbub as prospective bidders await the auctioneer to take his place on the rostrum. There are a large number of properties and parcels of land for sale. How many of those present are interested in Abbeydore Winery?

I have considered my sale strategy very carefully. I will not be the first to bid. I will let others open the bidding and bide my time. I know how much I can afford. Although my heart is wedded to the property, there is no point in spending every penny I have and then being unable to survive. I have carefully assessed my finances and know how high I can go.

I have never been a particularly religious person but, just at this moment, I feel an overwhelming urge to pray. So much hangs on today. My future will either be secured or I will be left in limbo.

Some of the men sitting near me look very well-heeled. Their corpulent bodies proclaim that they eat and drink well. If they are able to do this they can presumably spend money lavishly on other things - like property.

Are any of them interested in owning a failing winery? Might there be rich city-workers secreted amongst the audience wishing, like me, to escape the rat race and retire to the countryside and indulge a whim to manage a boutique winery?

There are no pinstripe suits or bowler hats; but then yuppies today are more likely to be seen wearing

designer T-shirts and chinos than suits. If only I
could see inside each person's head. Or, perhaps,
more to the point, at each person's bank balance.
Why does everything always come down to money?
Why can't these people realise I need a new start in
life and smile, nod and say, 'Yes, my dear. You have
it – and good luck to you.'

But that is simply asking for masculine favours. Why
should I play on my femininity to seek favours from
men? If I am to own Abbeydore Winery it will be
because I outsmarted the competition.

Stiffen your resolve, Jessica, and show you are the
equal of any man.

My mental keep-fit exercises are interrupted by the
auctioneer mounting the rostrum and calling the
assembly to order. He is a grey-haired man who
wears a dark suit with a rather ostentatious red
carnation in his left buttonhole. He brandishes a
wooden gavel in his right hand and defies gravity by
balancing a pair of half-moon glasses on the tip of his
nose.

'Gentlemen – and not forgetting the ladies, of course
– we begin with Lot Number One, a parcel of land at
Vowchurch, bordered by a stream and suitable for
equine use. Now, who will start me with this?'

He sweeps the hall with an imperious movement of
his head and waits for an opening bid. When it
comes, he sniffs as if he has just detected a foul smell

in the room. He does his best to hide his disgust at the low bid and waits for another bidder to enter the arena. Just as he is about to shake his head and declare Lot 1 has failed to reach its reserve price, a second bid is made.

Herefordshire bidders clearly think long and hard before committing themselves.

The parcel of land is eventually sold and the auction moves to the next lot.

Biding one's time would seem to be the preferred way of proceeding. I must keep my cool and not be hustled.

Derelict cottages, woodland, pastureland and fishing rights fall under the gavel before Abbeydore Winery becomes the property for sale.

'Lot 16: a well-established winery consisting of five acres of productive vines, a commodious farmhouse and ancillary buildings in the beautiful Golden Valley. Who would like to start me on this?'

His eyes survey the room for a prospective bidder. A silence ensues.

The man on the rostrum is not to be daunted. His eyes continue to sweep the hall to see who will be the first person to break cover. I feel the palms of my hands sweating. Although my insides are fluttering, I keep my resolve and wait for someone else to make the first bid. It will enable me to gauge the likely price at which the property will sell.

JESSICA'S VINEYARD

Just when it seems there is no interest whatsoever in Abbeydore Winery, a voice is heard from the back of the hall.

'£150,000.'

Angling around in my seat I see an older man holding aloft his auction card.

'I have an opening bid of £150,000,' announces the auctioneer somewhat superfluously.

This is a ridiculously low bid. Vineyards sell for £30,000 per acre. This bid covers only the cost of the land and takes no account of the house and outbuildings.

The eyes of the auctioneer sweep the room seeking another bid, but none is forthcoming.

Now is your chance, Jessica. There seems little interest in Abbeydore Winery. Confidentially and in a shrill take-it-or-leave-it voice that shows I mean business, I call out £175K.

Will it sow doubt in the mind of the man at the back of the hall? Will he think he is up against a woman who knows her mind and is not to be cowed? Will he crumble under my assertive bid?

'£175,000 from the lady on my left,' repeats the auctioneer.

He gives the man at the back of the hall his undivided attention. He focuses intently on him. He is willing him to increase his offer or else appear weak and foolish at being out-bid by a woman.

JESSICA'S VINEYARD

'It's against you, sir,' he calls from his elevated position on the rostrum.

He awaits a response.

There is a long silence before a plaintive voice issues from the back of the hall,

'£200,000.'

That is only half of what I am prepared to pay.

But, do I want to go for a killing or merely increase my bids incrementally?

Play it carefully, Jessica, I tell myself. There's no point throwing money away. Try another £25,000 and see how that is received. I want the man at the back of the hall to realise I am not a woman to mess with. I have the means to purchase this lot and I intend to do so.

Without waiting for him to catch his breath, I immediately call out, '£225k'.

I keep one eye on the auctioneer and the other on the man at the back of the hall. I see the woman sitting next to the man whispering in his ear. I like it. They are undecided. Whatever pre-sale plan they made has unravelled and they are thinking on the hoof. I sense the prize is within my grasp.

'£225,000 with the lady here on my left', declares the auctioneer as he keeps his eyes fixed resolutely on the man at the back of the hall.

'I have to sell,' he states unnecessarily.

JESSICA'S VINEYARD

Another long pause ensues before the voice at the back of the hall calls out '£250,000'.
The auctioneer immediately turns his attention to me. I decide to go for the kill. I not only want to eliminate the man at the back of the hall but give a clear message to anyone else in the room who thinks they can pick up a bargain to back off. I want this property and I am determined to secure it.
'£300k', I respond immediately.
A noticeable rustle passes around the room.
'£300,000, from the lady on my left.'
The auctioneer swings his attention back to the man at the rear of the hall. To my great delight I see the man shaking his head in defeat. He is beaten! He is withdrawing from the fight. I have out-bid him.
'Do I have any other offers?' asks the auctioneer.
My heart skips a beat. Are there other prospective vintners just biding their time and waiting to pounce? I still have money to spare but I would prefer to keep it for the things I will need to maintain my smallholding.
The all-seeing eyes of the auctioneer sweep the room but no response is forthcoming.
'Going for the first time at £300,000. I give fair warning. Going for the second time.' And then I hear the most wondrous sound. His gavel descends and the auctioneer calls out, 'Sold to the lady on my left for £300,000.'

JESSICA'S VINEYARD

My joy knows no bounds. I feel I want to hug the corpulent farmer sitting beside me. I want to emit a great whoop of joy to let everyone know I am the new owner of Abbeydore Winery. I have secured my very own property. I have achieved my dream. I have a place I can call home. I can begin a new life. I can bury myself deep in the Herefordshire countryside and pit my wits against the weather, the seasons and the vagaries of winemaking. I can be self-sufficient. I can be my true self, with no interference from others. This is where Jessica Pope's new life begins. Furthermore, I have secured an absolute bargain. A five-acre vineyard plus a house and a barn for a mere £300,000! I know that Herefordshire prices are a fraction of those in London, but, to secure a house and five acres of land for £300,000 is ridiculous! I was prepared to go up to £450,000. I have indeed secured a bargain! Furthermore, I now have cash in hand to trade in my BMW for a Land Rover, buy furniture for the farmhouse and purchase wine bottles, corks, labels and everything else needed to establish myself in the winemaking business.
Even if my first year is unsuccessful, I now know I can survive.
Having completed all the necessary paperwork, I leave the auction room with a spring in my step. In a very short time I will receive the keys to the property and my new life begins.

JESSICA'S VINEYARD

CHAPTER 2

There is something eminently satisfying about owing one's own property. It is said that a man's home is his castle. Leaving aside the sexist nature of the saying, it is true that owning a plot of land and the buildings on it provides a defence against the world. Here is my place of safety. Here is my place of permanence. Here is somewhere I can put down roots and become part of the surrounding countryside.
And what magnificent countryside!
As I throw open the casement window of my bedroom I see nothing but rolling landscape and expansive blue sky. No dark satanic mills here. No madcap dash to the office, catching the tube or dodging the crowds. No roar of traffic, wailing sirens or rubbish-strewn pavements. No graffiti disfiguring walls. No vagrants sleeping rough in doorways. No muggers, potential rapists or psychopaths. Just pure clean country air and the beautiful music of songbirds.
I have been transported to paradise.

JESSICA'S VINEYARD

I glimpse my vineyard to the far right of the house. It is flanked by trees and surrounded by pastureland and newly-sown wheat. Or is it barley? I really must learn the difference.

I have yet to meet my neighbours. All my time and energy have gone into furnishing the house in order to make it my home.

I could have bought fashionable furniture and fittings. I would have done so were I still living in London. But somehow my new home seems to call for solid rustic furniture.

Consequently, I scoured the county's antique shops and assembled a very acceptable solid oak dining table and four sturdy chairs, a dark oak dresser and linen chest, two comfortable fireside chairs, a chaise longue, a solid kitchen table, cupboards and wardrobes.

When I stumbled upon a four-poster bed I was sorely tempted to buy it. It certainly looked very grand; but I decided my bedroom was too small to contain such an ostentatious item and so I settled for a more modest oak-framed double bed instead.

My new home is furnished with rustic furniture, but I haven't stinted on comfort. I chose a wonderfully luxurious mattress for my bed and a full range of modern electrical appliances for the kitchen.

I've surprised myself with my do-it-yourself skills. I successfully fitted curtain rails and hung heavily

JESSICA'S VINEYARD

brocaded curtains to prevent the cruelty of winter from invading my little nest.

The walls look bare. I have no pictures to hang on them. There were many pictures on the walls of my former home but I decided I didn't want them here. I'm making a new start. I don't want to be reminded of the past. I want to make a new beginning. I have left my old life behind. The future beckons.

I inhale a deep lungful of Herefordshire's pure country air. A smile steals over my face. This is true living.

I leave my bedroom, descend the twisting stairs and prepare breakfast.

What shall I do today?

When I was at school we sang a hymn that began,

So here hath been dawning another new day,
think wilt thou let it slip useless away?

I may have forgotten the religious lesson it taught but I've always looked upon each new day as something to be used positively. In the past I was told what I should do. Instructions were issued from above - always by men. I was forced to do what others instructed. But now, I have no one to tell me what to do. I am my own master. Or should that be mistress? I can please myself from the moment I get up to the moment I go to bed. The feeling is exhilarating. I am mistress of my own destiny.

JESSICA'S VINEYARD

Spring is unfolding around me. The hedgerows are erupting into leaf. They are leaving their winter skeletal bones behind and shyly adorning themselves in new costumes of greenery. There is warmth in the sun. The birds are pleased. They trill their pleasure and urge others to share their excitement. Spring has begun its unstoppable forward march.
If I am to turn the loss-making Abbeydore Winery into a going concern I must join that forward march. Leaving the house, I climb into my recently-acquired Land Rover. It may be old and lack the kerb appeal of my previous BMW, but it is infinitely more practical for work around the vineyard and for transporting supplies to and from Abergavenny.
It splutters and coughs as it lurches into life, leaving a cloud of diesel fumes hanging in the air like a miniature atomic mushroom cloud.
I make for the vineyard. The lane is deserted save for the birds and the occasional rabbit that disappears into the hedgerow.
Rabbits: I must be on my guard against them; especially when planting new vines. Rabbits may make delightful characters in the books of Beatrix Potter but I have no intention of providing them with a source of food or a means to sharpen their gnawing buck teeth. Rabbits are not welcome in my domain.

JESSICA'S VINEYARD

I pull the Land Rover into the gateway of the vineyard and switch off the engine. The grass between each row of ascending vines is coming to life. I need to purchase a small tractor and mowing machine, capable of passing between the vines, to cut the grass. In the autumn the tractor can be used to gather in the grape harvest.

The previous owners must have owned such a vehicle but, alas, there was no tractor in the barn when I unlocked it and ventured inside. Indeed, the barn was devoid of practically everything except four large stainless steel tanks and a stack of old oak barrels.

A small second-hand tractor has to be my next purchase.

I scan the vines. The previous owners pruned them before the property was offered for sale. The horizontal branches are attached to wires with small twisted fastenings. Buds are forming: buds that will erupt into shoots surging upwards to the sun and trailing clouds of green glory in their wake.

The soil from which the vines draw nutrients and nourishment is being invaded by weeds. It is not only vines that grow in springtime, it would seem, but a rampant army of weeds as well.

I might as well make a start on weeding. It will give me an opportunity to examine the rootstocks and see if any replacements are needed.

JESSICA'S VINEYARD

It is slow work. I am glad of my large, broad-brimmed hat to provide protection from the sun. The sale particulars said that half the vines are Bacchus grapes and half Cabernet Sauvignon. My vineyard is able to produce both white and red wine. It seems a sensible arrangement. If one variety fails, hopefully the other will compensate.

A perusal of the previous owners' financial accounts revealed that the Cabernet Sauvignon vines were the weak link. They had failed to produce a vintage for the past five years. Does that mean they are past their best? Are the rootstocks so old they have lost their fecundity? Would it be best to grub them up and plant new vines?

There is no denying they are old. The sale particulars claimed they are over a hundred years old. But would previous owners have left them undisturbed for so long if they failed to fruit adequately? Is there some other reason why they've failed to yield a fruitful harvest?

If I grub up half the vineyard I will have to wait three or four years for new vines to establish themselves before I have a harvest. I cannot wait that long. Maybe I should see what happens this year before making any radical decisions.

I continue my slow upward progress on my hands and knees pulling weeds from around each gnarled and wizened rootstock.

JESSICA'S VINEYARD

I imagine the monks of Dore Abbey doing the same thing five hundred years before. They were no strangers to long hours on their knees. I've no idea how many hours Cistercian monks spent praying but it must have been a sizeable proportion of each day. Their knees must have developed callouses or else become immune to the hard surfaces on which they knelt. Perhaps mine will do the same.

Weeding is like an act of prayer. I am rooting out the bad and encouraging the good to flourish. The weeds are my sins and failings. I am uprooting and casting them aside to shrivel and die.

I try to recall the seven deadly sins. I know that one of them is lust - not that I am susceptible to that at present. I think another is anger. I've certainly experienced plenty of that during the past year. Alan was so unreasonable and difficult when I asked for a divorce. He went out of his way to make things as difficult for me as possible.

He claimed he earned the lion's share of our finances. He wanted to withhold my rightful share. He wanted to keep me financially dependent on him. I felt like a dog with a choking collar around my neck. The more I strained to get away the tighter the collar became. Some couples say they divorce amicably. Our divorce was certainly not amicable. Alan viewed me as his property. He had no intention of relinquishing his hold on me.

JESSICA'S VINEYARD

At first, I tried reasoning with him. I said there were no children to consider. We were not inflicting suffering on others. We had just grown apart. There was no longer any love in our relationship. We were bound to each other more by habit and inertia than by love and mutual affection.

But he would have none of it. He insisted I was behaving unreasonably. He said I was regressing and behaving like a spoilt teenager who wanted her own selfish way in everything. He said I did not know how well off I was with him. He claimed I would be lost without him.

That was the last straw! I was determined to show him I was quite capable of standing on my own two feet. I was not beholden to him for anything. I was a mature forty-year-old woman who knew her own mind. I could do whatever I wanted and there was nothing he could do to stop me.

We had some seismic rows. I became more and more angry at his patronising and pig-headed attitude. My anger boiled over in all sorts of petty ways. I ceased to iron his shirts. I pretended I hadn't noticed when a button came off his trousers. I selected television programmes I knew he hated. I was angry.

Am I still angry?

Well, perhaps not as much as then. I have proved I am quite capable of existing on my own. I am now the owner of a sizeable property in Herefordshire. I

JESSICA'S VINEYARD

have my own delightful home. I have an exciting future ahead of me. I am my own boss and can do exactly as I please.

I become so engrossed in pulling up weeds and seeing each one as a banished sin that I am completely unaware of someone advancing upon me from behind.

It is only when a shadow falls across the ground at my knees that I realise someone is standing over me. I emit a scream - not a blood-curdling scream but a nervous scream of surprise.

'I'm sorry to startle you,' says a deep voice from behind. 'I saw you working here and thought I'd come and introduce myself.'

I suddenly feel very foolish for my involuntary scream.

I turn around and see a pair of dirty boots inches from where I'm kneeling. I look up and see the craggy face and downturned mouth of a man. He is older than me. He wears threadbare working clothes. He has a receding hairline which, from my vantage point at ground level, throws his forehead into high relief. There is something strangely familiar about his face.

I hastily scramble to my feet in as ladylike a fashion as possible.

JESSICA'S VINEYARD

It is only when I am standing upright and looking directly into his grey eyes that I realise who he is. It's the man who bid against me at the auction.
Extending a hand he announces, 'Wilfred Spragg is the name.'
I pull the weeding glove from off my right hand and tentatively shake his hand. He has a very firm handshake. I sense he is a man who is used to having his own way and getting what he wants. His steel grey eyes bore into mine. No doubt he is trying to get the measure of me.
'Jessica Pope is my name,' I inform him.
He nods.
'I own the adjoining land to yours - Bellar's Pitch.'
'I'm pleased to meet you,' I say as I recover my composure and determine to be his equal. I then add for good measure, 'I am newly arrived here and have yet to explore the locality. Tell me where you're situated.'
'To the west of you. My wife and I have a smallholding a little further down the lane. We've been farming here for ten years: a few beef cattle, a few hens, a few pigs – you know, that sort of thing.'
I smile at his assumption that I know all about that sort of thing. There is no point in pretending that I do. It is better to come clean and admit my ignorance.

JESSICA'S VINEYARD

'I know nothing about that sort of thing,' I reply with a smile. 'I'm a newbie. I am here to make wine and nothing else. No livestock for me – just grapes.'
'Perhaps we can help each other,' he says. 'We've recently expanded into vines. We've planted three acres and are waiting to see how they do. Maybe we can help each other when it comes to harvesting and processing the grapes.'
I am not keen on having another man involved in my business affairs, although, it might be handy to have someone close at hand who could provide help if I found there were tasks I couldn't do on my own.
'That's very kind of you,' I smile.
Then, remembering the line from *Oklahoma* –
Territory folks should stick together, territory folk should all be pals
- I say, 'Perhaps you and your wife would care to join me for a meal next week. I would very much like to learn all I can about the district and I'm sure you know a great deal about the soil and the climatic conditions. I would very much like to learn from you.'
He gives me a long hard stare. He wants to know if I recognise him from the sale room.
When he realises there is nothing to be gained from concealing his interest in my land he says, 'Of course, we were against you in the sale room. We were hoping to get our hands on this parcel of land. We

thought it would make economic sense to extend our smallholding by incorporating your five acres into ours. But we lacked the resources of you city folk. You outbid us.'

I frown.

'I'm sorry I deprived you of your opportunity; but that doesn't mean we can't be good neighbours, does it? My offer of an evening meal next week still stands. You can tell me about your newly-planted vines. I'm keen to learn all I can.'

'I take it you've never grown grapes before?'

'Never: this is a new venture for me. But I'm very excited about it and am determined to work hard to make it a success.'

'Well, I can tell you for nothing, you won't have any success with those vines.'

He gesticulates towards the row of vines I am weeding.

'They're entirely the wrong variety to grow in this country. No one grows Cabernet Sauvignon in Britain. They need hot sun and plenty of it in order to ripen and produce grape juice. Britain doesn't have that sort of climate. You'd be much better grubbing them up and planting Bacchus or some other variety more suited to our northern climate. If my wife and I had been successful and purchased this land we'd have grubbed up the lot and started again from scratch.'

JESSICA'S VINEYARD

I am stung by this broadside. Why should he denigrate my vineyard and seek to undermine my confidence. He is Alan all over again.
But I am not to be cowed or deflected.
I give Mr Spragg one of my most radiant smiles.
'Well, I will have to see if I can succeed where others have failed,' I respond sweetly.
'You're wasting your time,' he counters. 'The Simpsons, who were here before you, couldn't make a go of it. They were experienced country folk. They knew what they were doing, and yet they couldn't make a living out of it. Mark my words, you'll find just the same. Those vines are useless. You're wasting your time tending such bad specimens.'
I have never been able to tolerate know-alls. I may not know much about vines but I have a sharp brain.
'How is it then, Mr Spragg, that these rootstocks have been here for a hundred years if, as you say, they are so unproductive? It can't be the vines that are at fault. There must be some other reason. And I intend discovering what it is and rectifying it.'
'Please yourself. You city folks have the means to play at farming. It's not a question of life and death for you if the harvest fails. I have to make a living out of my smallholding.'
I am stung by his suggestion that I am merely playing at viticulture. I am as much dependent on my vines producing a good yield as he is. I have no limitless

JESSICA'S VINEYARD

pot of gold to live on. I have got to make this vineyard work to provide me with a source of income.

'I, too, Mr Spragg, have to make a living out of this land. I'm not here to play at being a wine producer. I have to succeed in order to live, just like you.'

He raises his eyebrows in a doubtful gesture. I sense he does not like me. Nevertheless, he is my neighbour and I am determined to keep on good terms with him. Perhaps his wife is more amenable; and so I repeat my invitation to a meal the following week.

'I would be delighted if you and your wife could join me for a meal next week. I would very much like to meet Mrs Spragg.'

He purses his lips and thinks before saying, 'I'll have a word with her and let you know.'

He turns to leave, but, just as he is about to do so, he looks back at me and says, 'If you decide that Abbeydore Winery is not for you, I'm still interested in purchasing it.' Then, almost as an afterthought, he adds, 'Providing the price is right, of course.'

So saying, he turns and walks towards the gate leaving me puzzled.

I wish I knew what was going on inside his head. Does he dislike me as a person? Does he resent a woman gaining ownership of the land he desired? Does he treat all newcomers to the locality with

JESSICA'S VINEYARD

suspicion? If he is establishing a vineyard himself in the Golden Valley he will be my rival. Do I have anything to fear?
I return to my weeding with questions exploding inside my head like out-of-control hand grenades. Have I made the right decision to come to this place or am I destined to fail?

JESSICA'S VINEYARD

CHAPTER 3

The vines come alive under the loving caress of the strengthening sun. Buds appear from bare winter trusses like children peeping shyly from behind the folds of their mother's apron. All around, Nature is coming to life. The sap rises in the stem. The unstoppable life-force surges through all living things. Spring has begun its relentless forward march. Nothing can stop it. Even stones are pushed aside by the force of emerging plants as if they are mere specks of dust. The soil reveals its germinating seeds. The great march of spring has begun.

Of course, I knew about this from biology lessons at school. I knew the science, but I never experienced the reality. Living in a city one doesn't. The London plane trees don their summer greenery every year, but, apart from that, the silent march of spring goes unnoticed.

Now, seeing Nature erupt in all its glory, I cannot believe what I have missed all these years! I feel I have returned to my roots. I am reconnecting with the life-force that courses through my veins but of

JESSICA'S VINEYARD

which I have been blissfully unaware for so long.
This is real living! This is life as it should be lived!
I smile at my new appreciation of life and its
manifold wonders.

Not that everything is wonderful.

It took me five days of back-breaking labour to weed
the vineyard. No sooner had I completed the task
than new weeds began to appear where I started. It is
not just vines that bluster into life at this time of the
year but an army of unwanted weeds as well.

The grass between each row of vines is also growing
at an alarming rate. I need a tractor with a mowing
attachment to keep it under control: but not just any
tractor. It must have a narrow wheel-base to pass
between the vines.

I scan the internet and discover someone in
Shropshire who has a second-hand narrow-wheelbase
tractor for sale. He wants more for it than I wish to
spend. Despite my best efforts, he is unwilling to
reduce his asking price. He must know that vineyard
owners are desperate for such machinery at this time
of year.

I do, however, manage to extract a concession from
him. I insist he delivers the tractor to Abbeydore at
no extra cost.

The tractor duly comes with a grass-cutting
attachment and a trailer.

JESSICA'S VINEYARD

When my newly-acquired tractor arrives on a low-loader I demand a demonstration to prove it's in full working order; and, when all seems as it should be, I hand over the cash and clinch the deal.

I have never before driven a tractor, but it cannot be difficult. I follow the steps the seller showed me. I bring the machine to life and gingerly drive it around the farmyard. Easy, I reassure myself.

I recall that women, with no experience of farming, were drafted into the Land Army during the Second World War and soon became adept at driving tractors, bringing home the harvest and proving that women are perfectly capable of undertaking tasks previously considered the exclusive domain of men. I've joined the proud ranks of my former land sisters. I am firmly in the saddle and prepared for battle.

The battle comes the following day.

I decide to test my skills on my newly-acquired tractor by cutting the grass between the vines for the first time. Wearing jeans and a checked shirt and feeling every inch a country girl, I mount the tractor and bring it to life. Well, that is my intention. The reality is different. The tractor refuses to start.

Have I done something wrong?

I try again, but all I hear is a high-pitched whine. The engine refuses to start. I check to see if there is fuel in the fuel tank. There is. Perhaps I've flooded the carburettor. Alan would know instantly.

JESSICA'S VINEYARD

'Just like a woman to flood the carburettor,' he would say in that supercilious voice he uses whenever he wants to belittle me.

I stare at the parts of the exposed engine trying to decide where the carburettor is located. I seem to remember that the carburettor is where the fuel and air are mixed together. Did I once hear someone say that dirt from the fuel tank can cause a blockage in the carburettor? But where is the wretched carburettor?

Maybe it's an intermittent fault and I should try again.

I turn the ignition key repeatedly, getting angrier every time. Each time I'm answered by high-pitched screams of pain from the innards of the damned machine. I can feel my blood pressure rising. Have I been sold a pig in a poke? Did the seller know this machine was clapped out? Have I wasted my money on a piece of useless machinery?

I madly turn the ignition key hoping that my rage will act as a high voltage shock to dislodge whatever is preventing the engine from firing.

'Are you having trouble there?'

I swing around in my seat and see a lad in jeans and a T-shirt looking at me with a half-amused smile on his face. He has a large pack strapped to his back.

'What does it look like?' I angrily reply.

JESSICA'S VINEYARD

The last thing I want is some youth laughing at me. I probably confirm his unspoken belief that all middle-aged women are impractical.

'Can I lend a hand?'

He speaks with a foreign accent. His voice hints that he is Australian.

Even worse!

He probably thinks Pommies couldn't survive a day in the outback; that English women are only fit for embroidery, painting their nails and sipping cocktails and are completely useless when it comes to the practical essentials of life - like fixing an engine.

'I know a thing or two about tractors,' he continues in a distinctive Australian drawl. 'My dad used to have a machine very much like this and I spent most of my childhood tinkering with the old beast.'

I exhale and think rapidly.

I guess I have nothing to lose. If he can diagnose the trouble and fix it, that will save me calling out an engineer and incurring expense. I emit a deep sigh.

'OK. You're welcome to try.'

He slings the backpack off his shoulders and advances towards me. He walks with youthful confidence. This is no slouching adolescent but a young man in full control of himself.

I note that he has fair hair and blue eyes. He is well-tanned. In many respects he is the archetypical

JESSICA'S VINEYARD

Australian and could have stepped out of an
Australian soap opera set on Bondi Beach.
But what brings him to Herefordshire and to
Abbeydore in particular?
'You're a long way from home,' I offer as my
opening gambit.
He smiles a winning smile.
'I sure am. I'm on a gap year. I want to see as much
of the world as I can during that year.'
'But what brings you to Herefordshire and to
Abbeydore in particular?'
He laughs.
'I guess it's not exactly the centre of the universe. But
I wanted to see all of the UK. Everyone does
London, Edinburgh, Stratford-upon-Avon and Bath,
but I wanted to experience the full story – and that
includes the rural areas. And so I asked, 'Which is the
most rural county in England?' and I was told
'Herefordshire.' And so, here I am. I've walked
beside the River Wye. I've visited quaint black and
white villages and I've sampled Herefordshire cider.
Real good!'
He has an infectious manner of speech. There is a *joie
de vivre* about him which reminds me of myself when
I was his age. Back then the whole of life stretched
before me. There were no commitments; no ties; no
responsibilities. It was a time to explore, relish new

experiences, encounter new ideas and meet new people.
'Do you have any spanners and old rags?' he asks.
His practical question brings me down to earth and back to the confounded tractor.
'I've got a basic tool kit,' I reply, 'but I'm not sure it'll contain what you need.'
'Don't worry yourself about that. I'm used to improvising. We were miles from anywhere on my dad's smallholding and we got used to making do and mending. You'll be surprised what I can do with just a few basic materials.'
There is something very reassuring about him.
I go into the house and retrieve my tool kit. I've used it for jobs around the house but, as he will surely see, it is almost new.
'This is the best I've got,' I inform him.
'Right: let's have a look at the old beast and see what we can do. We'll start with the carburettor. That's often the cause of the trouble when an engine won't start.'
I note with envy the unerring way in which he immediately goes to a part of the engine and begins dismantling it. So that's the carburettor!
My basic set of spanners appear to provide the tools he requires.
'How long are you planning to spend in the UK?' I ask by way of conversation.

JESSICA'S VINEYARD

'That all depends. I'd like to spend summer in England. But, you know how it is ... I've only got limited finances and so I have to work my passage, as it were. Ideally, I'd like to get a job in England over the summer. That's one of the reasons I've came to Herefordshire. I was told there's plenty of summer work going in the hop yards and apple orchards.'
I note he doesn't include vineyards.
I would find an extra pair of hands very useful over the summer months – especially if those hands were mechanically adroit. But I have no means of paying him to work for me.
'This old lady can't have been cleaned for years!' he exclaims as he examines the disassembled carburettor he is holding in his hands. 'No wonder you had trouble starting the old girl! I'll give her a good clean and then, unless I'm very much mistaken, she should start a treat.'
He cleans the various components of the carburettor with the rags I provided and reassembles the unit.
'Now for the moment of testing,' he grins.
He jumps onto the tractor's seat, turns the key in the ignition and, as if my magic, the engine springs to life.
'Marvellous!' I shout above the roaring noise of the engine. 'You've got a magic mechanical touch.'
'I don't know about that,' he laughs. 'I do know, however, that this tractor isn't firing properly. It's

probably the points. If the carburettor was in such a poor state, it's a fair guess that the points are the same. It's not a big job to change them.'
I dither.
I'm at a crossroads.
Should I invite him to stay and attend to the points and, possibly, help me in the vineyard or should I resist male interference in my new life?
Do I really want someone else impinging on my solitude?
I came here to get away from men. Do I really want another man in my life?
And yet, there are some things I cannot manage on my own. This bloody tractor has shown me I know nothing about machinery.
Will I struggle with pressing grapes and manhandling wine barrels? Do I need an extra pair of hands?
I look at the young man sitting on the tractor. He is only a youth. I must be almost twice his age. I will have no difficulty exerting my authority over him and establishing a clear business employer-employee relationship. And, if at the end of the day, I don't like having him around, I can always send him packing. Backpackers are used to packing their bags and moving on.
I refocus and see he is looking down at his oily hands.

JESSICA'S VINEYARD

'Turn the engine off and come inside to clean up,' I call out. 'The least I can do is to offer you a mug of tea for the help you've given me.'
'Aha! Good old English tea! Where would we be without it?'
So saying, he descends from the tractor and, picking up his backpack, follows me into the house.
It's the first time I've entertained a man in my house. It's a strange sensation. I feel like a nun who has broken her solemn vows and allowed a man into her cloistered cell. I never intended men to enter this secret space. I console myself by saying 'This isn't a man. He's just a boy. And he's here merely to wash his hands and have a mug of tea'.
'Nice place you've got here,' he remarks. 'Have you been here long?'
Be careful Jessica. Don't go telling him everything about yourself.
'Not that long. Viticulture is a new venture for me.'
'That's exciting!'
Indeed it is, although I have to admit that some of the initial excitement is beginning to wear off as I come face to face with the practical reality of owning a vineyard.
'We grow a lot of grapes in the Clare Valley,' he says. 'When I was a school kid, I used to help with the harvesting. Great fun! How many acres do you have here?'

JESSICA'S VINEYARD

Not only is he mechanically minded but he has experience of viticulture. The more I discover about this boy, the more I am surprised. If I were a religious person, I might credit him with being an angel sent from heaven specifically to help me.
I need to make a decision. Shall I offer him a job over the summer months or shall I just be thankful for his help and wave him goodbye?
I procrastinate.
A chance like this might not come again, I say to myself.
Seize it and see what he says.
'I've got five acres. It's not that big but it's a lot for one person to manage. I could use some help. You've clearly got mechanical skills and, if you've had experience of harvesting grapes in Australia, you would be ideal helping with the grape harvest here when it comes.'
I watch his face intently. A smile spreads over it. But, before he can answer, I add, 'Unfortunately, I'm not in a position to pay you a wage, but I could provide free board and lodging. There's a room in the barn that could be yours if you'd like to give it a try.'
'That's extremely kind of you, ma'am,' he beams. 'And, as I've got nowhere else to go and no other offers, I'd be delighted to accept.'

JESSICA'S VINEYARD

'It would be a flexible arrangement,' I add, as my business acumen asserts itself. 'If, for whatever reason, we found the working relationship wasn't satisfactory, the arrangement would have to be terminated without any financial penalties.'
'That's fine by me,' he says, nodding his head gently in agreement.
Then, realising what I've done, I say, 'I've offered you a job, and board and lodging without even knowing your name.'
He laughs.
'My name's Jason. Jason Knightly.'
'And mine's Jessica. Jessica Pope.'
I reach across the table and shake his hand. I am surprised at the strength of his handshake. This is no weakling. This is an athletic young man.
'And now we'd better seal our new employment arrangement with a mug of tea and a slice of homemade fruitcake.'
'You make your own fruitcake?' he asks with incredulity, 'here in the depths of the Herefordshire countryside? Well, who'd have thought it? Trust my lucky stars to alight upon a place where there's homemade fruitcake!'
There is something about his manner that makes me feel he'll be easy to live with. He has the openness and enthusiasm of youth. Perhaps, at a psychological

JESSICA'S VINEYARD

level, I see him as the son I never had. His parents must be proud of him.

'Are your parents still alive?' I ask.

A frown passes over his tanned face.

'I'm afraid not. I suppose I'm what you'd call an orphan. That's one of the reasons I'm backpacking around the world. I've got no ties. No family responsibilities. I'm just a boy who's all alone and determined to see as much of the world as possible before I become an old man shackled with a mortgage, a nine-to-five job and a nagging wife.'

'Not all wives are nagging,' I reply, springing to the defence of my sex.

'I'm sure you were never a nagging wife.'

I am brought up with a jolt.

'What makes you think I've been married?'

His brows knit in anguish.

'I'm terribly sorry,' he stammers. 'I never meant to be rude.'

'You've not been rude. I'd just like to know what makes you think I've been married.'

'Well, I guess, it's just how I find you. There's no man around the place and so you can't be living here with a husband. There's no other woman around the place and so it's unlikely you're a lesbian. That only leaves one option: that you're divorced and attempting to make a new start in life in these beautiful surroundings.'

JESSICA'S VINEYARD

'You're very perceptive. You're also quite right. I am recently divorced and keen to make a new start. And that's all you need to know. Now let me show you the room in the barn. It needs some work doing on it but, with your practical skills, I'm sure that can soon be arranged.'

I lead the way to the barn and Jason follows.

We enter the large building. It is like entering a medieval cathedral. The slit windows high in the thick stone walls allow the bare minimum of light to enter the cavernous interior. It takes a few seconds for our eyes to adjust to the low light level.

Along one side of the barn are the gleaming stainless steel vats that will store the macerating wine at harvest time. Along the other side are rows of oak barrels stacked three high. These will contain the wine as it ages and absorbs the characteristics of the wood.

I lead the way to the far end of the barn where a flight of wooden steps lead to a mezzanine room. Pushing open the door of the room reveals an almost square space under the steeply sloping roof. There is just one window in the apex on the opposite wall. The light entering through the window reveals a completely empty space devoid of all furniture or fittings.

'I'm afraid it's pretty basic,' I say rather unnecessarily.

JESSICA'S VINEYARD

'Don't worry about that. I've dossed down in far worse places than this on my travels. I'll soon get this shipshape.'
Then, as he envisages living in the room, he asks, 'Would you have any objection to me fitting a tap and washbasin here?'
'None whatsoever. There's a water supply downstairs for the winemaking and there's drainage to the foul sewer.'
'What more could I ask?' he laughs. 'I'll have all mains services laid on here before you can say 'put a shrimp on the barby'.'
It's not my idea of good living, but he seems content with it. At least he won't have to shiver with cold as he will only inhabit the room for the summer months.
'I'll go and get some cleaning materials so we can spruce the place up,' I add, 'and I've got a few pieces of surplus furniture you can have.'
'It gets better by the minute!'
We spend the remainder of the day working on the attic room in the barn. He has a natural and unforced way of speaking. He tells me about his time at school, his youthful adventures in Australia and the dream of owning his own smallholding and living in tune with the rhythm of the seasons. It seems we have much in common.

JESSICA'S VINEYARD

By the end of the afternoon the attic room is habitable. It may not be luxurious but it's homely in a bachelor sort of way. Tomorrow I will take him to Abergavenny where he can purchase the plumbing bits and pieces he needs to install a washbasin and a downstairs toilet for his exclusive use. He also says he'll purchase the parts needed for the tractor in order to make it fit for purpose.

We adjourn to the farmhouse kitchen where I prepare supper. He offers to help, but I don't want a man interfering in my kitchen. I place a glass of wine – not Jessica's wine, as yet – in his hand and let him watch me as I prepare the meal.

'I spent my early years in Australia,' I inform him. 'My parents emigrated to Australia when I was a babe-in-arms; but things didn't work out and my mother returned to this country with me. My father decided to stay in Australia. My parents divorced and I lost contact with my father. I've no idea whether he's dead or alive.'

I pause and reflect.

'My father would be in his seventies now, if he's still alive,' I add. 'I don't suppose you've come across him? His name was Garfield Pollack.'

'I'm afraid not. But then, Australia's a mighty big country. The chances of stumbling across a specific person are pretty slim.'

JESSICA'S VINEYARD

Of course! Australia is a continent. It must have millions of inhabitants. How foolish to even think Jason might know my father!
'I had a childhood friend in Australia,' I continue. 'Her name is Celia Braithwaite. I don't suppose you've come across her?'
He laughs again and shakes his head.
'No, but I'll keep looking.'
'No need,' I reply. 'I've kept in touch with her over the years. I know exactly where she is.'
The conversation turns to childhood memories of Australia. Mine are somewhat hazy. I lived in Sydney, which was much like any other large city, but Jason grew up in the outback and has lots of tales to tell about snakes, poisonous spiders, droughts, storms, flying doctors and the enormous distances people travel to get from one place to another.
Abbeydore may be remote, but at least it's not as remote as the Australian outback.
We spend a convivial evening sitting at the kitchen table talking and then tackling the washing-up together.
It is only after he has left, clutching a torch and making his way to his attic room in the barn, that I realise how much I've enjoyed his company.

CHAPTER 4

The tractor is fixed. Jason replaced the points – whatever they are – and now the tractor positively purrs as it moves around the vineyard.
Jason is worth his weight in gold. Nothing is ever too much trouble for him. He has plumbed in a washbasin and toilet and fitted a light and electrical sockets in his attic room. Not that he spends much time there. He eats his meals in the farmhouse and spends the day undertaking jobs around the vineyard. He has cut the grass between the vines, weeded the rootstocks, forked in manure, replaced damaged Bacchus rootstocks with new ones (suitably staked and enclosed in plastic cylinders to prevent rabbits feasting on them), pruned the growing vine branches and sterilised the vats in readiness for harvest. This has left me free to research wine bottle suppliers, graphic label designers, retail outlets for our wine and the do's and don'ts of wine production.
It is while I am researching English wine prices on the internet that a car drives up in front of the farmhouse. At first I think it must be Jason returning early from his shopping expedition to Abergavenny;

JESSICA'S VINEYARD

but, when I look out of the window, I see not the old Land Rover but a pristine BMW convertible.
We have very few visitors. The postman is our most frequent visitor but, even he only calls once or twice a week. We are completely off the beaten track and unlikely, therefore, to attract passers-by.
It is surprising to see a gleaming metallic blue vehicle coming to a halt in front of the farmhouse. It's certainly not a local farmer's vehicle. The Spraggs drive a battered old Astra. I know that farmers are often richer than they pretend, but I know of no one in the locality with a car like this. I am puzzled. I wish Jason was here.
I abandon my trawl of the internet and focus on the man emerging from the car. He is tall. He wears a smart suit, a striped shirt and an expensive tie. His shoes look as if they are made from Italian leather. Hardly country wear! His silver grey hair is neatly brushed back over his head. He advances purposefully towards the front door of the farmhouse.
I am able to make out his facial features as he gets nearer. His forehead is deeply furrowed as if he is carrying a heavy burden of care. His eyes are deep-set under quizzical eyebrows. He is clearly used to warmer climes judging by his tan.
Rat-a-tat-tat snaps the knocker on the front door.

JESSICA'S VINEYARD

I never use the front door. It is kept permanently locked and bolted. And so, rather than wrestle with it, I exit the kitchen via the back door and walk around the house to confront my visitor sideways on. My unexpected approach startles him. He blinks before regaining his composure.

'Do I have the pleasure of meeting Mrs Pope?' he asks in a cultured voice that has been acquired if not on the playing fields of Eton then in very close proximity to them.

'Indeed.'

He knows me even if I do not know him.

Well, he knows my name. I suppose that could easily be obtained. The postman knows my name. The Land Registry knows my name. But he calls me Mrs. rather than the more generic Ms. Maybe my name is the sum total of his knowledge about me.

'I hope you don't mind me intruding on you in this way without prior announcement but I was anxious to meet you as I understand you have recently acquired Abbeydore Winery.'

He pauses awaiting a response.

'That is so,' I reply, keeping my conversation as laconic as possible without wanting to appear rude.

'I can see why you were attracted to this spot,' he says as a smile steals over his face. 'It is indeed a beautiful retreat, far from the madding crowd. I understand this was once part of the land worked by

JESSICA'S VINEYARD

the monks of Dore Abbey. They always picked the best spots. Take Evesham Abbey nestled in a loop of the River Avon; or Worcester on the banks of the River Severn; or Tintern on the banks of the River Wye. The monks were no fools. They knew instinctively where to put down roots and get the best out of the land.'

Am I to be subjected to a history lesson from this unexpected visitor? He clearly relishes his knowledge and cannot resist having a captive audience before whom to cast his pearls.

'I noticed, as I approached your house, that you have a large vineyard on the south-facing slope to the left: an ideal location for growing grapes. I expect the monks used the land for exactly the same purpose. They needed a constant supply of wine, of course, for sacramental use and also, no doubt, to stave off the coldness of winter and the isolated loneliness of living in such a remote location. It can't have been much fun renouncing all personal possessions, the pleasures of the conjugal bed and being subject to the unquestioning rule of an abbot, be he ever so benign. But then, what was the alternative? The abbeys were the only centres of civilisation in the Dark Ages. Where else could you be assured of a secure supply of food? Or a place to learn, read and write? And with private health and social care provided until you died? It must have been an attractive proposition

JESSICA'S VINEYARD

given the alternatives. Not that many flocked to Dore Abbey it would seem. I understand that, at the Dissolution of the Monasteries in 1536, there were only a handful of monks and they were a pretty unruly lot. Ah well, it's all water under the bridge. But at least some of their handiwork survives.'

He gives me an oily smile as if I were a piece of that handiwork.

I am unsure how to react. I've encountered many bores during my years in commerce. I either endured them, if I wanted to obtain something in their possession, or else I cut them short, if I deemed them time-wasters.

Who is this man? He would seem well-heeled and intelligent. He has taken the trouble to discover my name. He has driven to my remote smallholding in order to speak to me. There must be a reason he is standing here and regaling me with a history lesson on monastic life in the Middle Ages.

Play for time, Jessica. Allow him to unravel his verbal rope. Maybe he will hang himself.

'All very interesting, I'm sure, but …' and I allow my voice to trail off into a questioning silence.

'Quite so,' he replies straightening his back and preparing to come to the point and state the reason for his unheralded visit to Abbeydore Winery.

JESSICA'S VINEYARD

'You must wonder why I'm taking up your valuable time. Let me introduce myself. I'm Montague Smythe. You may have heard of me.'
I have not. I shake my head resignedly to register negativity.
He appears taken aback.
'Oh, I thought you might have come across my name as you're in the wine business. I write regular columns in the Sunday broadsheets. I write about wine. It's an endlessly fascinating subject, as I'm sure you'll agree. Every wine is unique. One never knows what surprise is awaiting one when one pulls a cork and inhales the bouquet of the wine within. It's like falling in love all over again – but with a different woman every time. You must excuse my similes but we wine writers have to resort to similes and metaphors in order to convey the richness and complexity of the wines we sample. How else will our readers appreciate the subtleties of the taste and tannins, the flavours and the acidity, the minerality and the lingering after-taste? Forgive my language. It is born from a lifetime writing about wine and wishing to share my passion with others.'
He looks at me with gleaming brown eyes under his beetle brows. He's willing me to share his enthusiasm and embrace him as a fellow pilgrim on the road to wine nirvana.
I do not embrace him.

JESSICA'S VINEYARD

I do not embrace men.

I cannot make up my mind if he is someone who might be useful to me or a nuisance looking for an audience before whom to perform.

If he does write about wines in national newspapers, he might be a person to cultivate and make use of when I come to market my Chateau Jessica vintage. I decide to keep the channels of communication open.

'You must forgive me,' I stammer. 'I am relatively new to winemaking and not *au fait* with the wine trade.'

He smiles a patronising smile.

How I hate patronising men.

'Well, we all have to start somewhere, I suppose,' he says with a supercilious smile. 'And you have chosen a very promising location to start, if I may say so. English wine is on the up. Our continental neighbours used to deride us and say we were a land without music and wine. But not any more! I am not qualified to speak about music, but I assert most strongly that we are no longer a land without wine. Some of our English wine is a match for any produced on the continent. Only the other day I opened a bottle of English white wine – no names, no pack drill – and it could have been a Chablis. Sheer rapturous ecstasy contained within a bottle that had never strayed from these shores! English wine is here to stay. It has a great future. One of the

JESSICA'S VINEYARD

beneficial effects of climate change is that the temperature in England is becoming more and more suited to wine production. Grapes, that one would have never thought of growing in this country, are now becoming viable. Tell me, what are your vines?'
His question takes me by surprise. I thought I was in for a long monologue about English wines.
'Half are Bacchus and half are Cabernet Sauvignon.'
He nods at the Bacchus but his eyebrows race to his hairline when I mention Cabernet Sauvignon.
'Good heavens! You're the first winemaker in this country that I've met who grows Cabernet Sauvignon. We may be experiencing climate change but I would hardly think we will have summers warm enough to ripen Cab. Sav. grapes. Tell me, how do they perform?'
I feel my confidence ebbing. Mr Spragg derided my Cabernet Sauvignon vines and said he would grub them up, and now Mr Smythe is casting doubt on them.
'I have yet to find out,' I reply in a confident voice that masks my true feelings.
'I hope you don't think I'm presumptuous,' he replies, 'but do you have a bottle of the Cab. Sav. I could purchase? I would be very interested to know what it's like. Even if it's not up to commercial standards, I might be able to detect latent potential lurking within its depths. A good wine is like a good

woman. It often needs coaxing. Sometimes that can be a very long process. But, if the potential exists, the foreplay is worth it.'

I really dislike this man. I want to slap him down and send him on his way with his tail between his legs; but he does offer an entree into the world of wine marketing. I would be a fool to tell him what I think of him and lose all chance of using him to my advantage.

'I'm afraid the previous owners removed all stock before they placed the property on the market. I've endeavoured to find bottles of Abbeydore Wine myself but without success.'

'Strange… very strange … I, too, have searched for Abbeydore wine and been unsuccessful. That can only mean one thing. It was so bad it was unsaleable. They must have poured the lot of it down the drain. In which case, you've got a challenge on your hands, Mrs Pope. Can you succeed where others have failed?'

I give him my most confident smile and say, 'I often do.'

'Well, I will be keen to observe your progress. If you don't, let me know. I may be able to help you. You see, besides writing about wine I've often toyed with the idea of producing it myself: on a small boutique scale, of course. Your five acres would be just the right size for me. If your business fails to turn in a

JESSICA'S VINEYARD

profit and you decide to sell I would be interested in purchasing it. Let me give you my card.'
Reaching into his wallet he produces a business card bearing his name, contact details and the moniker Master of Wines.
I have no intention of selling my vineyard but I take the card from him and store it for possible future use. It could be valuable to have a contact in the wine trade.
With a rather ostentatious bow, Mr Smythe bids farewell and departs leaving me wondering. He is the second person to express a wish to buy my vineyard. When Jason returns from Abergavenny I tell him about my unexpected visitor.
He laughs.
'It's not everyone who receives a visit from a Master of Wine within the first few weeks of purchasing a vineyard. I wonder what he knows that we don't?' he asks.
I shake my head in puzzlement.

JESSICA'S VINEYARD

CHAPTER 5

The days lengthen. Spring extends its green fingers into summer. Blackbirds forage feverishly for worms in the wet earth to feed their ravenous young. Cow parsley adorns the verges on either side of the lane, swaying in the gentle breeze, emitting its own unique fragrance. Honeybees leap from flower to flower sating themselves on the lavish feast prepared for them. Timid dormice quiver with anxiety or excitement and then scuttle for safety into ditches and hedgerows. Blades of grass miraculously change from being merely green to virgin green, verdant green, voluptuous green, green such as has never been seen before. Carpets of summer's bounty are unrolled from the never-ending storehouse of wonders as a salesman might unroll a carpet at the feet of a prospective customer. Dog roses flutter their delicate petals like the eyelashes of a young girl being asked to dance for the first time by a handsome young man.
Summer opens her arms and enfolds both Jason and me in a loving embrace. Smiles abound. We work in shirtsleeves and shorts.

JESSICA'S VINEYARD

We are growing comfortable with each other. We share the tasks around the winery and know, as if by telepathy, what needs to be done before it is put into words.

He is proving an invaluable help. It needs two people to undertake the heavy lifting tasks around the place. I could never manage on my own.

But it's more than that. I enjoy having someone I can bounce my ideas off. Dear old Hegel was right. You need a thesis and an antithesis in order to arrive at a successful synthesis.

Take sulphates.

I am resolutely against adding chemicals to my wine. I want Abbeydore wine to be organic. Jason agrees with me in principle. He says it's a good selling-point. But he's also realistic. He says that the winemakers of Australia discovered that sulphates act as a preservative and prevent spoiling and oxidisation taking place. They also act as protection against bacteria.

And so, do we want to be dogmatically organic or do we want to temper our aspirations and maintain the freshness and flavour of the wine to prolong its shelf life?

Perhaps the reason there is no Abbeydore Wine for sale is because the last owners failed to protect their wine from spoiling. I don't want to make the same mistake.

JESSICA'S VINEYARD

I could have stuck to my organic principles but Jason has made me inclined to play safe and use a small quantity of sulphates to ensure the wine is safely preserved.

The two of us spend most of the day together. Jason appears at seven-thirty each morning for breakfast. He lends a hand with the cooking. He is a dab hand at making omelettes. After we've done the washing-up, we embark upon the day's tasks. Sometimes it's tending the vines and removing unwanted growth and diseased foliage; sometimes it's cleaning the stainless steel equipment in the barn in readiness for the autumn grape harvest; sometimes it's driving into Abergavenny to stock up on provisions; sometimes it's simply relaxing on sunbeds in the backyard.

Jason is working on his tan. He likes to lie on his sunbed wearing just his shorts and soaking up the sun's rays. He has a fine athletic body – broad shoulders, an embryonic six-pack and long legs. He tans easily.

It is while we are having what Jason calls 'a resting day' that we hear the sound of a car approaching the house.

'Who can that possibly be?' I ask.

'Your guess is as good as mine,' he answers cheekily.

'Do you want me to go and find out?'

'Not in your present undressed state. I'll deal with it.'

JESSICA'S VINEYARD

Pulling on my sandals, I round the corner of the house just as a middle-aged man emerges from a sleek Jaguar. He could be a gentleman farmer from his appearance. He wears a tweed jacket and a loosely knotted knitted tie, corduroy trousers and brogue shoes. He advances towards me.
'Mrs Pope, I presume.'
I nod my head.
'Allow me to introduce myself. I'm Cecil Johnson: Councillor Cecil Johnson. I don't believe we've met before.'
We have not - and I'm not sure I particularly want to meet a representative from the County Council. In my experience, County Council officials usually spell trouble. They are obsessed with planning regulations, unauthorised surface rainwater runoff into foul sewers, light pollution, taking children into care and such like. What have I done to warrant a visit from a County Councillor?
When I moved to remote and isolated Abbeydore I thought I would be spared the attention of interfering officialdom. But, it doesn't matter where one goes, it always sniffs one out.
I shake my head to indicate I have no recollection of ever meeting him.
He gives me a smile. It is a pitying smile. He clearly thinks I am the loser for not knowing him.

JESSICA'S VINEYARD

'You must excuse me intruding on your rural
paradise. Is it convenient to talk?'
I think of the sun-bathing he has interrupted and of
the scantily-clad Jason on his sunbed, but I can
hardly use them as excuses for not wishing to talk
with him. I have no desire, however, to invite him
into the house and so I say, 'What about?'
He gives a forced laugh.
'Yes, it must seem strange when an unknown man
appears on your doorstep and wishes to speak with
you. Of course, I try and visit as many of those in my
ward as I can - and not just at election time.'
He laughs at his little joke. I maintain a stony face.
'I wonder if we can go indoors as the thing I wish to
speak about is of a confidential nature.'
'But you haven't told me what it is,' I reply. 'And
anyway, there's no likelihood of anyone overhearing
us here in the depths of the countryside, is there?'
This is clearly not the answer for which he was
hoping. 'Alright, if that is what you prefer.' Then,
taking a deep breath and straightening his back he
says, 'I want to make you an offer for your property.
I know that you recently purchased it at auction for
£350,000 but I am willing to double that and offer
you £700,000 for the site.'
He pauses and looks me in the eye.
I feel an irresistible urge to laugh, but I repress the
urge and merely smile.

JESSICA'S VINEYARD

'It's not for sale,' I say.

'Everyone has their price,' he responds. 'Tell me what you're willing to sell for.'

'It's not for sale,' I repeat.

He frowns.

'I've seen the sale particulars and this place hasn't made a penny for the past five years. You'd be much better accepting a generous offer from me, cutting your losses pocketing your profit and moving to better things: perhaps purchasing a vineyard that does make a profit.'

'Why are you so keen to purchase my vineyard?' I ask.

'Well, certainly not to grow grapes,' he haughtily replies. 'I've no wish to waste time and energy tilling the land. No. I'm interested in your five acres because of its location.'

He looks me in the eye.

'I've been looking for a south-facing plot of land in a secluded location for some time so I can build a house for my wife and myself. We need somewhere far from the madding crowd, so to speak. You see, County Councillors are at the beck and call of every Tom, Dick and Harry. Few people realise how little private life we have. And private life is precious. I need somewhere off the beaten track, away from the pressures and demands of other people, where I can

JESSICA'S VINEYARD

relax and unwind. Your smallholding would be first class. It's just what I'm looking for.'
He gives me a wide smile.
He wants me to feel sorry for him – the poor, overworked, unpaid politician buffeted this way and that by the unremitting demands of his job, unable to escape and find rest. He's playing on my femininity. He thinks I am a sympathetic and understanding woman with a warm heart. He thinks that all he has to do is play gently on my heartstrings and I will roll over and purr. Wrong!
'I'm sorry Mr Johnson, but my property is not for sale.'
He frowns
'I realise that my offer must have come as something of a surprise. If someone appeared on my doorstep and offered me a large sum of money for my house, I would naturally recoil. It's not the sort of thing one expects to happen. Perhaps you need time to think it over. A hundred per cent return on your original capital outlay is not to be sniffed at. It would take years to achieve a similar return from your vines. And think of all the hard work you will have to put in to get anything approaching such a return on your capital investment! My proposal offers you all the rewards with none of the hard work. It's a very attractive offer.

JESSICA'S VINEYARD

'I'm sorry, Mr Johnson, but my property is not for sale.'

He frowns and a streak of exasperation appears on his face.

'May I ask if you have any previous experience of winemaking?'

He is now attempting to undermine me. He probably knows I am a complete novice and this is his way to sway me and make me more receptive to his offer. There is no point in prevaricating.

'I am a complete novice,' I answer with an ear-to-ear smile on my face. 'I have come to Abbeydore on a mission. I am determined to master the art of winemaking and turn this vineyard into one of the best boutique vineyards in England.'

He laughs.

'I applaud your ambition. I wish there was more of your entrepreneurial spirit in this country. It's what we need to get the economy growing and increase the prosperity of the nation. But, I'm sure you don't need me to tell you that 90% of all new start-ups end in failure. I understand that the previous owners of this smallholding were incapable of turning in a profit. The odds are stacked against you. Of course, you're welcome to see if you are more successful than them, but what happens if you're not? You'll be stuck with a smallholding that no one wants and you'll take a heavy financial hit. That's why I urge you to seriously

JESSICA'S VINEYARD

consider my offer. It's a once in a lifetime offer. Something like this is unlikely to come your way again. Let me give you twenty-four hours to think it over and then we'll talk again.

'You're wasting your time, Mr Johnson. My property is not for sale.'

Then, seizing the initiative, I ask, 'Why are you so interested in acquiring my land? There must be hundreds of other south-facing parcels of land in this rural county.'

'Indeed there are – but not in such remote and isolated spots as this. It is privacy and seclusion I seek. I've been unable to find anything that remotely compares to your location. That's why I'm prepared to pay well over the odds to acquire it.'

It is true: his offer is well over the odds – too much so, as far as I am concerned. There is something not quite right about it.

'From my knowledge of local government,' I reply, 'I have always understood there are strict planning regulations as to where one can and cannot build a house. This is an agricultural smallholding and not a brownfield site crying out for development. I think it is highly unlikely you would ever get planning permission to build a house on the site of my vineyard.'

He gives me a pitying smile.

JESSICA'S VINEYARD

'Mrs Pope: that would be perfectly correct if it was you that was applying for planning permission to build a house here; but I am in a somewhat more privileged position. I sit on the County Planning Committee and, although there are restrictions on where new houses can be built, I can pull strings and achieve results where you could not.'
How I hate this man! The more he says the more I loathe him.
'There are wheels within wheels,' he smilingly continues. 'I have no doubt I could secure planning permission if things are gone about in the right way: all of which means that now is your chance to maximise your initial investment. Accept my generous offer whilst it's on the table. No one else will be able to match it. No one else is in my position. But my offer cannot remain on the table for ever. If you categorically refuse it, I will, of course, have to look elsewhere.'
'My property is not for sale,' I reiterate with all the emphasis I can muster.
He makes a herculean effort to contain his frustration. He clearly thinks women are illogical, stubborn and maddening. He feels he has made an unrepeatable offer and yet I have refused it. Frustration is etched all over his face.
'Very well,' he says, regaining his composure with a supreme act of self-will. 'Maybe this has come as a

shock to you. Why don't you have time to think it over? One's natural reaction is to recoil at the unexpected. It is only with the benefit of hindsight that we see the sense in what was offered. I'll let you sleep on it before I get in contact with you again.'
'You're wasting your time, Councillor Johnson,' I tell him. 'I have no wish to sell.'
He grimaces, shakes his head in frustration, turns and retraces his steps back to his gleaming Jaguar.
I stand and watch as he swings his car around and disappears down the lane leaving me highly bemused. When I return to Jason sunbathing in the backyard, I say more to myself than to him. 'There's something very strange going on here.'
He looks up at me from his recumbent position. 'What's strange?' he asks.
'I've had three offers in the past four months from people wishing to purchase this vineyard. Strange! Very strange!'

CHAPTER 6

Life is idyllic. I have never known life so wonderfully stress-free. From the moment I pull back the bedroom curtains to the moment I go to bed at night I experience nothing but joy. There may be terrible things going on in the world for all I know, but I am blissfully unaware of them. I live in my own microcosm with just the birds, the trees, the vines and Jason for company.

I sing to myself as I move around the house. There is something liberating about living so close to the rhythm of nature. The days unfold with unerring regularity and nothing disturbs my peace.

I understand why monks and nuns joined religious communities to escape from the world. I have my very own enclosed community here at Abbeydore. It is my place of peace and tranquillity.

I have my work. I have my dreams. I have all that is necessary for abundant living.

I laugh when I think of the frantic life I used to live! I must have been mad battling with crowds on the underground, racing against the clock to get to the office on time, missing out on meals to meet deadlines, chasing money, shouting into telephones, worried, anxious, exhausted and oblivious to the wonders that were all around me had I just had time to stop and stare.

I have found real contentment and joy by turning my back on the rat race and escaping to the country. This is where true living is to be found. I have never felt happier. This is where I belong.

'You sound like a cat that's just consumed a saucer of cream,' Jason jests as he enters the kitchen for his breakfast and hears me singing to myself.

'Well, what's not to be happy about on such a beautiful summer's morning as this?'

'Yeah! The weather certainly acts as a good barometer of our feelings.'

'But it's not just the weather,' I reply. 'It's the peace and the solitude; the absence of strife and worry. It's living in tune with the rhythm of nature. It's living life as it should be lived.'

He smiles at my enthusiasm. I have no idea what he's thinking.

Does he see me as a pathetic middle-aged woman desperately trying to cling to her lost youth? Or can he understand why I feel and behave as I do? He never betrays his thoughts. He smiles and goes along with whatever I say. He's very easy to live with. He's accepting and easy-going.

He never complains of isolation.

JESSICA'S VINEYARD

Most young men would want to mix with others of their age. But Jason seems perfectly content with his mezzanine room in the barn and sharing the tasks around the house and the vineyard.

'The rhythm of nature unfortunately includes the natural breeding cycle of rabbits,' he laughs. 'We've got real trouble with the vermin at the top of the vineyard. The new Bacchus shoots that we planted last week have been attacked mercilessly by the local rabbit population. Those rabbits are completely out of control. We need to do something before it's too late.'

I read stories of Peter Rabbit and Cottontail Rabbit when I was a small girl and have always thought of rabbits as cuddly adorable creatures; but now I'm a viticulturist my outlook has changed. I realise that rabbits are a real pest. If it's a battle between my vines and rabbits, my vines win.

'What do you suggest?' I ask.

'I know you don't like harming wildlife,' he grins, 'but we've got to be realistic. Unless something is done, the rabbits will destroy all the hard work we've put into the vineyard. Either they go or the grape harvest goes.'

I don't need convincing. I agree that something has to be done – but what?

My unspoken question is answered before I put it into words.

JESSICA'S VINEYARD

'There's nothing for it but to purchase a rifle and some cartridges to cull the pests.'

'But I've never fired a rifle in my life!' I exclaim. 'And as for hitting a rabbit, I think the odds would be heavily weighted in the rabbits' favour. I would never be able to kill a rabbit.'

He laughs.

'You may not be able to do so, but I've had plenty of experience with a rifle. I was reared with a rifle in my hands in Australia. I'll put a stop to the carnage those rabbits are causing in no time at all.'

I consider what he says. There must be more humane ways of catching rabbits. But then, what do you do with them once you've caught them? You either have to kill them or let them go loose. If you let them go loose they breed and produce yet more rabbits. A rifle seems the only solution.

'OK. We'll get a rifle and you can demonstrate your shooting skills.'

He looks intently at me.

'I can't apply for a firearms certificate,' he says. 'I'm only twenty and a foreign national. I'd never get a licence. You'll have to apply for it. The police won't raise objections to a woman of your age, living in the country, wanting to own a rifle to control vermin.'

I'm not sure I like the phrase 'a woman of your age' but I know what he means. Women of my age are not in the habit of going around the countryside

JESSICA'S VINEYARD

blowing the brains out of other people. I should be considered a safe pair of hands.

'OK. I'll deal with the paperwork but you must advise me what to buy - and you'll have to be the person who uses it.'

'It's a winning partnership,' he replies with his wide captivating smile.

Our age difference means we should have a mother and son relationship, but it doesn't feel like that. I am never conscious of the twenty years that separate us. We have grown comfortable with each another and the age difference has ceased to exist. Jason keeps me feeling young. His openness and willingness to embrace new challenges rubs off on me. I've become more daring and carefree.

He says I am always laughing.

It is true. My former woes are behind me and I am experiencing a new sort of living. I am deeply happy. And when one is happy, the natural thing to do is to laugh.

My laughter may also be due to Jason. Whenever he sees me looking at him, he raises his adorable eyebrows and gives me a smile. My face must mirror and reflect his youthful smile.

I sometimes see him staring at me intently. I would love to know what is passing through his mind. Am I an enigma?

JESSICA'S VINEYARD

Does he struggle to understand why a woman like me should want to bury herself in this hidden corner of Herefordshire?

Has he noticed the first wisps of grey hair appearing at my temples? I really must do something about them the next time I go into Abergavenny.

Does he see the pains of the past etched on my face or has my new-found happiness erased them?

Does he wonder what I was like when I was his age? I like to think I was attractive. I never had difficulty attracting boys' attention. Alan claimed he had to fight off the competition in order to claim me as his wife.

I sigh. If only he had failed, things might not have turned out as badly as they did.

His relentless persistence to drive others away was the same persistence that spelled disaster for our marriage. He brooked no competition. He was an egotist. He was so used to getting his own way that he became intolerable to live with.

If only I had been more astute when I was Jason's age I might have seen through him and saved myself the heartache and misery that followed.

But then, I think to myself, if things had not turned out the way they did, I would not be here in the beautiful Golden Valley with Jason.

Jason possesses the qualities Alan lacked. He is easy-going. He does not worry about money or

JESSICA'S VINEYARD

possessions. He enjoys life. He laughs and smiles. He carries none of life's baggage on his back. He is clever with his hands and no slouch when it comes to solving problems around the vineyard. Jason is everything that Alan was not - and I could not be happier. My partnership with Jason is infinitely more satisfying than the one I shared with Alan.

*

We are now the owners of a 35mm Bolt Action Rifle. It was not easy to obtain. Jason insisted it was the correct rifle we required. I had to go through a complicated form-filling process, obtaining a passport photograph from the local photographer in Abergavenny, furnishing a good character reference from my former employer and being interviewed by the local constabulary.

I think the local bobby was somewhat bemused that a single woman, with no shooting experience, should want to own a 35mm Bolt Action Rifle; but Jason had primed me what to say. He told me to tell the policeman there were muntjac deer invading the vineyard; that way, he said, I would be more likely to convince the police I needed such a weapon.

Well, it worked. I duly obtained a firearms licence. It permits Jessica Pope to own and use a 35mm Bolt Action Rifle. I haven't the slightest idea how to use it but Jason says he will take care of that side of things.

JESSICA'S VINEYARD

He stores it in his attic room. Every so often, when I am undertaking work around the buildings, I hear the retort of the gun as he eliminates another rabbit.
It is while he is on one of his shooting expeditions that I have an unexpected visitor.
No one is more surprised or shocked than me to see Alan emerging from his car and striding towards the farmhouse. Of all the people in the world, he is the last person I expected to see – or want to see!
I feel my blood pressure rising. Why has he sought me out? Why is he invading my idyllic paradise? Why is he here to remind me of the past, to stir up painful memories and contaminate my place of sanctuary? What right has he to come here disturbing my peace? I came to Abbeydore to escape from him; and now, like some malign spectre, he has re-appeared.
I wanted a clean break. I deliberately concealed my new address and all contact details so he would be unable to trace me. I do not want to see him. And yet, here he is striding purposefully towards my front door to destroy my peace.
He looks just as he always did: resolute, sure of himself, confident and assertive. How I loathe him!
Rat-a-tat-tat hammers the knocker.
It is the knock of a man who is not to be thwarted. The sound pierces my soul. It is the sound of nails being driven into a coffin. It is the retort of a

JESSICA'S VINEYARD

machinegun snuffing out life. It is the hammer blows of fate.

I have no intention of allowing him to cross the threshold and enter my personal space and so I exit the back door and walk around the house to confront him sideways on.

He sees me out of the corner of his eye and spins around to face me.

His face is set in a granite stare. His thin lips stretch tight in a cruel line. His blue-grey eyes bore into me. The scowl lines on either side of his nose look more pronounced than ever.

Not a word is spoken. We stare at each other. It is not a loving look. There is no smile of recognition playing around the corners of his mouth. There is no joy at seeing someone he has not seen for a long time. It is a stare devoid of all warmth.

His eyes scan me from head to foot. He is weighing me in the balance and forming an opinion.

He has an opinion on everything and everyone: usually it is a superficial opinion. An opinion based on outward appearances, prejudices and his own blinkered outlook on life. He maintains a silent gaze for what seems like eternity.

I have no intention of being the first to speak. I did not invite him here. I resent his intrusion into my sacred space. There is no welcoming hospitality for him here.

JESSICA'S VINEYARD

He eventually breaks the silence.
'Quite the country-loving girl, I see.'
He has the hardest job to utter the words whilst masking his contempt.
I hold my tongue. He will have more to say. He always has.
'You've taken some finding, but at last I've tracked you down. You couldn't have found a more out-of-the-way place if you'd tried.'
I am not interested in knowing how he has tracked me down. I just want him gone.
'Why are you here?' I demand.
'That's not a very friendly greeting,' he replies. 'We were married for nearly twenty years. I presume that gives me some justification for being here.'
'I told you when we parted that I never wanted to see you again,' I snap. 'Don't you understand? I want a clean break so I can re-start my life. The last thing I want is for you to dog me and intrude upon my new life.'
'It doesn't seem such a great new life to me,' he says in the superior voice he uses for those he considers his inferiors. 'An isolated dwelling in the middle of nowhere, with no transport links, retail outlets, centres of entertainment or even a local pub. I noted that *The Neville Arms* looks as if it's been shut for years.'

JESSICA'S VINEYARD

'Perhaps I no longer need any of those things to be happy.'
'There's no way anyone could be happy in a backwater like this,' he retorts. 'It's just escapism. You're running away from reality and trying to create a rural utopia that's as outdated as the parish pump or an outside privy.'
Then, with a rare flash of humour, he says, 'I suppose you're going to tell me you've got an outside privy.'
'I have everything I need to make me happy,'
'You won't be happy when the Council Tax demand comes through the letterbox – or the water rates, or the electricity bill or the car insurance or road tax or the broadband bill – assuming you can get broadband in this back-of-beyond place. Its then that reality will hit you and you'll realise you have to work in order to live. You can't just hide away and turn your back on the world.'
He treats me as though I were a little child. He assumes I have failed to think things through. He thinks that, because I'm a woman, I'm impractical. He thinks I need him to lecture me on the basics of life. Well, I don't.
'I am quite capable of standing on my own two feet and looking after myself,' I tell him.
He gives a sneering laugh.
'The trouble with you was that you were never practical. You lived in a fantasy world. Your head was

JESSICA'S VINEYARD

always full of unrealistic dreams. You were never anchored in reality. It was always me that had to keep you grounded. We would have been bankrupt if I had let you have your head and follow your dreams. Life isn't like that. You have to keep your feet firmly planted on the ground. It's all very well having aspirations. We all have those. But they've got to be achievable aspirations.'

'Thank you for the lecture,' I reply with a sigh. 'Unfortunately, your aspirations and mine were never the same. You wanted to make headway at work, constantly exchange the car for a new one, make more money, extend the house and so on. Those weren't my aspirations. I wanted to do something worthwhile with my life. I wanted to do something tactile. I wanted others to derive pleasure and enjoyment from my work. I wanted to enrich the lives of others rather than merely line my own pocket. But you could never see that. You thought it was all pie in the sky. And that's why I had to get away. I needed to break free. I needed to put my aspirations to the test if I was to discover real happiness.'

'Well, there's not much chance of doing that in this god-forsaken hole.'

'That's where you're wrong. I have everything I need here in order to succeed. I have five acres of land and I intend making beautiful wine. It will be my wine:

JESSICA'S VINEYARD

Jessica's wine. It will bring a smile to the face of others. It will be raised in toasts at anniversary meals, weddings and christenings, Christmas parties and dinner parties. My wine will produce joy and happiness in the lives of others.'

'As impractical as ever!' is his damning verdict. 'What do you know about wine production? It's a scientific process. Men spend years training and refining their skills in order to make good wine. What do you know about wine-making? Absolutely nothing! You're on a loser. You may as well admit defeat now rather than waste hours and hours of effort producing something that is undrinkable and unsaleable.'

How I would like to hit him! Why does he always try to put me down? His denunciation is intended to deflate me. He wants me to think I was better off with him than struggling to make a living here.

Well, he's wrong! Rather than deflate me, his words have the opposite effect. I am even more determined to succeed. I'll show him. I'll prove that my airy-fairy dreams are capable of being transformed into reality. Abbeydore Winery will be a success.

'The proof of the pudding is in the eating,' I reply with Delphic mystery. 'We must wait and see what I am capable of producing.'

Just as he is about to give me another salvo from his portfolio of life experience, Jason appears around the corner of the house with the rifle under one arm and

JESSICA'S VINEYARD

a brace of dead rabbits on the other. He looks taken aback.

'Sorry to intrude,' he says. 'I didn't realise you had a visitor.'

I give him a radiant smile. He could not have appeared at a more opportune moment. I was wondering how I could get rid of Alan and now, as if in answer to prayer, Jason has arrived to terminate the unwanted tête-à-tête.

'You're not intruding,' I smile. 'Come and meet Alan. Alan was my former husband. He has appeared quite unexpectedly but is just about to leave.'

Jason advances towards Alan to shake his hand before realising he's holding a brace of rabbits.

'Oh, excuse the appendages,' he laughs. 'I've just been reducing the rabbit population.'

'And who might you be?' demands Alan with a concentrated frown and a none-too-friendly tone in his voice.

But before Jason can reply, I say, 'This is Jason, my business partner. We manage Abbeydore Wineries between us.'

Alan gives Jason his most withering look.

'I see now why you're so happy in this backwater. You have your own little gigolo to keep you company.'

I am filled with indignation.

JESSICA'S VINEYARD

'How dare you!' I shout. 'Jason is a gap-year student and he's assisting me at the winery before he goes to university.'

'No doubt,' replies my infuriating ex-husband. 'Two of you holed up in an out-of-the-way place like this must have lots of fun together.'

'I think it's time you left,' I say to him.

He gives me a withering smile.

'I guess three's a crowd,' he says, as he prepares to leave. But he cannot resist one final salvo before he goes.

'Be careful, young man,' he directs at Jason. 'This woman is set for a fall; and when that happens, there's no saying what the fallout will be.'

And with that he turns on his heel and strides to his car.

Jason and I stand in silence, side by side, and watch him go.

'Well, what do you make of that?' he asks.

'He has no right to come here disturbing my peace,' I say, fighting back my tears. 'Everything was going so well until he appeared. And then, he comes out of the blue and undermines my confidence.'

I am unable to hold back my tears. I sob inconsolably.

An arm enfolds me. I feel myself drawn gently across the broad chest of the man standing beside me. I hear the words 'Don't cry'. The words are soft and

JESSICA'S VINEYARD

comforting. They are words of compassion and empathy. They sound like words of love.
I become aware of the rifle sandwiched between us and emit a weak laugh.
'This is a dangerous position to be in,' I say in an attempt to regain my composure. 'That gun could go off at any moment and put an end to all my troubles.'
He looks into my eyes and says, 'Don't upset yourself. I'll make sure no harm comes to you.'
He is so kind and trusting. A wave of passion surges through me. It is as sudden as it is unexpected. I have not felt like this for years. I pride myself on being a rational person. I am usually guided by my brain rather than my heart. I managed to keep a firm grip on my emotions throughout the acrimonious divorce proceedings, but now, all the pent-up emotions within me swell to the surface. I can no longer maintain my detached and resolute exterior. Suddenly the floodgates are open. The barren desert of my soul is flooded with warmth and light. Streams flow in the desert. The parched landscape is revived after years of drought. New shoots emerge. Love flows through my veins.
I reach for his head and draw it to mine. I place my lips on his and kiss them.
He does not resist. I hear a dull thump as the brace of rabbits and rifle fall to the ground.

JESSICA'S VINEYARD

He puts his arms around me and we enfold each other in a long passionate embrace. His lips are soft. So is his skin. His eyes are closed as we bend and sway to the music of love. It is a moment of exquisite beauty. This is what has been lacking from my life for so long.

Who would have thought that I would find love in the depths of the Herefordshire countryside? Who would think that such a fine, good-looking boy would walk into my life and, in a matter of weeks, transform my life?

The loving kiss is the outward expression of the happiness Jason has brought into my life since he first appeared so unexpectedly all those weeks ago. I revel in his company. I adore his winning smile. I love his Australian accent. I am in awe of his practical skills. I relish having him around. He is so good for me.

There may be a twenty-year age gap between us but I am unaware of it. Either he is more mature than his years or else I have regressed and become a twenty-year-old girl again. Whatever the psychology, the age-gap makes no difference. I know I love him and, judging by the passion of his kiss, he must love me.

I wanted to escape from the world when I purchased Abbeydore Winery; but I have no calling to be a celibate nun. The Cistercian monks that lived at Dore Abbey may have been happy living without members of the opposite sex, but I am not of that ilk. I need to be loved. I need to be valued and affirmed. Alan was incapable of doing either of those for me. But Jason is different. He looks up to me. He admires my free spirit. He appreciates my desire to turn dreams into reality. He must sense in me the idealism of youth. I am not willing to kowtow to a dominant partner. I am a woman who wants to embrace the unknown and run with it.

The twenty-year age-gap is no impediment to a loving relationship. It is enriching. We bring different perspectives to bear – he, the unsullied enthusiasm of youth, and I the experience of middle-age. It is a winning combination. Already we have transformed Abbeydore Winery into a get-up-and-go business poised to maximise wine production and ambitious to produce the very best wine we can.

I cannot possibly do this on my own. I need Jason's help. I need him by my side. I need to bounce ideas off him and to turn to him for help and support if things go wrong.

He is proving adept at supporting me. His ready shoulder and enfolding arms speak more than a thousand words. His strong embrace and gentle words communicate protection and safety. His rapturous kiss speaks of love.

Our lips eventually part and we gaze into each other's eyes.

JESSICA'S VINEYARD

I am suddenly overcome by embarrassment.
'I shouldn't have done that,' I stammer.
'Why ever not?' he asks in astonishment.
'Because I'm taking advantage of you.'
'Nonsense,' he replies. 'I'm a big boy and quite capable of taking care of myself.'
'But you came here to help at the winery. You didn't come here to be seduced by a middle-aged woman.'
He laughs. He has the most infectious laugh. It's a laugh like a sun-filled day in June. It's a laugh that makes sunflowers smile. It's a laugh that causes the corn to ripple and wave in the fields.
'Why are you always referring to yourself as a middle-aged woman?' he asks. 'I never look upon you in that way. You are simply Jessica – the kindest, most genuine person I've ever met.'
Then after a moment's pause, he adds, 'Perhaps it's me who has seduced you. After all, you were here on your own before I intruded on your privacy. I am the interloper.'
I smile at him.
'Thank you for intruding,' I whisper.
I then add, 'I thought I would be happy with my own company here, but I was wrong. I am not made to live the life of a solitary hermit. I need to be loved. You have stepped into my life so unexpectedly. I will always be grateful for that.'

JESSICA'S VINEYARD

That night, Jason abandons his attic room in the barn and shares my bed.

JESSICA'S VINEYARD

CHAPTER 7

I may have felt happy in the past, but my happiness is now of an entirely different order. I am in love. I share the beauties of Abbeydore with someone else. I no longer have a self-centred happiness but a shared happiness. I am not striving to please myself: I want to please Jason as well.

I sometimes think we are like a couple of lovesick adolescents in danger of regressing into childhood. Yesterday I was hosing down the Land Rover when Jason crept up behind me and tickled my ribs. I swung around and soaked him with the hosepipe. This then developed into a play-fight to see who could get their hands on the hosepipe. We both got soaked in the process.

'You beast!' I cried out. 'Just look at me! I'm soaked to the skin.'

'You look as if you've emerged from the depths of the ocean,' he laughed. 'My very own mermaid!'

'You'd better watch out,' I shouted, 'Mermaids lure unwitting sailors to their destruction.'

JESSICA'S VINEYARD

'This one has travelled halfway around the world and has no intention of being lured to destruction by a Herefordshire mermaid.'
And with that he aims the hosepipe at me and gives me another dousing.
I cannot help noticing a sadistic glint in his eye.
'You beast! I'll catch my death of cold!'
My matted hair sticks to my face and my shirt clings to my body like a cold compress. I must look like a drowned rat. My efforts to make myself look young have vanished and I am exposed for what I really am: a forty-year-old woman on the inevitable downward slope to old age. I suddenly feel very dejected.
Jason sees the transformation come over me. He drops the hosepipe and moves quickly towards me, embracing me in a cold and wet hug.
'I'm sorry,' he whispers. 'I shouldn't have done that. It was just a bit of fun – but it went too far. Come. Let's go inside and clean up.'
The two of us shower together.
This time, the water is hot and the playing is of an entirely different nature. We frolic and soap each other in the close confines of a shower designed for only one. We do so to the accompaniment of squeals and laughter.
Alan and I never did anything like this.

JESSICA'S VINEYARD

Jason is growing in confidence. Our new relationship has given him permission to assert himself.

He particularly enjoys going on treks with his rifle. It's not something I wish to do, even if he invited me to join him. I would derive no pleasure seeing living creatures killed. But he appears to enjoy putting his shooting skills to the test and returning home with game destined for the casserole pot.

Whilst he is out, I busy myself around the house. I enjoy preparing meals for the two of us. It so much more satisfying sharing a meal with someone else than eating on one's own. It takes time to prepare a good meal. When I was working in the city, most of our meals consisted of convenience food. I now have plenty of time to prepare more ambitious meals.

I like to impress Jason with my culinary skills. It is said that the way to a man's heart is through his stomach – not that Jason has much of a stomach. He is as lean as a garden rake. But he does enjoy fine dining at the end of a day's work.

We eat by candlelight. We have yet to produce our own wine to accompany our gourmet fine dining but I dream of the day when we will sit together and raise a glass of my very own vintage to celebrate our successful partnership.

It is while I am chopping onions and garlic for a sauce to accompany Rabbit Wellington that I see a shadow pass across the kitchen window. Before I can make out who it is, there is a knock on the back door.

I may have said before that we have very few visitors at Abbeydore Winery and so this is a rare occurrence. I open the door and find Mr Spragg on the doorstep. I have not seen him since I first moved to Abbeydore. He may be my neighbour, but our paths never cross. This is not surprising, really. Jason and I keep ourselves very much to ourselves. We have no need to socialise. So long as we have each other we do not need anyone else.

My neighbour looks as gaunt and unfriendly as ever; but I am not intimidated by him. I am happy. I am very happy, and so I give him a big smile.

'Mr Spragg: how nice to see you. Our paths don't seem to have crossed since I moved here. Do come inside and I'll make a pot of coffee.'

I motion for him to enter my kitchen, which he does without a word.

'Do have a seat,' I say, indicating one of the chairs at the kitchen table.

He sits and I wait for him to speak. He must have a reason for visiting me.

His eyes rove around my kitchen. He is taking everything in, no doubt to inform his wife on his return.

JESSICA'S VINEYARD

He is a taciturn man. His years of working on the land have made his skin leathery. It is not the smooth leather of a horse saddle or a briefcase but the wrinkled leather of a pickled walnut. His eyes peer from under shaggy eyebrows. His mouth has a downward trajectory and his forehead resembles a harrowed field.
'I came to see if you'd had second thoughts about selling,' he says in a deep cavernous voice.
I almost laugh.
His voice is like a voice from the underworld seeking to suck me down into its miry depths. His words are risible, but I manage to hold back my involuntary laughter.
'What makes you think I might have changed my mind?' I ask.
He eyes me suspiciously. I sense malevolence. There is a long pause before he says, 'Maybe the romance has worn off and you find you don't like living in the country. It's not to everyone's taste – especially if they're townies and not used to country ways.'
I bestow one of my most generous smiles upon him.
'Have no fear, Mr Spragg. I'm enjoying every moment of country living'.
He gives me a hostile stare before asking, 'Even if the land hasn't made a penny since you bought it?'
'One hardly expects a vineyard to yield revenue until after the harvest has been gathered in and the wine

fermented and bottled. Surely you know that, Mr Spragg.'

He is not to be deflected.

'Grapes don't grow themselves. You have to know what you're doing.'

'Quite so,'

And then, wishing to change the course of the conversation I ask, 'How are your vines performing, Mr Spragg?'

There is a long pause. It seems he is not going to answer.

Perhaps he regards my question as a gross intrusion into his business activities. Perhaps he feels bound by some unspoken protocol that forbids the sharing of sensitive business information with competitors. Perhaps he is searching for an answer that is truthful and yet hides the true condition of his business.

I turn to make the coffee whilst he considers his answer.

It is only when I turn to face him again and raise my quizzical eyebrows that he says, 'My vines are newly planted. They're not ready for commercial wine production.'

'Ah!' I exclaim, 'And so your vineyard will not make a penny this year … and maybe not next year … or even the year after. Is that why you're so keen to get your hands on my vineyard?'

JESSICA'S VINEYARD

If looks could kill, a murder would have occurred in the kitchen of Abbeydore Winery.
I have rarely seen such a murderous look in someone's eyes.
'I have other forms of income,' he replies gruffly. 'I'm not dependent on grapes like you. I can survive the lean years.'
Then, with a rare burst of eloquence, he adds, 'You've put all your eggs into one basket. If your harvest fails, you fail. The Simpsons couldn't make a living out of it and you won't.'
'If you're financially secure,' I reply, 'I don't see why you need to acquire my land.
He gives me a masculine stare. It's a stare I've seen so often. It says must I really spell this out to you? Are you really such a dense woman that you can't see the logic in my offer? Have I got to spend my time explaining how the world of commerce operates?
'Miss Pope,' he begins, clearly thinking I am an unmarried woman. 'You do not appear to appreciate economies of scale. If two people grow grapes side by side they need two tractors, two wine presses, two sets of storage vessels, two bottling machines and two marketing strategies; whereas, if all the grapes are grown by one person it only needs one tractor, one wine press, one set of storage vessels, one bottling machine and one marketing strategy. Moreover, it's easier to obtain retail outlets for a large quantity of

wine than for a small amount. Do I make myself clear?'

'Absolutely,' I answer. 'But perhaps I'm not interested in turning in a big profit. Perhaps I've come to Abbeydore to produce a boutique wine that won't make me rich but will enable me to enjoy a simple lifestyle in beautiful surroundings.'

He gives me a withering glance. I probably confirm all he has ever thought about women. They are unrealistic, irrational and impossible to deal with.

I smile and ask, 'Do you take sugar in your coffee?'

He gives a dismissive shake of his head.

I do not want to be at loggerheads with my neighbour and so I adopt a conciliatory approach. 'Should I change my mind,' I add, 'I'll give you first option on buying my land.'

He sniffs. He then changes the conversation by asking, 'Did you have a visit from that Mr High and Mighty fella in the blue BMW the other week?'

My sales skills immediately kick in and, rather than answer his question, I ask, 'Why? Did you?'

'He was looking for you, he said. He wanted to buy some Abbeydore wine. I told him he'd be lucky. No wine's been produced at Abbeydore Winery for years. I told him I've recently planted three acres of vines but he didn't seem interested. It was Abbeydore Wine he wanted. Did he find you?'

'He did. He knows a thing or two about wines and we had quite an interesting conversation.'

'I don't like strangers snooping around here. They're usually up to no good. Why's he interested in Abbeydore wine?'

I have no intention of telling him of Mr Smythe's credentials or his connections with the wine trade.

'Perhaps he's clairvoyant,' I answer, 'and foresees great wine flowing from my vineyard in the future. In which case, I will certainly not be putting my land back on the market.'

'Great wine, be damned!' retorts my not-very-friendly neighbour. 'Them Cabernet Sauvignon vines will never fruit in a month of Sundays. The English climate isn't designed for them as anyone with any sense will tell you.'

'We seem to have had this conversation before, Mr Spragg,' I reply somewhat wearily. 'The rootstocks are over a hundred years old. They must have fruited in the past, and fruited well, in order to have remained all this time; otherwise they would have been grubbed up and thrown into the fire.'

'That's exactly what I'll do when I get my hands on them.'

'If you get your hands on them, Mr Spragg,' I reply, with the emphasis on the word 'if'.

'You'll soon see you're wasting your time here,' he says as he drains the last dregs of coffee from the mug in his hands. 'The sensible thing to do is to cut your losses. Sell to me now and you won't regret it. I'll match what you paid for it at auction Take my offer while it's on the table. It's a take-it-or-leave-it offer. A man can't be fairer than that. You'll never get another offer like it. Take it while you can.'

'I'm very sorry, Mr Spragg, but my smallholding is not for sale – not now, not ever.'

He pushes his chair back and rises to his full stature. It is only then that I realise how much taller he is than me. He could easily overpower me if he wished. A tremor of fear runs through my body. I wish Jason was here.

His unblinking eyes bore deep into my soul.

'Very well,' he says through clenched teeth. 'If that's the way you want to play it, so be it. But I'll tell you this for nothing. You've made a big mistake. I usually get what I want, if not my fair means then by foul. You'll live to regret that you opposed Wilfred Spragg.'

And with those menacing words he moves towards the door.

But he has not finished.

'And tell that lad of yours to keep off my land. If I see him on my land with that rifle of his I'll treat him as a dog worrying sheep. He may have an assault rifle, but I've got one just as powerful and, believe you me, I'm not averse to using it.'

JESSICA'S VINEYARD

With that he exits the kitchen without bothering to close the door behind him.
I clutch the kitchen work surface.
I am quite shaken.
I moved to the country to escape confrontation and angst and now it has invaded my very home. What have I done to antagonise my neighbour? I feel very vulnerable. I wish Jason had been here. Wilfred Spragg would not have been so belligerent if there had been another man in the house. I fight back my tears.
I have to wait more than two hours before Jason returns. He holds a brace of pheasants in one hand and the rifle under his other arm.
'Look what I've bagged,' he proudly declares. 'I didn't know there were pheasants in this part of the world. I'll hang them in the barn and allow them to mature and then I'll pluck and gut them and we can have Pheasant Veronique.'
I laugh at his boyish enthusiasm.
'What on earth is Pheasant Veronique?'
'I don't know,' he replies jauntily. 'I've just made it up. But I bet you'll work wonders and produce a feast fit for a king.'
'I see that now you have royal aspirations.'
'And I elevate you to the position of my queen.'
We both laugh and hug each other.
I suddenly feel much safer with Jason around.

JESSICA'S VINEYARD

'I hope you didn't shoot those pheasants on Farmer Spragg's land,' I ask with a worried look on my face.
'Does it matter where I shot them?' he asks.
'Well, yes, it does. I had an unexpected visit from Mr Spragg whilst you were away and he's none too pleased with you trespassing on his land. He threatens to shoot you if he catches you doing it again.'
Jason emits a great laugh.
'It's just like the Australian outback here!' he roars. 'Shoot or be shot.'
I don't share his light-hearted humour.
'I'm not joking,' I tell him. 'Mr Spragg is not a happy man. He dislikes me and wants to see the back of me. There's no saying what he might do.'
'Now don't go worrying your head about him,' replies Jason with a serious look on his face. 'He's just sore he didn't get your vineyard at the auction and he's envious of you. He thinks you're going to show him up. You'll be making beautiful Abbeydore wine whilst his attempts come to nothing. You've nothing to worry about. Put him out of your mind. And don't worry about me. I'm quite capable of looking after myself.'
He gives me one of his big reassuring smiles.
There is something very reassuring about having Jason around. I don't know how I would cope without him,

CHAPTER 8

Breakfasts get later. Neither of us is in a hurry to embark upon a new day. We much prefer remaining in bed together.
There are different degrees of happiness. There is the happiness that comes from finding a lost object, perhaps a piece of jewellery or a misplaced book. There is the happiness that comes from stumbling unexpectedly upon a beautiful landscape or a glorious sunset. There is the happiness that comes from meeting someone one has not seen for a long time. But none of these forms of happiness compare to the happiness I am experiencing at present. My happiness is the summation of all other forms of happiness. I have discovered what I have been searching for throughout my life – a person I can truly love. I have discovered a thing of rare beauty – a young man who is handsome, intelligent and loving. I have met the person who has been missing from my life until now. All other forms of happiness are subsumed in my present all-enveloping happiness, which knows no bounds.

JESSICA'S VINEYARD

It is ten o'clock before we've cleared away the breakfast things and are ready to embark upon a new day.
The vines are producing fruiting shoots from their gnarled and twisted laterals and it is time to prune and ensure that each lateral is securely fastened to the retaining wires. It's a big job and will occupy many days.
I have assembled a packed lunch to take to the vineyard so we don't have to break off from the task at midday. I imagine agricultural labourers doing this in the past and I like to maintain rural customs.
'You have the most fanciful notions,' smiles Jason shaking his head in disbelief.
'No I don't. I just like to continue country customs. It's no use moving to the country and then not following the country way of life. It's the customs and practices of the countryside that give it its distinctive character. They make it a special place. They make it different from elsewhere. I'm determined to preserve as many country traditions as possible.'
'Well I hope that doesn't involve straining grapes through old pairs of stockings or stuffing rag into the neck of wine bottles.'
He is being deliberately facetious.
'I said I wanted to preserve country customs: I didn't say I wanted to return to the Middle Ages. The

JESSICA'S VINEYARD

monks of Dore Abbey may have resorted to crude methods of winemaking – although I doubt if they had access to ladies' stockings – but I intend using the very latest scientific know-how when it comes to wine production.'

'That's good to hear – even if it means we've got to have lunch sitting on the hard ground under a tree in order to maintain your country customs.'

I laugh as I swing the Land Rover through the gateway and into the vineyard. But my laughter is abruptly cut short.

'Holy cow!' shouts Jason. 'What's been going on here?'

The two of us freeze in our seats. We stare in speechless horror at the sight before us. It is as unexpected as it is horrifying. The wires supporting the vines have been attacked mercilessly. They have been cut. Some wires lie on the ground like felled soldiers on a battlefield. Some hang limply from the posts like downcast victims of a firing squad. Some curl like broken springs from a clockmaker's workshop. Some coil around vines like suffocating tendrils. Some straddle aisles like saboteurs' trip wires.

The beautiful and peaceful Abbeydore Vineyard has been transformed into a crime scene.

'Who on earth has done this?' yells Jason.

JESSICA'S VINEYARD

I am too numb to reply. All my hopes and dreams are pinned on this five acre vineyard. This is where I hope to find fulfilment. This is my new life. It lies in tatters. The serpent has entered my Garden of Eden and done its worst. An unimaginable malignant wickedness has invaded my paradise. My hopes and dreams are in ruins. Life is no longer good. Evil stalks the land. It has sought me out and discovered me even in this remote location.

'Who on earth has done this?' screams Jason for a second time, although this time his voice is more bewilderment than rage.

Get a grip, I say to myself. I must not become overwhelmed by feelings of inadequacy and despair. You're a sensible woman, Jessica. You've dealt with setbacks and difficulties in the past. You can cope with this. After all, it's only a few strands of wire that have been cut. It's not as though your home has been burnt down or you've suffered a life-changing injury. And you're not alone. You don't have to deal with this alone. You have Jason to help you. He is sitting beside you. The two of us can overcome this setback.

I eventually find words. They are hollow words devoid of all emotion. They fall from my lips like an undertaker's salutation.

'I don't know,' I whisper, 'but somebody's got a grudge against me.'

'Clearly,' he answers. 'But who?'

JESSICA'S VINEYARD

A picture of Mr Spragg invades my consciousness. He was none too friendly when he visited me recently. He didn't take kindly to my refusal to part with Abbeydore Vineyard.
But is he so envious of me that he would resort to this? Surely not! Unless it's part of his plan to make me sell up.
'Is it that bastard who wants to get his hands on your vineyard?' asks Jason.
There is real anger in his voice.
'If it's him, he'll find he's crossed the wrong person,' he continues.
'We mustn't go jumping to conclusions,' I reply, seeking to lower the emotional temperature and bring some logic to bear on the situation. 'It could be any one of a number of people.'
'Like who?'
I inhale and take a deep breath. It pains me to say my next words but I cannot escape their possible truth.
'It might be Alan.'
'What? Your ex-husband?'
I hang my head abjectly. 'He clearly doesn't want to see me succeed. He poured cold water on my winemaking plans. He might well do something like this to ensure my business fails and show that he's right. He'd then have the satisfaction of saying, 'See I told you so'.'
'What a bummer!'

JESSICA'S VINEYARD

But my natural sense of justice finds it difficult to believe it is Alan.
Alan may be power-driven and single-minded but I have never known him stoop to criminality. Cutting wires in a vineyard is a criminal act. Surely he wouldn't resort to such underhand behaviour?
'Don't let's be too damning,' I reply with the faint glimmer of a smile at the corners of my mouth. 'It would be very out of character for Alan to behave in this way.'
'If it's not him, who else could it be?' demands Jason.
I shake my head.
'I know so few people here.'
My words sound lame, but they are true. I have made no attempt to cultivate friends or acquaintances. My entire focus has been to get away from people. I came to this isolated place to sever all ties with those I previously knew. I wanted to be alone. I wanted to be undisturbed. I wanted to be left to live life without interference or disruption. I came here to find peace. But even here, in this earthly paradise, there is no peace. It is as if I am pursued by some mythical beast whose sulphurous breath is seeking to choke me. Have the fiends of Canary Wharf discovered my hideaway? Have they sharpened their claws and come after me. Have those I outmanoeuvred in the business world tracked me down and come to exert their revenge? Might pinstripe-suited men, who

shrugged and pasted a whimsical smile on their faces when they discovered they had been outsmarted, have returned with fangs bared and talons sharpened to claim their prey. Have the infinite resources of technology been harvested to discover my whereabouts?

An image of Henry Jackson-Jones comes into my mind. He was really sore when I pipped him to the post and secured the contract we were both after. I don't think I've ever seen a man so angry. He railed at me. He accused me of the most despicable things. He claimed I had resorted to bribery and supplying sexual favours in order to secure the contract. He was heinous. He made all sorts of threats. At the time they were very disturbing but, with the passing of time, nothing came of his threats and life continued as before.

But perhaps his hatred of me has continued and he has discovered my whereabouts.

I cannot escape. Even here in remotest Herefordshire I have been tracked down and he has launched a merciless campaign to annihilate me.

'Any idea who it could be?'

Jason's words reach me from across the universe.

Any idea who it could be?

Yes, of course. It could be anyone of a dozen men I out-manoeuvred in my previous existence. I cannot remember them all. Henry Jackson-Jones is just one of many. They merge into anonymous players on a chessboard, moving this way and that in the hope of pulling off a deal only to hear me whispering 'Checkmate'. Anyone of a coterie of city businessmen could hold a grudge against me and be seeking revenge.

Jason is staring at me with a worried look on his face. 'Are you alright?' he asks.

I emerge from my nightmare and give him a wan smile.

'I'm OK,' I lie.

Taking a deep breath I say, 'I was just thinking of those I crossed in the business world before I came to Abbeydore. There must be many who hold a grudge against me. There was one man in particular: Henry Jackson-Jones. He took a particular dislike to me. I used to shrug off such hostility. I put his attitude down to sour grapes. He'll get over it I used to say to myself. Well, perhaps he hasn't. Perhaps his resentment has been festering and now he's out to get revenge. This could be the past catching up with me.'

'Oh come off it!' exclaims Jason. 'Do you honestly think that city types from London would come all this way to rural Herefordshire in the dead of night to cut wires in a vineyard? Get real!'

He's right, of course. Deep-seated psychological guilt has a way of intruding in the most irrational ways.

JESSICA'S VINEYARD

Whatever commercial dealings I had with others are now a thing of the past.

I frown and attempt to think logically.

Perhaps this is not an act of revenge but a strategic act.

'It must be someone who wants to drive me away from here. It must be someone who thinks that, if they make my life unbearable, I will move away. It must be someone who wants to get their hands on this vineyard.'

It is then that I recall the unexpected visit of Montague Smythe. He was interested in acquiring Abbeydore Vineyard. Would he stoop to such a mean act?

'Any idea who it might be?' persists Jason.

Montague Smythe is like a genie emerging from a bottle. I recall how suave and smartly dressed he was – hardly the type to prowl around under cover of darkness with a pair of wire-cutters in his hands.

He put himself to considerable inconvenience to track me down and was very interested in Abbeydore wines. He claimed he wanted to buy a small vineyard to indulge a personal whim to make his own wine. That was strange. He didn't look like the sort of man who would want to dirty his hands.

Tending a vineyard involves hard manual work, as I am discovering. I cannot see him undertaking heavy manual labour. Perhaps he wished to own a vineyard whilst having others undertake the day to day running of the place. If so, would he want to risk damaging the vines by blatantly cutting the wires supporting the lateral growths? It doesn't make sense. Jason stares at me waiting for an answer.

'I was thinking of the Master of Wines who called unexpectedly not long after I moved here. The more I think about him, the more strange his visit seems. To be a Master of Wines requires a long apprenticeship. You have to build up an international knowledge of wines and be able to pinpoint exactly where a wine comes from. It's not a qualification that's easily obtained. You have to be able to identify wines in blind tastings, to the extent of pinpointing the exact chateau where a wine originates. Why would someone who is able to identify a Chateau Lafitte be interested in producing wine in Abbeydore? It doesn't make sense.'

'Perhaps it's not the wine he's interested in. Perhaps it's the location. This is a very isolated spot. Anyone looking for an out-of-the-way hideaway would have difficulty finding somewhere better than this.'

'But why would he want a hideaway?'

'I don't know. But judging from what you've told me, he sounds more like a businessman than a winemaker. Some businessmen buy wine as an investment, I understand. They use insider knowledge to identify good vintages and then store

the wine for years before selling it at a substantial profit. Perhaps your Mr Smythe wants an out-of-the-way place to store his cache of wine and he's scouring rural Herefordshire to find somewhere remote and secluded.'
I shake my head and laugh.
'I hardly think our barn would make a very secure storage place for aging wine. Wine investors use secure cellars to squirrel away their investments. They're more interested in underground military storage facilities at disused airfields than a barn in rural Herefordshire. I hardly think Mr Smythe would want to risk depositing an expensive hoard of wine in this remote location where anyone could break in and steal it with impunity.'
'Perhaps you're right,' he replies. 'But, if it isn't Smythe, who else could it be?'
Another individual comes into my mind.
'Do you remember that man from the County Council who wanted to buy this place? He said he wanted to build a house here.'
'Is he the fella that asked you to name your price?'
'Exactly! That didn't ring true at the time and it still doesn't. There must be lots of suitable isolated sites for building a house in Herefordshire. What's so special about Abbeydore Vineyard? Why was he prepared to pay well over the odds to acquire it?'
'It's probably all to do with his position on the

JESSICA'S VINEYARD

Planning Committee. In Australia, you'd be surprised at the number of back-handers given by unscrupulous entrepreneurs to get planning permission for their dubious money-making schemes.'
'Maybe in Australia – but surely not in rural Herefordshire!' I exclaim.
'Human nature is the same the world over. You scratch my back and I'll scratch yours.'
I shake my head at his youthful cynicism.
'Perhaps I ought to report Councillor Johnson to the Local Authority Ombudsman,' I suggest.
'Yeah, and the local CID to see if he's got a pair of wire-cutters hidden under the seat of his Jaguar.'
Jason's mention of the police brings me back with a jolt to the scene of the crime confronting us.
'Let's go back to the house and phone the police', I suggest.
'A fat lot of good that will do!' he replies. 'Do you think they'll send a police car, with flashing blue lights, speeding to Abbeydore to investigate cut wires? Not a chance! All it will mean is that we're kept hanging around twiddling our thumbs in the hope they might eventually appear. We'd be much better assessing the damage and making a start on repairs.'
I agree. I prefer action to inaction any day.

JESSICA'S VINEYARD

We leave the Land Rover and, beginning with the first row of vines, inspect the carnage inflicted on it. The lateral vines have yet to develop swelling bunches of grapes. If they had, the weight of the fruit would inevitably cause the branches to snap and break. We are fortunate that the vines have suffered no irretrievable damage. It is the supporting wires that demand attention.

I examine the cut wires. Sherlock Holmes would immediately identify the wire-cutters used, the date of their manufacture and the retail premises from which they were purchased; but, alas, I don't possess his forensic skills. As far as I can see, the wire has been cut cleanly with no tell-tale clues as to the implement used.

Remembering the detective stories I read as a child, I carefully examine the ground for footprints. But, either we have had little rain lately and the soil is comparatively dry or else the perpetrator kept his feet on the grass whilst moving around the vineyard. I find no tell-tale clues as to the size of the footwear our enemy wore.

I reach the same conclusion as Jason: the police would be unable to advance matters one iota.

The sun burns down upon us as we begin the task of prising metal staples from wooden posts to free the damaged wires before replacing them with new taut wire. We then affix the lateral vine branches to the new wires. It is a slow job. By lunchtime, we have repaired just two rows.

'I wonder how long it took The Enemy to perform his dastardly deed?' asks Jason as we sit down under a spreading oak tree to eat our lunch.

'What makes you think it's a 'he'?'

'Well, I can hardly imagine a woman prowling around here in the dead of night with a pair of wire-cutters in her hand intent on criminal activity.'

'Never underestimate a woman,' I reply. 'Some of the wickedest criminals have been women. Think of Myra Hindley or Rose West.'

'Sure – but didn't they have male accomplices? If a woman is involved in this, she almost certainly had a man helping her.'

He's right. I cannot envisage a woman undertaking such a task on her own. What's more, I cannot think of any woman who would want to harm me in this way.

The more I think about it the more convinced I am that someone wants me to fail. Could it be the Simpsons, the previous owners? They were unable to make a success of Abbeydore Winery. Perhaps they want to ensure I am unable to do so.

But that would indicate a very mean spirit. Would anyone indulge in criminal activity simply to see someone fail as they had failed? I don't think so. After all, they escaped from their failed business with my money in their pocket. I was their salvation rather than their enemy.

'I'm at a loss to know who has done this,' I say with a resigned shake of my head. 'All I know is that someone wants me to fail. That only makes me more determined to succeed.'

'That's the spirit, old girl.'

'Not so much of the old girl, if you don't mind.'

I pretend I am offended.

Jason puts his arm around me to reassure me. All thoughts of vineyard vandals and lunchtime picnics are forgotten as he practises his very own type of tender loving care.

Alan never made love to me out-of-doors. He restricted all love-making to the bedroom.

But Jason is so much more relaxed than Alan. He's a free spirit. He has blown into my life like an unexpected breath of hot air from the Sahara. He makes me giggle with girlish glee whenever we make love. He has discovered my erogenous zones and exploits them mercilessly. Not that I mind, of course. There is something liberating about making love with Jason. The years fall away and I am a young girl once more.

Clouds float overhead in the sapphire sky. The soft whispering leaves of the oak tree hum a love refrain. The sweet-smelling grass is our featherbed. Birds fly overhead and see our bodies entwined below. They

are welcome to their voyeurism. I have no secrets to hide from the birds. I am as free as them. My flight of rapture may not last as long as their flight across the heavens but it soars higher than anything they are capable of achieving. Worry and anxiety cease exist. I have discovered bliss and nothing else matters.
Jason is good for me.
I cannot image coping on my own with the vandalism that has occurred. Jason is my tower of strength. With him by my side I feel I can face anything. His youthful physicality and optimism are exactly what I need in my new life.
I am becoming increasingly dependent upon him. Does he know this? Can he see through the confident exterior I project and discern a fragile woman clinging to a dream by her fingertips? Does he regard our lovemaking as a release for his own sexual desires or does he do it to please me?
'Tell me what you're thinking?' I whisper from beneath his outstretched body.
His hands gently move my hair to the side of my face before replying, 'I was thinking how beautiful you are.'
'You fibber! Any beauty I once possessed has long since disappeared. I'm now a careworn woman midway through her life.'
'Nonsense! You belittle yourself. Your beauty is the talk of the Golden Valley. That's why men come

running to your doorstep. They want to catch a glimpse of the most beautiful and seductive woman in the district.'

'Now you're trying to flatter me … or flatten me, if you continue to rest your weight on me like this.'

'Are you implying I'm overweight?'

'Nothing could be further from the truth. You have the most wonderful athletic body: beautiful bronzed legs, bulging biceps, expansive chest and other impressive parts that modesty prevents me from mentioning.'

He tickles my ribs and sends me into spasms of uncontrollable laughter.

'Stop it!' I shout. 'What would Mr Spragg say if he saw us now? He'd be scandalised.'

'He'd be green with envy that it's me on top of you and not him.'

I shudder at the thought of Mr Spragg lying on top of me and quickly dismiss the image from my mind.

'Nevertheless, I think lunchtime lovemaking is over and viticulture calls,' I say.

We haul ourselves to our feet, adjust our clothing, grab a quick bite to eat and then embark upon the afternoon's work of replacing more of the damaged wires and affixing the sagging lateral vines to the new wires.

By the end of the afternoon we have repaired a quarter of the damaged vineyard.

CHAPTER 9

Smoke triggers deep primordial fears and dark indelible memories from the past.

Smoke issuing from terraced chimneys on dark November nights, infusing the air with coal tar, spiking the frost and beckoning a fireside chair, warm slippers, family laughter and comfort.

Smoke belching from factory chimneys, depositing grim on pavements, walls, and windowpanes, as bodies trudge through the bronchial air to earn a living.

Smoke belching from the funnel of a steam train, wheezing and puffing, with distant memories of waving farewell to a favourite aunt as the hissing, snorting, pounding and angry train disappears from sight leaving only smoke lingering in the air to mark its departure.

Smoke wafting heavenwards from a wood fire in a forest on a still autumn day: acrid, pungent wood-smoke, trailing tales of axe, saw and strenuous manual labour.

JESSICA'S VINEYARD

Long forgotten days sitting beside a campfire with friends, toasting marshmallows, as pervasive smoke drifts aimlessly upwards and out of sight.
Sudden changes in wind direction causing smoke to billow wildly, swirl and impregnate clothes with its acrid smell.
The sudden slap in the face of a billow of out-of-control smoke bringing tears to the eyes.
Smoke aimed by the beekeeper at the disturbed dwellers of a hive - capable of turning on him and wreaking unimaginable vengeance were it not for an overwhelming fear of losing their home to fire and preferring to foolishly sate themselves with honey rather than attack the fire-raiser.
The smell of smoke is so evocative.
It opens a picture-storybook of my life.
I don't doubt that the sense of smell is the most powerful of our five senses. It encapsulates and rekindles memories long forgotten. It triggers a vast arsenal of buried treasures and emotions.
Perhaps that is why I have always liked the smell of smoke. It is the incense of Mother Earth, wafting heavenwards, trailing smiles and laughter in its wake.
And so, when I awake in the night and detect a faint smell of smoke, I am not alarmed.
With my eyes closed, I attempt to identify the source. Is it coal smoke or wood smoke? It is difficult to tell.

JESSICA'S VINEYARD

The bedroom window is slightly ajar and the smoke, if such it be, only reaches my nostrils intermittently. It gives me no cause for alarm. Indeed, I inwardly smile as I recall scenes from my childhood irrevocably associated with its unique smell.
I am in that strange half-asleep-half-conscious state that precedes sunrise and the beginning of a new day. My bed is warm. Jason is sleeping peacefully by my side. I am happy and content.
The distant perfume of wood smoke merely adds to my contentment.
Yes, it is wood-smoke, I decide: the pungent smell of branches burning on a campfire, logs radiating heat on an open fire, brash consumed in a forest clearing. Wood smoke.
I don't know how long it takes for my mind to sense danger but I suddenly experience a complete change of mood. I sit bolt upright in bed and inhale deeply. There is definitely an acrid smell of wood smoke in the air. But where is it coming from?
Although Jason and I often burn discarded vine branches in the vineyard, we haven't done so since we repaired the vandalised wires a week or so ago. The lengthening days and the gradually increasing temperature mean we no longer need a log fire in the house in the evenings.

JESSICA'S VINEYARD

We have no near neighbours. It cannot be smoke wafting from an adjoining property. And so, where is the wood smoke coming from?
I slip out of bed and creep silently to the window to see if I can locate the direction of the smoke.
A shudder of dread races through my body.
I freeze.
It is as though I have been struck by a sudden blast of arctic air. The warmth of the bed is instantly transformed into the shivering horror of fear.
The barn is on fire.
Clouds of smoke issue from under the eaves. It is as if a mythical giant from a grotesque nursery story is inside the barn blowing clouds of smoke and brimstone from his inflated cheeks. The poisonous sulphur is billowing out of the narrow window slits and under the lower courses of the roof tiles. The malignant giant appears to have no need to inhale. He relentlessly exudes clouds of smoke into the early morning air.
This is no time to stand in frozen horror. This is a time for action.
'Wake up, Jason! Wake up! The barn's on fire.'
The figure in the bed moves and then sinks back into oblivion.
'Jason. Jason. Wake up!' I cry as I tug his arm to rouse him.

JESSICA'S VINEYARD

'What's the matter?' he mutters in a half-asleep voice. It has the unspoken codicil, 'Why are you waking me when I am in such a deep sleep?'

'Jason, Jason. The barn's on fire.'

My panic-stricken words eventually connect with his brain and he springs from the bed.

'What's happening?' he asks.

'The barn's on fire. Clouds of smoke are pouring from under the eaves. We must do something.'

What do you do when you live in the depths of the countryside and a building is on fire? I have no idea where the nearest fire station is located. It might be Hereford or Abergavenny. But I know I have to summon help.

'I'll phone the fire brigade,' I announce with a sudden surge of determination.

'It'll take hours for them to get to this remote location,' he says.

'I know, but I've got to alert someone to what's happening,' I answer.

I need help.

I have a deep, unformed suspicion this is no accident. Even if the fire brigade is unable to save the barn, they should be able to discover the cause of the fire. I need to know why my barn is on fire.

While I dial 999 and summon the fire service, Jason shouts, 'I'll pay out the hose. We'll see if we can extinguish the fire ourselves.'

JESSICA'S VINEYARD

I am so relieved I am not facing this emergency alone.

What would I do without Jason? He doesn't show the slightest sign of panic. He's down-to-earth and practical. He's a tower of strength. I don't know what I'd do without him.

But as these thoughts race through my head, a new fear overwhelms me.

What if I lose him? What if his attempt to douse the fire claims his life? What if he's overcome by smoke and collapses in the barn?

'Jason: be careful,' I shout. 'Don't do anything foolhardy.'

But he's gone. I have no way of knowing if he's heard me.

The voice at the other end of the telephone is asking for my post code and address.

'Do you know your *what3words* grid location?' asks the anonymous voice. 'It greatly helps us to locate rural properties.'

I have no idea what she's asking. I repeat my post code with increased urgency and ask, 'How long will it take for a fire engine to arrive?'

'Don't worry, madam,' says the anonymous voice. 'I've put a call out to our fire officers at Ewyas Harold. As soon as they get to the station they'll head straight to your property. I see it's 2.1 miles away. It should take approximately 5 minutes.'

'Does that mean they'll be here in five minutes?' I demand frantically.
'They'll be with you as soon as is humanly possible,' comes the reply. 'Ewyas Harold is staffed by retained firefighters. They'll be on their way to the fire station at this very minute and an appliance will be with you in approximately five minutes from then. Are there any people in the barn? Is there any risk to human life?'
My thoughts turn immediately to Jason.
'There's Jason', I stammer, 'I must go and see if he's alright.'
So saying, I drop the telephone receiver and dash across the farmyard to the barn.
My eyes rapidly adjust to the darkness. The air is full of thick acrid smoke but I can see no flames.
What flammable material is there in the barn?
Wooden barrels and the wooden roof timbers.
The fire must be prevented from reaching the roof timbers. If the timbers ignite the entire roof will collapse.
Any wild surmise as to what is causing smoke to billow from under the eaves and through the high slit windows is swept away by a panic-stricken realisation that I don't know where Jason is. Barns can be rebuilt. Jason is irreplaceable.
'Jason, where are you?' I scream into the choking, smoke-filled night air.

JESSICA'S VINEYARD

There is no response.
He said he was going to pay out the hosepipe.
I make for the outside water tap. As I do so, I trip over something on the ground. It is the hosepipe. This will surely lead me to Jason.
I stumble forwards following the pipe towards the barn shouting all the time, 'Jason! Jason!'
The nearer I get to the barn the more hysterical I become.
Surely he hasn't entered the barn? To do so would be suicidal. He will be instantly overcome by the enveloping clouds of choking smoke. No one would be so foolish!
But Jason is impetuous. He never senses danger. He has all the impetuosity of youth. Whereas I would stop and think of the consequences, he fearlessly rushes in, casting caution to the four winds, impelled only by an inner determination to achieve the goal he has set himself.
Oh Jason! You mean more to me than a barn! It's you I want saved not an old building.
'Jason! Jason! Where are you?'
No answer.
I reach the doors of the old barn. They are open. I see to my horror that the hosepipe disappears into the barn.
I stand at the entrance unsure what to do. Should I follow the hosepipe or remain outside?

JESSICA'S VINEYARD

One part of me wants to go to the assistance of Jason. If he's overcome by smoke inhalation, I must rescue him.
The other part of me says, 'Don't be a fool, Jessica. There's no point in both of you perishing'. I quickly stifle this thought.
Life without Jason would be impossible. My life and his have become so inextricably entwined that I do not think I could live without him. He has become my rock. I depend on him. I need him. He has opened a new chapter in my life. He has shown me what it is like to be loved and accepted. He has opened the doors of paradise for me and I cannot envisage life without him. If he dies, there is no point in living. I would rather die with him. It was not just Romeo and Juliet who were unable to face life apart. I don't think I could survive without Jason.
I clutch the edge of the old barn door and call out for the last time, 'Jason! Jason! Where are you?'
Then, just as I am about to plunge into the thick smoke in search of him, he appears like a ghost emerging from a tomb. The lower part of his face is obscured by a dirty, oily rag that he's tied around his head. Only his eyes and blackened forehead are visible. Tears are streaming from his eyes and he is coughing uncontrollably.
'Jason! Jason! You fool!' I scream at him.

JESSICA'S VINEYARD

But my scream is not so much of anger as of relief. He is alive. He has not been overcome by smoke inside the barn. He has survived.

'Whatever made you go inside that barn?' I demand, as I clutch his arms and attempt to steady him as he coughs and staggers like a drunken man on a pitching and rolling ship.

I pull the oily rag from his face so he can inhale fresh air. His clothes reek of wood smoke, but I don't care. He could smell like the London sewers and I wouldn't care. He is alive. That's all that matters.

It is then I realise that the smoke is no longer billowing from under the stone roof tiles and out of the narrow slit windows.

'Jason! You've done it! You've saved the barn! Look! Smoke is no longer pouring out of the building. I don't know what you've done, but you've doused the fire.'

He looks into my face through his tear-filled eyes and says, 'Didn't you think I'd fix it?'

There are no words to express my love for him. I throw my arms around his smoke-infused body and hug him. I loved him before, but now I know my love for him is absolute. The thought of losing him made me want to lose my life. He means more to me than anything else in the world. He is marvellous. I know that he would do anything for me. He was even willing to risk his life in order to save

JESSICA'S VINEYARD

Abbeydore Winery. It cannot be the barn that propelled him. What possible connection could an Australian youth have with an old barn in the depths of the countryside? No: it was because it was my barn that he put his life on the rails and sought to rescue it. He did it for me. His devotion to me is beyond question. We feel as one towards each other.

I give him another hug. Then, as the thought of losing him returns to haunt me, I demand, 'Whatever were you thinking when you went into that burning barn? It was an act of suicide.'

He gives me a wan smile.

'No act of suicide, Jessica. I've no intention of dying. I've had experiences of fires before. We often get them in the outback. The important thing is to keep your mouth and nose covered with a wet cloth at all times. That way, you can still breathe, even in thick smoke. I knew that if I could reach the seat of the fire with the hosepipe I could direct water on it and then beat a hasty retreat. And that's just what I did.'

'Oh Jason! I don't know what I'd do without you. You may be half my age but I think you're infinitely wiser than me. You seem to know more about life than I ever will. But I still say you were a fool to venture into that barn. You could easily have been overcome by smoke and then what good would your heroism have been?'

He looks at me and smiles.

'Don't worry on my account. I'm perfectly capable of looking after myself.'

He has proved that without doubt.

My thoughts then turn to the cause of the fire.

'Where was the fire?' I ask, 'and what was burning to produce so much smoke?'

'I'm afraid we've lost two or three barrels. The fire was at the far end of the stacked barrels. Whatever started it had a ready source of timber on hand to fuel the fire. I guess we were lucky the barrels had been used for storing wine. They must have been wet or damp inside and that prevented them going up in flames. However, the dampness produced the thick clouds of smoke you saw billowing from under the eaves. We were very lucky.'

Just then, the still night air is disturbed by the distant sound of an emergency vehicle's siren.

'That will be the fire brigade,' I sigh. 'They won't have much to do when they get here. I reckon you've done their work for them.'

'Guess so. I told you not to bother them. I knew they'd be no help. The important thing is to act quickly before a fire gets established. If we'd waited for them to arrive, the roof timbers would probably have gone and the entire roof collapsed.'

I am not so sure, but I hold my tongue. I certainly have no wish to take away kudos from Jason for the wonderful feat he has pulled off.

JESSICA'S VINEYARD

Our conversation is cut short by the deafening siren of the Ewyas Harold fire tender as it skids to a halt, with lights flashing, beside the barn. Four fire-fighters jump from the tender.

'Where's the fire?' asks the foremost fire-fighter. His features are barely distinguishable under his large white helmet.

'It was in the barn,' I answer, 'but I think you've arrived too late. Jason has managed to douse the flames and save the barn.'

The fire officer casts a quick glance at Jason before asking, 'Is anyone in the barn at present?'

'No. There are only the two of us living here and we're both present and accounted for.'

While he is talking, his colleagues pull on breathing apparatus and prepare to enter the barn trailing a hose and carrying a powerful searchlight.

'Where's the main electrical fuse box?' asks the white helmet.

'Just inside the barn, on the left,' answers Jason, 'but you don't have to isolate the electrics. I did that before I entered the barn.'

The white helmet focusses his attention on Jason. 'That was smart thinking, young man, even if your actions were extremely foolish. You should never enter a burning building. It's a job for trained professionals. We're equipped with oxygen cylinders.

JESSICA'S VINEYARD

You could easily have been overcome by smoke and perished in there.'
'But I didn't,' replies Jason with a cheeky grin.
The white helmet shakes his head in disbelief. His action speaks more eloquently than words. It says I'm wasting my time talking to this cocky youth. He thinks he knows it all. He wouldn't be so cocky if we were now giving him artificial respiration and struggling to revive him. The youth of today! They think they know it all!
Without another word the white helmet returns to the fire tender, pulls on his mask and oxygen cylinder and advances towards the barn. He disappears inside.
'There's nothing for them to do,' says Jason. 'The fire's been extinguished. There's only a few smouldering pieces of cooperage left to show there ever was a fire in there.'
A shiver passes through my body. I suddenly become aware of the temperature. Until now, all thoughts for my own comfort were far from my mind, but now, in the moment before dawn, I realise I am still in my nightclothes. Jason sees me wrap my arms around my body in order to keep warm.
'Why don't you go into the house and put some warm clothes on?' he suggests. 'Perhaps you could make some mugs of tea whilst I remain here and attend to the firefighters.'

JESSICA'S VINEYARD

It sounds like a sensible suggestion, but I am torn. It would be good to put on some warm clothes and drink a steaming mug of hot tea, but I also want to know what the fire officers think was the cause of the fire. My innate curiosity triumphs over my discomfort.

'Just put your arms around me to keep me warm,' I say. 'I want to speak to the fire officer to discover what caused the fire.'

'I can do that,' he answers. But a stubborn streak in me resists his offer.

'No: I want to speak to the fire officer myself,' I answer.

'Please yourself.'

We stand in silence in the chilly early morning air waiting for the firefighters to emerge from the barn. When they do, I immediately ask the white helmeted officer, 'What was the cause of the fire?'

His face is partly hidden by his large helmet and only partially illuminated by the headlights of the fire tender. Nevertheless, I can distinguish an anxious look on his face.

'It would seem it was caused by an electrical fault,' he declaims in a sepulchral voice. 'Has anyone been undertaking electrical work in there recently?'

A shiver runs down my spine. Jason wired plug sockets and a light in the attic room when he first moved in. But that was weeks ago. Surely any fault would have manifested itself before now. I look at Jason and wait for him to answer.

'Sure,' he replies. 'I wired some plug sockets and lights so I could use the attic room as my berth when I first came here.'

'And did you leave live cables loose behind the barrels?'

'Well, there was no point fixing them to the walls. This is a barn and not a domestic dwelling. I just did what was necessary to get power to my attic room.'

'Well, your cowboy electrics could easily have resulted in the complete destruction of this barn.' Then, turning to me, he asks, 'Did you know there was a quantity of old hessian sacks and linen sheets behind those barrels?'

How could I know? The barrels were stacked against the wall of the barn. I never had any reason to look behind them.

'We certainly didn't put them there,' I answer. 'It must have been the previous owners who left them there.'

'But you must have known they were there, young man, when you did your cowboy electrics,' declares the white helmet.

'Sure. I saw them; but I was more concerned with getting my attic room habitable than clearing out rubbish left by the previous owners.'

JESSICA'S VINEYARD

'Well, your negligence meant there was a ready supply of flammable material on hand to ignite an electrical fire from your trailing cable. A flaw in the cable must have produced the heat that ignited the flammable material and that in turn ignited the wooden barrels. It was a classic case of shoddy workmanship resulting in a potentially disastrous fire.'

Then, turning to me, the white helmet says, 'You are extremely lucky madam, to still have a barn. I would suggest that, in future, you only permit qualified tradesmen to undertake work at your property.'

Then, as his parting salvo, he says, 'As soon as my men have finished dousing down, we will return to our beds. I will issue a full report and it will be up to the Chief Fire Office to decide whether or not you are charged for this call-out.'

And with that, he turns on his heel and disappears once more inside the barn.

My shivering has now become unstoppable.

'Come. Let's go inside,' I say. 'I need something to warm me up and steady my nerves.'

Jason follows me. He is sullen. He does not take kindly to criticism.

As soon as we are in the warmth and comfort of the house I turn to him and give him a radiant smile.

'Don't worry about what the Big White Fire Helmet said. I think you were marvellous. You showed great courage in tackling that fire singlehandedly. You can't be held responsible for an electrical fault. There's nothing to say that, even if the wiring had been undertaken by a qualified electrician, it mightn't still have caused a fire. Perhaps a rat or a mouse nibbled through the cable. It's not your fault. You're not to blame.'

He looks at me with his begrimed face and pursed mouth. He looks so young and vulnerable. He needs loving. I throw my arms around him and envelop him in an expansive hug. He responds by placing his arms around me.

It's time to put the thoughts of my heart into words. 'Jason: when you went into that barn I thought I'd lost you. I thought you'd been overcome by the smoke and collapsed. It was then I realised what you mean to me. You are worth more to me than a hundred barns. I could live without a barn and without this vineyard. I do not need either of them. But I know that I cannot live without you.'

He looks into my eyes.

'What are you saying?'

'I'm saying you mean more to me than anything or anyone else in the world. Since you came into my life you have brought me nothing but joy and happiness. I thought I could be happy living in a beautiful and remote spot on my own, but I was wrong. I am not made to be alone. I need companionship. You are the most wonderful companion. You bring a smile to my face. You make me feel young again. You excite me with your courage and daring. I love your laughter. I love your Australian accent. I love your physicality and prowess. Jason: I have fallen head over heels in love with you.'

He continues to stare intently at me.

'So, what are you saying?'

'I'm saying that, although there is a great difference in our ages, and I must appear a shop-soiled reject that's been put out to grass, I love you with all my heart. I want us to be together for ever. Promise you'll never leave me.'

He continues to scrutinise me with his unblinking eyes.

What is he thinking? Why won't he speak? What's going through his mind?

Eventually he says, 'I guess age doesn't come into it when two people fall in love. I like your company. I like being with you, but you've got to understand: I've got my life stretching before me. I've got to decide what I'm going to do with my life.'

I catch my breath. This is the brush-off. He's trying to find words that will let me down gently. He doesn't want to hurt me, but neither does he reciprocate my feelings.

Oh Jessica! What have you done? Why have you allowed your heart to lead you to yet another emotional disaster? The pain this time will be worse

than before. I have been given a glimpse of heaven and now it is about to be snatched away from me.
'My year backpacking was to give me time to find myself and decide what I'm going to do with my life,' he continues. 'I had no intention of settling down and becoming domesticated. I was a free spirit and I wanted to experience as much of life as I could.'
It's just as I thought. A young man of his age, with so much going for him, is not interested in a woman like me. I may be good for a few weeks' fling, but then he'll pack his bags and move on. I was a fool to think otherwise.
'I never thought, when I came to this rural corner of the world, I'd meet someone like you,' he continues. 'You are like no other girl I've known. The girls I knew back home in Australia were out for a good time. They wanted fun and excitement, but they had no depth. They didn't know what life was really like. They hadn't experienced pain and hardship. They didn't know about scaling the heights and conquering fear. They were shallow, and I knew I could never tie myself to someone like that. But you are different. You set yourself a goal and are determined that nothing will make you deviate from the course you've set yourself. You have ambition and resilience. You are just as much a free spirit as me.'
Where is this leading? Is it all part of the soft landing he is preparing for me? Is he listing my good qualities

JESSICA'S VINEYARD

before politely saying goodbye? Is this his way of salving his conscience at leaving me on my own?
'And so, I've come to realise that good chances don't come your way that often. You have all the qualities I admire in a woman. I've no doubt I could live with you very happily for the rest of my life. But, if I'm to turn my back on all the possible girls I might meet in the future, I've got to be sure that our relationship is secure. I don't want to jettison my future chances for a relationship that is short-lived.'
I can hardly believe my ears! He is not giving me the brush-off. He is serious. He is willing to bind his life with mine providing it is a serious and lasting relationship.
'Oh, Jason!' I exclaim in wonderment. 'We think as one."
He looks into my eyes and then, as if I am watching a slow-motion film sequence, he gradually sinks down to the ground on one knee and keeping his eyes firmly fixed on mine asks, "Jessica: will you marry me and be my wife?"
We look into each other's eyes. I see past the besmirched, sooty face that is before me and into his serious and penetrating eyes. Jason probably sees a face that has furrowed lines on its forehead and crows' feet around the eyes, but, hopefully, he also sees the passion and love I have for him shining bright and strong.

JESSICA'S VINEYARD

I place my hands on either side of his face and plant my lips on his. Our kiss is the seal on our partnership. I give myself to him and in return he gives himself to me. I could never have imagined such a thing!
Only a short time ago I walked out on Alan and vowed I would never have anything else to do with men. I deliberately searched for a place in the depths of the countryside, far away from men, where I could live my life undisturbed my masculine interference. And just when I thought I was safe, a man appears in my life and completely sweeps me off my feet.
Jason is unlike any other man I have known. He is a free spirit. He is not encumbered with cares and concerns about money, ambition and fame. He is the most natural and easy-going person I have ever met. He possesses the unrestrained freedom of youth. He makes me feel like a young girl again. Maybe I was destined to fall in love with someone younger than myself.
Most women marry men who are either the same age as themselves or else older than them. Perhaps they are inwardly seeking a father-figure who will offer them security and protection. Well, I've tried that and it doesn't work. Alan sought to exert parental control over me and I rebelled. I am not as other women. I do not want to be dependent on a man who is older

than me. I want to experience the unrestrained freedom that goes with youth.

Jason makes me young again. He rejuvenates me. He sweeps away my anxieties and concerns and throws open the doors of freedom. Perhaps, at a deep psychological level, he fulfils an innate maternal instinct within me. Perhaps I see him as the son I never had – someone on whom I can shower my love and affection. But who cares what the underlying reasons are for our mutual attraction! The fact of the matter is we are in love and willing to pledge ourselves to each other for the remainder of our lives. What could be more wonderful? It is the summation of everything for which I have ever dreamed. I am in heaven!

JESSICA'S VINEYARD

CHAPTER 10

The grapes hang in tight clusters on the vines as the summer sun kisses and caresses them like a mother suckling her baby and watching her offspring grow imperceptibly day by day. The pea-green skins of the Bacchus grapes and the yet-to-ripen red skins of the Cabernet Sauvignon grapes expand as moisture from the ground and warmth from the sun perform an intricate balancing act in which each complements the other.

As the Bacchus grapes increase in size, so each grape's skin is stretched. It becomes translucent. Veined flesh conceals the inner seeds placed there by Mother Nature to propagate the species. But no seeds will fall to the ground in Jessica's vineyard. The seeds here are destined for the waste bin. Crushed seeds add bitterness to wine. I have no need of grape seeds. It is the flesh of each grape I covet: succulent, juicy, luscious flesh exuding the nectar of the gods that I can ferment into wine: Jessica's wine. Wine that has its very own characteristics and bouquet. Wine that draws minerality from the soil of my south-facing vineyard; that magicks a distinctive character

JESSICA'S VINEYARD

from Abbeydore's unique combination of sun and rain; that lingers on the palate and lodges in the memory for ever.

The red Cabernet Sauvignon grapes are altogether different. They have a life of their own. They are not destined to remain green. They aspire to become deep ruby red. They reach out to the sun and implore the rays of the heavenly sun to focus upon them. The rain feeds their roots but it is the sun that draws the life-giving moisture from the ground and into the embryonic grapes causing them to swell with pride. As they swell they blush, like an adolescent girl beholding her budding breasts for the first time. Will they remain half-formed and the subject of derision or will they swell to voluptuousness and excite wonder and rapture?

I hope it's the latter.

I can hardly contain my excitement and wonder at having become Mrs Jessica Knightly.

Immediately after the barn fire, Jason and I made an appointment to see the Registrar of Births, Deaths and Marriages. Births and deaths did not concern us: we were focussed on marriage. Having pledged to work as a team, it seemed the logical thing to make the arrangement a legal one.

As a husband and wife team, we now put our combined efforts into making Abbeydore Winery a successful commercial enterprise. We share together the hard work and the hoped-for rewards. It is a marriage of equals. I am in my seventh heaven. I have never been as happy as I am now.

My marriage has given me new confidence. My self-esteem has rocketed. I am married to a wonderful Adonis. He is handsome. He is virile. He is innovative. He is unencumbered by worldly concerns. He is fun. He's all I've ever wanted in a man. And he's mine. The two of us will live our lives in perfect harmony till death us do part.

I have developed a new spring in my step. I am unencumbered by the past. I am open to new ideas. When Jason suggests installing an irrigation system in the vineyard, I instantly agree.

We have toiled long and hard to bring the vineyard to the threshold of productivity. Jason says we need to ensure that our hard work is not wasted on account of the vagaries of the English weather. He says he has knowledge of irrigation systems in the Clare Valley and they are not difficult to construct; and so, we now have our very own irrigation system. It ensures that our vines receive a constant supply of water, even when there is no rain. He thinks that the absence of such a system was probably why the Simpsons failed to turn in a profit during their tenure of the vineyard. We certainly don't want to follow their disastrous path and so I am only too pleased to go along with Jason's suggestion.

JESSICA'S VINEYARD

The two of us trailed miles and miles of black piping up and down the rows of vines before Jason connected the lengths of pipework to the main pipe that we connected to the old disused well at the rear of the farmhouse.
'All that's needed to complete the job is a small electric pump,' declares Jason. 'I know a place in Abergavenny where I can get just what we need.'
So saying, he climbs into the Land Rover and disappears down the narrow country lane in the direction of Abergavenny.
He has not long gone before a sleek Jaguar pulls up outside the house. I've seen the car before – and I've seen the man who emerges from it. It is Councillor Johnson. What on earth does he want?
I wish Jason was here.
There is an authoritative rat-a-tat-tat on the front door knocker. I leave the house via the kitchen door and walk around the outside of the building to confront my unwanted visitor sideways on. This time, he is prepared for my unorthodox approach.
'Ah Mrs Pope!' he beams with effusive bonhomie whilst extending his right hand for me to shake.
'Actually, it's Mrs Knightly,' I reply.
His eyebrows rise in surprise. He is clearly disconcerted.
'I'm sorry,' he utters, 'I thought your name was Jessica Pope.'

JESSICA'S VINEYARD

'It was,' I reply, secretly pleased at his discomfiture. 'But I've recently re-married. I am now Mrs Knightly.'

'Allow me to congratulate you,' he replies, as he rapidly regains his composure. 'I hope that you and your husband will have a long and happy married life together.'

He is thinking on his feet. I can almost see the cogs turning inside his head. My new marital status has clearly unhinged his plans. He is struggling to know how best to proceed. But he is not a County Councillor for nothing. He quickly adapts to the new situation.

'In view of your new marital status, perhaps it would be best if we shared this conversation with your husband.'

How I hate men who think they can only do business with husbands and brush wives aside like unwanted dust on a piece of furniture! He's clearly a man's man. He is much more comfortable dealing with men than a person of the weaker sex, as I am sure he would term me.

'My husband is not at home at present,' I reply, wishing very much that he was.

He frowns and then inhales deeply before saying, 'Very well.'

Then taking another deep breath he launches into his spiel.

JESSICA'S VINEYARD

'You'll remember that, when I called on you some while ago, I expressed an interest in purchasing your property. You said at the time that it was not for sale. I quite understood. You had only recently acquired it and, no doubt, had plans and high hopes for turning it into a successful winemaking business. Perhaps I was a little rash in pressing my case too vigorously. But the fact of the matter is I am still very interested in your property.'

'I told you then and I tell you now, I am not interested in selling.'

'Quite so. But I understand that things have taken a somewhat ominous turn since we last spoke.'

'What do you mean?'

He gives me an oily smile. He considers me an absolute simpleton with no conception of the way politics work.

'In addition to serving on the County Planning Committee, I am also a member of the County Fire and Rescue Service Executive. As such, I receive regular reports about incidents to which the Fire Service is called. I saw that one of those incidents was here at Abbeydore Winery. I was naturally concerned.'

His expression of concern is as false as crocodile's tears.

'I understand you experienced a fire in your barn. It would be a great pity if an ancient barn, dating back

JESSICA'S VINEYARD

to the Middle Ages, were to go up in flames. Not only would it be a great loss to local heritage but I guess it would seriously impact your business. Without business premises it would be impossible to ferment and bottle wine. You had a very lucky escape, if I may say so. I know it's said that lightning never strikes twice in the same place; but one never knows if and when another unforeseen catastrophe might occur that could place your business in even greater jeopardy.

'In view of the close encounter with disaster that you experienced, I wondered if you might be willing to reconsider my offer to purchase your property.'

The oily County Councillor assumes another persona. He no longer wears a smart Saville Row suit and silk tie but is clad from head to foot in black. He wears silent plimsolls on his feet. He moves stealthily in the shadows. He creeps around my barn under cover of darkness. His gloved hand conceals a torch. He is intent on mischief. He is a fireraiser. He has come to Abbeydore with malice aforethought. He is intent on scaring me and driving me from the Golden Valley.

'So, Mrs Knightly …?'

He looks intently at me awaiting an answer.

I blink and banish the malignant image that has invaded my mind.

JESSICA'S VINEYARD

'There was an electrical fault in the barn. It has now been rectified,' I reply, determined to keep my words factual to disguise the seething anger that is in my heart.

'But this is a very isolated spot,' returns the man holding an imaginary trident in his right hand and trailing a black tail behind him. 'You were fortunate that the Fire Service was able to get here in time and save your barn; but what if it had been your home, and you were inside it and asleep? The consequences could have been disastrous.'

'We will have to be more careful in future,' I reply with a smile.

He frowns.

'My offer still stands,' he answers. 'I'm willing to purchase your property for twice the price you paid for it. It's an unrepeatable offer.'

When he sees I am not about to budge, he says, 'Why don't you discuss it with your husband? The money would enable the two of you to embark upon your new married life in a place of your own choosing. A new marriage: a new start. What could be more appropriate?'

He does not seem to understand that Abbeydore Winery is my new start in life. It is here I met Jason. It is here that I want to put down roots and spend the rest of my life. I have no desire to start all over again. This is my home and this is where I intend to stay.

'I will certainly discuss your offer with my husband,' I say, 'but I have no doubt he will be of the same mind as me. We have no wish to sell Abbeydore Winery.'

'Very well,' he answers with a deep sigh. 'But if your circumstances change, you must let me know. I can often pull strings and get things done. I'll keep in touch with you.'

Then, before I can tell him he is wasting his time, he turns and retraces his steps to his sleek Jaguar and glides away to the purring sound of a very expensive engine.

Although he has gone, he remains firmly lodged in my mind. There is something about him I do not like. He made his knowledge of the barn fire sound plausible, but did he know more than what was in a Fire Service report? And what about the severed wires in the vineyard? Could he have had a hand in that? He doesn't look like a criminal; but then, some of the wickedest gangsters have cultivated suave and impressive façades. He disconcerts me.

Why is he so intent on acquiring Abbeydore Winery? Why has he paid me two visits within the space of four months? What does he know that I don't? I don't like it. I am unable to get him out of my mind.

JESSICA'S VINEYARD

I spend the next couple of hours moping around the house mulling over the unwelcome visit from Councillor Johnson.

When Jason returns I lose no time telling him about my encounter with the County Councillor.

'Perhaps we're sitting on an oil well here at Abbeydore,' he laughs. 'Or perhaps it's an ideal site for fracking. Or maybe there are rich gold seams running beneath the vineyard.'

His laughter dispels my anxiety.

'Well, whatever's below the surface, I hope it's good for grapes,' I smile. 'I'm not interested in oil, gas or gold. I just want ripe, succulent grapes that can be made into exquisite wine.'

'I'm with you there,' he replies. 'And this pump from Abergavenny should help ensure we do just that.'

So saying, he shows me the electric pump he has purchased.

Later in the day he calls me to the wellhead to see the pump in action.

'I hope you've wired this properly so we don't have any fires in the future,' I say sardonically.

'Don't worry your head about it,' he answers. 'This little beauty will run for years with no trouble.'

True to his word, as soon as he switches on the pump, water begins to surge along the main pipe to the irrigation pipes in the vineyard. It's a triumph of inventiveness.

JESSICA'S VINEYARD

I could never have conceived such a scheme myself, let alone executed it. But then, marriage is all about sharing, and Jason shows no reticence in sharing his ideas to make Abbeydore Winery a successful enterprise.

I am sharing my life with a genius. His inventiveness is infectious. He makes me look at new ways to nurture our business. I revel in his company. How could I ever have thought I could live on my own? I need a companion to stimulate and excite me. Jason ensures there is a constant smile on my face.

If I were living at Abbeydore on my own I would be seriously worried.

The cutting of the wires in the vineyard was no accident. It was a deliberate act of vandalism. Who hates me so much as to perpetrate such a crime? Who wants to ensure I am unsuccessful and my winery fails? What have I done to provoke such hostility?

If I were here on my own I would be seriously worried.

This is a very isolated location. A single woman would be extremely vulnerable. I might in all probability accept Councillor Johnson's offer and beat a hasty retreat to safety. But, thankfully, I am not alone. I have Jason as my lifelong soulmate. I don't have to face the future alone.

JESSICA'S VINEYARD

The fire in the barn might have been accidental or it might not. If someone is seriously intent on driving me from Abbeydore they might resort to arson. Councillor Johnson is correct: if I had lost the barn my chances of making wine would have gone up in smoke. There is no way I could ferment and process wine without the barn. If the barn went up in flames I would be finished.
There is something very untoward and unnerving happening here and I don't know what it is.

CHAPTER 11

In many ways, married life doesn't differ greatly from what went before. Jason and I share the tasks around the farmhouse and we spend our days tending the vines and preparing the equipment in readiness for the grape harvest.
The grapes are swelling nicely thanks to our new irrigation system and the remarkably fine summer weather we are experiencing at present.
We are toying with the idea of using the ripasso technique with the red grapes. It will involve a secondary fermentation. The pomace of leftover grape skins and seeds will be added to the first fermentation for an extended maceration. This should produce a medium-bodied wine with a good alcoholic content. But it will be a gamble. It is something they do in Italy - but Italy has a much warmer climate than England. If we pull it off, we would have a wine of great depth and colour. But will it work given our climate? We decide to defer a decision until we see how the grapes ripen.
Jason is as energetic as ever. I sometimes wish I had his youthful energy. He is particularly focussed on

reducing the rabbit population. They don't appear to be a nuisance to me, but then, I don't have his experience of the great outdoors. He claims that rabbits have to be kept constantly under control, otherwise they take over and our newly-planted vines will become their principal source of food.
He disappears for long stretches during the day with the rifle slung over his shoulder. He invariably returns with a brace of rabbits in his hand and a smile on his face.
'Rabbit casserole in red wine for dinner tonight,' he grins as he deposits the game on the kitchen table.
'But not, alas, with our own red wine,' I answer with a wry smile.
'Don't go worrying yourself about that. It's just a question of time before those Cab Sav grapes are the size of gobstoppers and the colour of liquorice. Then, we'll have the best red wine in England. And your *lapin au vin* will be the talk of the neighbourhood'.
I somehow doubt it. We have no dealings with our neighbours. Even the Spraggs at the adjoining property seem to have vanished. Not that I mind. I prefer Jason and me being together without outside interference. When you're in love you don't need anyone else. I have Jason and that's all I want.
We divide the household tasks between us. Sometimes I drive the old Land Rover into

JESSICA'S VINEYARD

Abergavenny to stock up on provisions and sometimes Jason undertakes the task. It is while he is away in Abergavenny that I have an unexpected visitor.

I may have said before that we have very few visitors at Abbeydore. We are completely off the beaten track. The narrow lane that leads to our property goes nowhere in particular. Consequently, there is no passing traffic. That is part of the magic of the place. The arrival of a visitor is, therefore, an unusual occurrence.

I first become aware that someone is approaching the farmhouse as I am standing at the kitchen sink washing up the breakfast things. I catch sight of a movement out of the corner of my eye through the kitchen window. No sound accompanies the movement. It is not a vehicle that is approaching. I look more closely. It is a person on a bicycle.

I watch intently as the figure gets closer. It is clearly no sporting cyclist clad in Lycra spandex and hunched over drop handlebars on a speed test but someone on an ancient black bicycle with a wicker basket attached to the front. As the moving figure approaches the farmhouse I see it is a young man on the bicycle, with a mass of unruly tasselled hair. He is wearing a sports jacket and a pair of grey flannel trousers. The bottoms of his trousers are held in place by a pair of cycle clips.

JESSICA'S VINEYARD

I am usually good at placing people. I can usually tell if someone is well-heeled or poor, clever or stupid, working class or middle class, ill or healthy, integrated or unhinged, studious or dissolute - but this figure defies categorisation. He is certainly not fashion conscious. What young man nowadays wears a sports jacket and grey flannel trousers? He cannot be well-heeled to ride such an old fashioned bicycle. He cannot care greatly about his appearance to allow his tasselled hair to be so out-of-control. He is a conundrum.

Oh dear! Why do I always have visits from such people when I am on my own? I wish Jason was here to support me.

Taking a deep breath, I abandon the washing-up, leave the kitchen by the back door and walk around the farmhouse to confront my visitor sideways on. He sees me as he removes the cycle clips from his ankles.

'Oh, hello,' he stammers, 'I didn't see you coming. You must forgive me. I'm a bit hot and flustered. I didn't realise it was such a hot day. There are so many inclines around here.'

I surmise he has called for a drink of water to quench his thirst. If so, I can hardly refuse him. Perhaps it is better to offer him a drink before he asks for one.

'Would you like a glass of water to cool you down?' I ask in a neutral voice.

JESSICA'S VINEYARD

'Oh I say, that would be frightfully kind of you.'
He is well-educated. Perhaps he is a well-educated
buffoon. I came across plenty of them during my
working life: boys born into wealthy families with
sawdust between their ears. They were sent to private
school to acquire a frightfully posh accent whilst
failing to be separated from their sawdust. Could this
be an educated nincompoop?
I have no intention of inviting him into my house
and so I say, 'Please wait here whilst I get a drink for
you.'
'Thanks awfully,' he answers.
When I return with the glass of water I see he is
attempting to smooth his wild hair into some
semblance of normality but without much success.
'That looks awfully good,' he says as I hand the glass
of water to him.
I watch as he devours the contents in one continuous
swig. His large Adam's apple bobs up and down like
a cork in turbulent waters.
'Wonderful!' he declares on emptying the glass.
He looks at me and gives me a wide smile but shows
no sign of leaving. His need of a drink was clearly not
the reason that brought him to Abbeydore Winery.
I wait for him to explain himself.
He clears his throat.
'You must wonder what I'm doing on your doorstep,'
he declares with another wide smile.

JESSICA'S VINEYARD

I do indeed wonder, but I have no intention of asking. I wait for him to explain himself.
'I'm undertaking field studies.'
He pauses. He clearly wants me to enquire the nature of his field studies, but I have no intention of doing so. I do not want to encourage him. He has arrived unannounced and uninvited and I have no intention of getting into an in-depth conversation with him about whatever it is that interests him. I merely raise my eyebrows and wait for him to enlighten me.
'Yes, you see, it's for my PhD. I'm frightfully interested in medieval barns. I always have been - ever since I was a young lad. My pater used to take me to look at old tithe barns and I suppose the bug bit me at a very tender age. I've never been able to pass an old barn without wanting to look inside. They are all so different. The medieval masons knew what they were doing. Their handiwork has spanned the centuries. Their work has stood the test of time. The Herefordshire School of Stonemasons is my speciality. Have you been to Kilpeck and seen the magnificent stone carvings there? Absolutely unique! They developed and fine-honed their skills to perfection. Kilpeck appears in all architectural books. But, of course, the masons undertook work elsewhere. And that's what interests me. I'm investigating the other buildings in Herefordshire on which they worked. Now, as I'm sure you know, you

JESSICA'S VINEYARD

have a medieval barn here at Abbeydore. It may well be the work of the Herefordshire School. I would be immensely grateful if you would allow me to take a look at it. I promise not to take up your valuable time. I would just like an opportunity to take a few measurements and photograph the roof beams and other interesting features. So little is known of the vernacular medieval barns of Herefordshire! You would be doing me a great favour if you allowed me to have a peep inside your barn and you would also be contributing to the greater advancement of human knowledge and understanding.'

I can tell he is an enthusiast. I will not get rid of him easily. Perhaps the best course is to allow him access to the barn so he can satisfy his curiosity. But I have no intention of giving him free rein. If he is to enter our barn, I will be his shadow. I also intend to establish the ground rules.

'I am willing to show you the interior of our barn but you must understand that I am a busy woman. I cannot allow you unlimited access. I am willing to give you fifteen minutes. Can you work within that parameter?'

He frowns and blinks. He would clearly like longer, but I am unbending. I might have been more amenable if he had taken the trouble to contact me beforehand and arrange a visit; but, turning up, out of the blue, with no prior warning, makes me think he has no entitlement to more than fifteen minutes of my time.

'That will concentrate my mind tremendously,' he replies. 'I sometimes become so absorbed in the architectural details that I lose all track of time. I shall have to work extra hard to keep to the strict timetable you've set.'

I lead the young man to the barn and open the large double doors just wide enough for us both to enter.

'Oh I say!' he exclaims on stepping inside the dimly-lit building. 'What an absolute beauty! Just look at that arcade post with its upstand: definitely the work of the Herefordshire School. I would recognise that anywhere. And look at those purlins clasped by ashlar pieces! A marvel of the medieval carpenter's skill! You are so lucky to own such an exquisite medieval masterpiece. I congratulate you!'

He casts his eyes around the barn and takes in not only the expansive timber roof but also the corbel stones, slit windows, stone walls and flagstones.

'I see you're using the barn for wine production,' he says somewhat superfluously. 'I'm sure the men who built this cathedral of stone would be delighted that you are using it six hundred years later for a similar purpose for which it was constructed. Now tell me, are there carpenters' marks on the timbers?'

I have no idea and I have no intention of climbing a ladder to discover if there are.

JESSICA'S VINEYARD

'I am a winemaker and not a builder,' I answer. 'I confine my activities to ground level.'
'Quite so! And what a magnificent ground you have. These flagstones must be contemporaneous with the rest of the barn. Look how they've been worn and fashioned by the hundreds of feet that have passed over them through the centuries!'
So saying, he produces a hand torch from his shoulder bag and begins to sweep the floor with its beam of light. It seems a strange thing to do for a man who is interested in medieval barns. I would have thought his interest would lie in the construction of the walls and roof.
'Tell me,' he says, 'does this barn have a crypt? So many medieval buildings have subterranean cellars that are every bit as interesting as what is above. I've seen undercrofts with barrel vaults, groin vaults, rib vaults and even a pitched brick barrel vault. Truly amazing! Does your barn possess an underground treasure chest?'
'It does not, I regret to say.'
A look of disappointment tinged with exasperation steals over his face.
'That's a pity,' he replies as he continues to sweep the beam of his torch across the flagstones. 'Perhaps you would permit me to take some measurements and some photographs.'
I glance at my wristwatch in a purposeful manner.

JESSICA'S VINEYARD

'I'm frightfully sorry to be taking up so much of your time,' he stammers, 'but I would like to record the interior of your magnificent barn.'

'You have ten minutes of your allocated fifteen remaining,' I state in my most autocratic voice. 'I suggest you get on with it as quickly as possible.'

He produces a camera from out of his shoulder bag in some confusion, and begins walking around the interior of the barn taking photographs. I thought he would want photographs of the interior features of the barn – the stone walls, the corbels, the roof timbers and so on – but he seems more interested in general views of the barn from as many different angles as possible. He sinks to his knees for many of his photographs. He is a strange young man.

I get the impression he would willingly spend the entire morning inside my barn if I permitted it; but I am bored by his presence. He has told me nothing I did not already know about the barn. I have had enough of him after fifteen minutes and want him gone.

I give a discreet cough before calling out, 'Time up! I've got other things to do this morning and so I must ask you to leave.'

Then by way of a polite sop I say to him, 'I hope you've got all you need for your dissertation. You must let me know if your PhD is ever published. I

JESSICA'S VINEYARD

would be interested to see how my barn compares with other medieval barns in the district.'
With one last photographic blink of the camera's shutter he turns and follows me out of the shadowy barn and into the bright morning sunlight.
It is only then that I realise I do not know the young man's name.
'Tell me,' I demand, 'what's your name?'
'Quinten Stretcher,' he stammers. 'My ancestors must have stretched and softened fur pelts to have a name like that. Alas, I am absolutely no good with my hands and that's why I occupy an ivory tower in academia.'
He smiles at his little witticism as he replaces his cycle clips around his ankles.
'Thank you so much for letting me look inside your magnificent barn. That's another one down: just forty-eight to go.'
And with that, he wobbles out of sight on his ancient bicycle leaving me in a reflective mood.
When Jason returns from Abergavenny I tell him about our unexpected historical visitor.
'I guess it takes all sorts to make the world go round,' he comments. 'People get excited about all sorts of queer things. I don't think I could get excited about an old agricultural building – but there you are. We're all different.'
I nod my head and life goes on.

CHAPTER 12

Midsummer comes and goes. The days are long. A feeling of somnolence descends upon the countryside. Insects linger on plants as if loath to make the effort to move on. Flowers stand motionless in the heat of the sun, swayed neither by a breeze or a desire to see more of their habitat. The early morning dew dissipates under a cloudless sky leaving the freshly laundered grass gleaming in the sunlight. No birds are to be seen. They must think it's too hot to rummage for food. Their need for nourishment is replaced by a need to remain cool amongst the shady branches of the canopied trees. Summer trails lassitude in her wake.

Jason and I spend long hours on the sun loungers at the rear of the house. It is our little corner of Paradise. He wears the skimpiest shorts I've ever seen on a man and, as a result, has an almost all-over tan. His bronzed body and athletic physique make him the most adorable male anyone could wish to meet.

He urges me to go topless and acquire an all-over tan just like him, but I am not so keen. My body doesn't possess his youthful physicality. My breasts are beginning to sag and show their age. No longer do I have the pert and firm breasts I had when I was a twenty-year-old girl. I prefer to keep myself covered. I don't want him to lose interest in me. I prefer to hide my body under the bedsheets where lovemaking is more private.

Our bedroom is unconscionably hot during these summer days. We are experiencing an unusually hot summer. The experts say it's the result of climate change, but I'm not convinced. There have been very hot summers in the past. I think the present hot weather is part of a natural cycle. Extremes of temperature recur from time to time. My mother told me that the summer of 1947 was uncommonly long and hot – and that was after the uncommonly cold winter when snow remained on the ground from December until March.

Well, whatever the reason, we are currently experiencing a heatwave. This is great news as far as the vines are concerned. We need plenty of hot Mediterranean sun to ripen the Cabernet Sauvignon grapes. But the heat does make it difficult to sleep at night.

We keep our bedroom window open to allow the night air to circulate around the room; but, even so, I find it difficult to sleep when it is so hot. Jason doesn't appear to be similarly affected. I guess he's

JESSICA'S VINEYARD

used to the excessive temperatures of Australia. He sleeps peacefully through the night whereas I am constantly going to the bathroom for yet another drink of water.

It is on one of these nocturnal journeys that I glance out of the open bedroom window.

There is a full moon and the area in front of the house and towards the ancient barn is lit by a strange luminous light. It bathes Abbeydore Winery in ethereal beauty. I have never before seen our property looking so otherworldly. The bright colours of daytime are replaced with shades of silver and grey. Black shadows fall to the ground where the beams of the moon are unable to penetrate a tree or one of our buildings. It is a study in black and white with every conceivable shade of the two monotone colours. It is a magical sight and I stand in a trance, overwhelmed by the beauty of the silent moonlit scene spread out before me.

I don't know how long it is that I stand gazing at the magical landscape. It may be just a few minutes or it may be longer; but something causes me to snap out of my trance. There is a movement at the far corner of the barn. At first, I am unsure if it's a shadow cast by the nearby tree. Perhaps the night air has caused the tree's branches to sway and make a shadow creep imperceptibly backwards and forwards over the ground.

JESSICA'S VINEYARD

But I am not aware of any breeze. Indeed, the night is uncommonly still.

I focus my eyes on the far corner of the barn to see if the movement reoccurs. Sure enough it does.

The far corner of the barn is perhaps two hundred yards from the house. I strain my eyes to see if I can make out the cause of the movement.

It is then that I have the shock of my life.

There, in the shadows, at the far corner of the barn, is a hooded figure. It is stationary. Although it does not move, it sways rhythmically. It appears hunched. I watch dumbfounded. Every so often the hooded figure ceases to sway and pulls itself erect.

It is a monk. Well, I presume it is a monk. It wears an ankle-length habit that appears to be fastened around the waist with a cord. It has a cowl pulled over its head making it impossible to see if the figure has a face or is some ghostly apparition.

But what strikes me most forcibly is the colour of the monk's habit. I always thought monks wore black habits, but this monk is wearing a white one. Or, at least, I think it's white, although the moonlight may be playing tricks on me and simply making it appear white.

It's then that I recall the history lesson I was given by the Master of Wines. He said the monks of Dore Abbey were Cistercians who wore white habits.

JESSICA'S VINEYARD

My smallholding was once part of Dore Abbey. White robed monks would have been a familiar sight here five hundred years ago. But not anymore! A shiver runs through my body. I don't believe in ghosts. Perhaps that's because I've never encountered one before. Could this be the moment my unbelief changes into an acceptance of the supernatural? Is this my Damascus Road experience? I focus intently on the shadowy, swaying figure at the far corner of the barn. The ghost stories I read always had supernatural beings gliding noiselessly over the ground with their feet barely touching the surface. But this apparition is not gliding. It is riveted to the spot. It sways and then pauses before swaying again. My mind goes into overdrive. Whatever is this strange apparition? Did a monk from Dore Abbey meet a grisly end here? Is this his spirit rising from the ground and swaying in a paroxysm of anger at the injustice done to him? Is he seeking revenge?

Then another thought assails me. Could this hooded figure be the malignant spirit that wreaked havoc in our vineyard? And set the barn alight? Both of these things happened at night under the cover of darkness. Could this spectral being be intent on yet more mischief?

A shudder passes through my body. If this is the being that wreaked havoc in the vineyard and almost destroyed the barn, what else might it do? And what is it doing now?

The questions bombard my mind. I need help.

'Jason! Jason! Wake up!' I hiss through barely parted lips.

The sleeping figure in the bed stirs, rolls over and prepares to drift back into a deep sleep.

'Jason! Jason!' I hiss more urgently.

I don't want the apparition at the far corner of the barn to hear my voice.

'Wake up! There's someone or something prowling around outside.'

He stirs; but it is only when I move across the bedroom and shake him that he finally awakens.

'What's the matter?' he enquires blearily.

'There's a figure over by the barn.'

'A figure?'

'Yes – like a monk from Dore Abbey.'

'Don't talk daft,' he retorts. 'There are no monks at Dore Abbey. Your dreadful Henry the Eighth got rid of them all.'

'I tell you there's a figure in a monk's habit near the far corner of the barn.'

With a great sigh of exasperation, he pulls himself out of bed and staggers to the window.

'Look! There!' I whisper, pointing to the far corner of the barn.

'Holy cow!' Jason whistles through his teeth.

JESSICA'S VINEYARD

The figure is rooted to the spot where I first saw it. It bends and then straightens upright. The light of the moon causes its habit to emit an ethereal glow.

'It must be some spirit from the past come back to haunt us,' I say with a shudder.

'Don't be daft,' he says for the second time.

I'm not sure I like being called daft. I'm a very level-headed woman. I'm certainly as sensible and logical as any man. I am perfectly aware that there are no white robed monks at Abbeydore in the twenty-first century and so the logical conclusion must be that this is a being from the past unable to find rest. It must be re-visiting its former habitations desperately searching for a place to rest.

'There's no such thing as disembodied spirits,' asserts Jason. 'It's a man – and he's up to no good.'

So saying, he turns on his heel and moves back towards the bed. Reaching under it, he brings out the bolt-action rifle he uses for shooting rabbits.

'What are you going to do?' I ask anxiously.

'I'm going to see whether our monk can take a bullet. That should prove beyond all reasonable doubt if he's real or otherworldly.'

'Don't be a fool, Jason,' I stammer. 'If it's a person disguised as a monk and you kill him, you'll be guilty of murder and you'll be sent to prison. I don't want to see you in prison.'

He nods.

JESSICA'S VINEYARD

Thank goodness he sees the sense in what I am saying.
'OK. But a warning shot over his head should be enough to frighten him off – if, that is, it's a real person. No man is going to hang around with bullets whizzing overhead. If that monk remains riveted to the spot I'll buy your explanation, but I somehow doubt it.'
Raising the barrel of the rifle he takes careful aim.
'Make sure you don't hit him,' I plead. 'You mean more to me than a dead midnight prowler. I don't want you sent to prison for murder.'
'Don't worry! I've had plenty of practice with rabbits. I'm aiming at the corner capstone of the barn just above his head. Just watch him jump!'
And with that there is a terrific explosion as the rifle discharges. The bedroom resounds to the gun retort and a smell of graphite fills the room.
But it's not the bedroom that holds my attention. It is the ethereal figure illuminated by the moon at the corner of the barn.
I don't think I've ever seen anything vanish so quickly. One moment the figure is clearly visible, the next moment it's gone.
At first, I think that Jason must have shot the monk and he's lying prostrate on the ground; but, as I peer more intently through the dispersing graphite haze, I

JESSICA'S VINEYARD

see there's no figure on the ground. The being has vanished.

'What did I tell you?' Jason asserts. 'That was no supernatural being. It was a person of flesh and blood dressed in a monk's outfit.'

'But why would anyone want to do that in the middle of the night?'

'I don't know,' he replies slowly. Then, after a momentary pause for thought, he says, 'There's something very strange going on here and I mean to find out what it is.'

So saying, he moves back into the bedroom and pulls on his jeans and a sweater.

'What are you going to do?' I ask anxiously.

'I'm going to see who it is that's prowling around our property in fancy dress.'

And with that, he picks up the rifle and makes to leave. But I catch him by the arm. I don't trust him with that gun. He's young and impetuous. There is no saying what he might do if he finds someone prowling around outside.

'Wait!' I command. 'If you're going on a search mission, I'm coming with you. Two pairs of eyes are better than one.'

This is not the real reason for wanting to accompany him but it's the best I can think of on the spur of the moment.

'Just wait while I pull on some clothes.'

JESSICA'S VINEYARD

I can tell he's frustrated by my insistence to accompany him, but I am determined he shall not go out into the night alone with his deadly rifle. I have no wish for Abbeydore Winery to become a crime scene and my husband condemned to life imprisonment for murdering an unarmed practical joker.
As soon as I am dressed we go downstairs and out into the moonlit night by the back door. A solitary owl hoots in the distance; otherwise all is perfectly still.
I grab our powerful handheld lamp as we pass through the kitchen, but there is no need to use it. The farmyard is flooded with the silvery light of the full moon.
We move slowly towards the barn.
I grip Jason's elbow and whisper, 'On no account are you to fire that rifle. You can use it to scare the intruder, but you are not to fire it. Do you understand?'
I am terrified he will regard the robed and cowled monk as just another rabbit and his natural instinct will be to fire without thinking.
He does not respond.
We advance stealthily on the barn. I feel my heart pounding in my ribcage. I half-expect to find a figure slumped in the shadows bleeding to death but there is no one on the west side of the barn. We inch

towards the corner of the barn like a couple of cowboys in a western stealthily advancing upon a band of gung-ho outlaws.

With our backs pressed against the stone wall of the barn we listen for the tell-tale sound of breathing that might tell us where our nocturnal intruder is hiding. But no sound do we hear. Then, suddenly, with the rifle cocked, Jason springs out and rounds the corner of the barn with the rifle extended horizontally. He remains motionless for a couple of seconds before lowering his weapon and whispering, 'There's no one here.'

We are now in shadow. He beckons me to follow him along the west side of the barn with a finger over his lips to indicate we do so in silence.

We creep along the wall of the barn until we reach the other corner of the building. Once again, there is a tense pause before Jason springs forward with the rifle pointing into the shadowy darkness. No sound is heard. No movement is detected.

Jason gives a deep sigh.

'Whoever was playing silly buggers has scarpered,' he declares before adding, 'Lucky for him.'

I, too, think it extremely lucky that no one has been fatally injured as a result of our nocturnal escapade.

'Who do you think it was?' I ask.

'Your guess is as good as mine.'

JESSICA'S VINEYARD

'And what was he up to?' I continue. 'It looked as if he was rooted to the spot at the corner of the barn.' So saying, we retrace our steps to the place where the apparition appeared. With the aid of the lamp we see that the ground has been disturbed. Indeed, there is a pile of earth against the wall of the barn and a small hole in the ground.

'Holy Michael!' emits Jason. 'Whoever it was has been digging here.'

'That would account for the swaying action I saw from the bedroom window.' I confirm. 'It must have been the action of digging followed by a period of rest before the person embarked upon another bout of digging. But what was he hoping to find?'

'I don't know. But whatever it was it looks as if he was unsuccessful.'

He pauses and thinks before saying, 'I tell you what: we'll return here tomorrow and take over where he left off. If there's something hidden here we'll be the ones to find it and not this practical joker in a monk's habit.'

What he says makes sense. Also, the night air is making me feel cold.

'Let's go back to the house,' I suggest 'and I'll make some tea.'

We retrace our footsteps back to the farmhouse and, as we sit at the kitchen table warming ourselves with our mugs of hot tea, I say, 'I wonder what the person was searching for? Do you think there might be hidden treasure here? Dore Abbey must have been a very wealthy place in its heyday. It must have possessed lots of gold chalices and plate and such like. Perhaps the abbot or whoever else was in charge, heard about Henry VIII's plans to dissolve the monasteries and decided to bury the abbey's treasures where the Crown couldn't find them. We know that this house and barn once formed part of the abbey's curtilage and so, perhaps, this is the place where the treasures are buried.'

'I think you've been reading too many Enid Blyton stories,' he smiles.

'But why else would anyone want to dig at the corner of our barn under cover of darkness in a monk's habit?'

'I think the monk's habit was merely a disguise,' he answers. 'I don't think the digger had anything to do with Dore Abbey. It was just a convenient way of ensuring he couldn't be identified. He might also have thought that, if he was spotted, he would be mistaken for a ghost and whoever saw him would be too frightened to raise an alarm.'

I hold my peace. I'm not willing to admit that I mistook the figure for a supernatural being. There are some things that are better left unsaid.

JESSICA'S VINEYARD

'But why would anyone want to dig by our barn in the middle of the night if they weren't searching for buried treasure?'
Jason frowns.
'I don't know,' he answers slowly. 'There's something very strange going on here. Perhaps we'll know more tomorrow when we undertake our own excavations.'
And with that we drain the tea from our mugs and return to bed.
But I cannot sleep. The events of the night swirl around in my head.
I'm so glad I have Jason with me. I don't think I would cope on my own with a midnight prowler, vandalism in the vineyard and a potentially devastating fire in the barn.
When I moved to Abbeydore I thought I was escaping from the angst and cut-throat competition of the business world and Alan's increasingly oppressive behaviour; but I seem to have walked into a nightmare. Where is this going to end?
I eventually drift into a restless sleep.
I stand before the abbot in the chapter house of Dore Abbey. His towering figure sits erect in the abbatial chair. He has his mitre on his head. His eyes bore into my soul. What have you done with the abbey's treasures? he demands. Remember your vow of poverty. You are forbidden to own possessions. Everything here is held in common. You have

robbed your brothers. You have succumbed to the sin of covetousness. Your name shall be blotted out of the book of the living. Expect no mercy. You shall be cast out into the nethermost flames of hell. The sin of Ahaz has overtaken you. You have set your acquisitive sights on our vineyard. It has been in this community's ownership for centuries and now you come along and lay your hands upon it. You have seized our vineyard and appropriated what is not yours. You have stolen the holy treasures for which your brothers toiled long and hard to adorn this House of God. And how do you repay your brothers? You abuse your calling. You seize our property. You exalt the secular over the sacred. You turn a deaf ear to the dominical command to lay not up for yourself treasures upon earth where moth and rust doth corrupt and where thieves break in and steal. You are a worm and no man. We cast you out. We expel you. We drive you into the wilderness to live with the wild beasts. We condemn you to the fate of Jezebel. May the dogs tear you limb from limb so that only your skull and the palms of your hands remain. May your corpse be as refuse on a field.
'Help! Help!' I scream as I sit bolt upright in bed in a paroxysm of fear and dread.
'Whatever's the matter?' asks a distant voice

JESSICA'S VINEYARD

'I didn't steal your vineyard. I bought it with my own money.'
'Whatever are you talking about?'
'It's mine - legally mine. You have no claim on it.'
'Jessica, whatever's the matter?
The mention of my name acts as a pin inserted into a balloon. I instantly deflate and shrivel.
Jason sits up in bed and puts a reassuring arm around me.
'Whatever's the matter?' he asks in his confident Australian voice.
I hang my head and sob quietly.
'There, there! You've had a bad dream. It's all the excitement of the night, I guess. There's nothing to worry about. Things will look different in the morning.'
And with that, he draws me to himself. I lay my head on his chest and feel his rhythmic breathing and the steady beat of his heart.
How fortunate I am to have him as my husband. He is my rock. I would be lost without him.
I cling to him and eventually drift back into sleep. When, at five o'clock, the first light of morning enters our bedroom, we get up and embark upon the new day. There is only one thing on our minds: to investigate the ground at the far corner of the barn As soon as we have breakfasted, we make our way to the scene of the previous night's excitement.

JESSICA'S VINEYARD

The bright morning sun exposes a hole approximately two feet in diameter and about one foot in depth with a pile of freshly dug soil piled against the wall beside it.
'Well, our night visitor didn't dig very deep,' laughs Jason. 'You must have spotted him soon after he began digging. My bullet clearly put an abrupt end to his nocturnal activity. Let's continue where he left off and see if we are more successful.'
Without more ado he begins to wield a spade. The ground is very hard. I can well understand why the hooded figure made heavy weather of it. Jason has to repeatedly pause to get his breath before embarking upon another bout of digging.
The hole grows in diameter and depth but nothing of any interest appears.
'This ground hasn't been disturbed since the barn was built in the Middle Ages,' Jason declares. 'The earth is so tightly packed I don't think it's ever been disturbed. I'm afraid your theory about a hoard of treasure buried here looks highly unlikely.'
'But what if this isn't the correct place?' I suggest. 'What if it's buried somewhere else around the outside perimeter of the barn?'
Jason shakes his head, not so much in disagreement as to signify he has no intention of digging around the entire perimeter of the barn in the forlorn hope

there might, perhaps, just possibly, be buried treasure hidden there.

I laugh. He is correct. It would be a tremendous waste of time and energy.

'OK,' I say, 'We'll just keep our eyes and our ears open in case our midnight friend returns. We'll let him do the hard work.'

'I don't somehow think we'll be seeing anymore of him,' says Jason with a grim face. 'Only a madman would risk prowling around here at night now he knows someone in the house has got a rifle and is not afraid to use it. I don't think we'll be disturbed by our monk any more.'

And he was right.

CHAPTER 13

We constantly discuss the mysterious hooded figure that appeared at Abbeydore Winery under cover of darkness, but to no effect. We can find no plausible explanation for the figure's appearance or its strange activity.
Meanwhile summer is morphing into autumn. The leaves on the vines are losing their chlorophyll and imperceptibly changing into every conceivable shade of russet, bronze and yellow. It's an artist's paradise. How I wish I could capture the colours of our vineyard on canvas!
I like nothing better than walking to the top of the vineyard and gazing upon the rows of vines flowing down the hillside in all their mellow autumn beauty. It is beauty tinged with sadness. I know that in a very short time these beautiful leaves will be gone. They will fall to the ground and be trampled underfoot, leaving just the bare black branches of the vines to weather the winter months. Nature is so transient. Its beauties are so short-lived. Here today and gone tomorrow. I find this so sad.

JESSICA'S VINEYARD

Not that my life is sad! I am currently on cloud nine. Life is good. I have an Adonis for a husband. My vineyard is about to yield its first harvest. The wonderful summer weather means that both the Bacchus and Cabernet Sauvignon grapes have ripened to perfection. All doubts about my ability to manage a successful vineyard are banished. I am poised on the brink of a successful career as a winemaker. My courage and resourcefulness have paid off. My break with Alan has been vindicated. Things are going my way and I could not be happier. I know exactly what Keats meant when he said,

Season of mists and mellow fruitfulness,
Close bosom-friend of the maturing sun;
Conspiring with him how to load and bless
With fruit the vines that round the thatch-eves run.

My vines may not run around thatched eaves but they are loaded and blessed with succulence and fecundity.

I fondle the bunches of grapes hanging proudly in clusters like jewels on a royal diadem. They are my grapes. I have succoured them and tended them and brought them to this glorious state. They await only my command to yield their sweet juice in the winepress.

Ten bunches of grapes produce one bottle of wine. Ten handfuls of summer sun, pure well water and soil minerals are about to be captured in a bottle. Ten

JESSICA'S VINEYARD

bunches of grapes will soon produce a bottle of
nectar and ambrosia, making glad the heart, lifting
spirits, lowering cholesterol, reducing the risk of
cancer, keeping the memory sharp and the body slim
– or, at least, that's what the experts say.
But I don't need scientists to tell me that wine is
good for me. I know it from my own experience.
What can be better than to share a bottle of wine
with a group of friends? To savour a wine's
individual character, its bouquet, its lingering after-
taste, its composition, its similarity to other fruits and
tastes? Every bottle is an adventure. There is no
saying where it will lead. It may be a good adventure
or a not-so-good one. But that's the fun of it. Every
wine is unique. Abbeydore wine will be unique. There
is nowhere else in the entire world that has the same
climate, soil structure, rainfall, altitude and vines as
Abbeydore. My wine will be as personal and unique
as me.
I fondle my grapes with a great sense of pride. I have
nurtured them and brought them to the pinnacle of
perfection. Each bunch encapsulates the toil and
hard work that has gone into producing such fine
succulent specimens. They are the fruit of my
labour. My crown jewels. My Hatton Garden rubies
and emeralds. They are my offspring. I caress them
with all the love a mother bestows upon her children.

JESSICA'S VINEYARD

Jason does not share my poetic susceptibilities. He says he would rather fondle a woman's breasts than a bunch of grapes. I notice that he says 'a woman's breasts' rather than 'your breasts'.

Every day we examine the grapes. It is important to harvest them at exactly the right time: if we pick them too soon, the acid levels will be too high, the sugars too low and the tannins too aggressive. If we pick them too late, the sugar levels will be too high, the acids too low and the tannins will have evolved to a point where they will not provide the wine with its required structure.

The Bacchus grapes are more advanced than the Cabernet Sauvignon grapes and so we decide to harvest them first. The skins of the white grapes have changed from deep green to translucent yellow and have become much thinner. They are plump, juicy and easy to pull from the cluster.

We have two-and-a-half acres of Bacchus grapes. That's a large area to harvest and so we begin the task at daybreak.

Jason summons our trusty tractor and trailer to life at 7.00.am and we head for the vineyard. We take it in turns to inch the tractor between the rows of vines whilst snipping bunches of grapes from the vines. It is important not to damage the skins and protect the grape's juice content from oxidisation. It is slow work but immensely satisfying. I smile as I see the

JESSICA'S VINEYARD

harvested grapes gradually filling the baskets in the trailer.

As soon as the trailer is full, we return to the barn to transfer the contents to the crushing machine, in order to destem the fruit, before transferring it into the wine press to produce the must. Our press can take four tonnes of crushed grapes at a time. We need to press the grapes as quickly as possible in order to get the juice off the skins without crushing the seeds.

Once we have picked four tonne of Bacchus grapes, Jason remains in the barn overseeing the crushing and pressing process whilst I take the tractor back to the vineyard to continue harvesting the grapes.

The task is much slower doing it alone. I have to continually break off from snipping bunches of grapes to advance the tractor along the row. I understand now why harvesting has traditionally been a community activity. The more people that are involved, the quicker the task can be completed. But, although it is hard work doing it singlehandedly, I would rather do it on my own than have other people around.

We break off from work at 1.00.pm for a short lunch break.

'I always thought that wine was a fun thing,' declares Jason, 'but I'm beginning to change my mind.

There's not much fun crushing and pressing grapes.

JESSICA'S VINEYARD

It's darn hard work lifting those baskets into the press and transferring the must into the fermenting tank. I just hope it's going to be worth all the effort.'
'Who's the doubting Thomas now?' I ask with a sly grin. 'I thought you were the positive one.'
'Maybe I'm thinking there's an easier way to earn a living.'
'Don't lose heart. This is bound to be the hardest part of the process. We've just got to grit our teeth and get on with it. There'll be plenty of time to relax and put our feet up once the must is fermented and safely stored in barrels.'
My words do not appear to have the desired effect. Jason doesn't normally shy away from hard work. Perhaps it's because he's working on his own in the barn and is cut off from the warmth of the sun and beautiful countryside all around. Perhaps he resents the fact that he's become the equivalent of a factory worker whilst I'm enjoying the delights of the great outdoors.
'Do you want to swap roles?' I ask in an attempt to revive his spirits. 'I could do a stint in the barn whilst you continue harvesting.'
He gives me a wry smile.
'As attractive as that sounds, I don't think it would be very practical,' he replies. 'Have you lifted one of those baskets above your head and felt the weight of those grapes?'

JESSICA'S VINEYARD

He shakes his head.
'I know you're a very independent woman,' he says, 'and you think you can do anything a man can do, but believe me, you'd struggle to manhandle these grapes. Better leave it to me.'
So saying, we go our separate ways – he to the wine press and me to the vineyard.
My joy at harvesting our magnificent crop is tinged with regret that, the more trailer journeys I make to the barn, the more gruelling work I make for Jason. I love him dearly and don't like to see him struggling; but I am a viticulturist. Womanly sentiment cannot override practical necessity. We must gather in the harvest as quickly as possible.
We toil all afternoon and into the evening – he in the barn and me in the vineyard. The first of the fermenting vats slowly fills with beautiful white grape juice and its exquisite perfume fills the barn.
It is the scent of summer flowers mingled with autumn fruit. It is the nostalgic smell of a childhood sweet shop, a tube of sherbet sucked through a liquorice tube and a hand thrust into a bag of dolly mixtures. It is the perfume of a department store's cosmetic department assailing the nostrils as soon as one enters the premises. It is the wafting fragrance of a lemonade factory. It is a smell like none other.
We toil long and hard inside the barn.

JESSICA'S VINEYARD

I wonder how many times others have done the same? Did the Cistercian monks experience the same sense of satisfaction and pleasure in this barn as me when they pressed their grapes and conveyed the must into their fermenting vessels?
Did they drink white wine or were they only interested in mead?
Perhaps they only grew red grapes to make wine for sacramental use on the altar in the abbey.
Thinking about monks causes my mind to return to our nocturnal visitor who so unsettled me some weeks ago. I shiver and immediately banish all thoughts of monks. This is the twenty-first century. We are producing wine for the British retail market and not for some medieval monastic community. Abbeydore wine will sit in the cellars of wine merchants and on the shelves of boutique wine shops alongside other English wines. I must not lose sight of that. Our hard work is necessary to achieve this end.
As the last rays of light fade and night gradually steals across the vineyard, we decide to call it a day. We have harvested approximately a third of the Bacchus grapes. Two more days' hard work awaits us – and then we have to turn our attention to the Cabernet Sauvignon grapes.
We collapse around the kitchen table, thoroughly exhausted.

JESSICA'S VINEYARD

'Whose turn is it to cook tonight?' asks Jason.
'Clearly not you, judging by your exhausted condition.'
Although he is only half my age and is incredibly fit, the day's work in the barn has taken its toll on him.
'Go and have a shower whilst I rustle up something to eat', I say.
As I prepare a makeshift meal, I ruminate on Jason's character. He's always the strong and dependable one. He was not fazed by the fire in the barn or frightened by supernatural ghosts in the night. He's the positive and forthright person in our marriage. But today he appears disheartened. I know that no one likes strenuous manual work, but he is strong and energetic. He should be able to take a stint of manual labour in his stride.
When he reappears, I tackle him about his subdued demeanour.
'I guess I'm just not used to hard manual labour,' he replies ruefully. 'Today has come as a bit of a shock to the system. It's made me realise just how much hard work goes into a bottle of wine. Perhaps I'll be a bit more appreciative in future when I savour a glass of wine.'
He's right. There is a great gulf between the romance of wine and the hard work that goes into producing it.

JESSICA'S VINEYARD

'Well, I'm sure we'll sleep well tonight,' I reply, 'and then, hopefully, we'll awake refreshed and ready to tackle the next trounce of Bacchus grapes.'

*

The remainder of the week is devoted entirely to bringing home the Bacchus grape harvest, crushing the grapes, transferring the must into the press, and the juice into the fermenting tanks. It's hard work and occupies every available hour of daylight. We even continue well into the evening each day, working in the barn under bright fluorescent lights. By the end of the week, two of our large fermenting vats are almost full and we are able to add sulphur dioxide to the must to prevent the juice from spoiling.

We carry out daily tests to monitor the fermentation process. To do this, we extract a small amount of fermenting wine from a tap at the bottom of each tank and then climb a ladder to take a sample from the top. We test each sample with a hydrometer and monitor the rate at which the sugar in the grape juice is converting into alcohol.

White wine normally has an alcoholic content of between 9% and 14%. We have to decide when our wine has attained its optimum alcoholic constituency. I wish I had someone knowledgeable to advise me. There are professional winemakers with cultured and sensitive palates who hire out their services to

JESSICA'S VINEYARD

vineyards and advise on the precise moment to cease fermentation and transfer the wine into barrels. But I cannot afford such professional services. My production is so small as to make the involvement of a professional winemaker uneconomic. I have to make my own decisions. I may not be a Master of Wines but I am capable of telling a good wine from a bad one.

I like my white wines crisp. I dislike the buttery and creamy white wines that are produced through long aging in oak barrels. I want Abbeydore White Wine to be clean and fresh, with just the optimum amount of acidity and a subtle fruit flavour. The bouquet should be full of promise and lure the wine-drinker onwards, filling him (or her) with expectancy and a foretaste of heaven. Well, that's how I would like it to be: whether or not I can achieve it remains to be seen.

Jason has recovered from his week of toil in the barn and regained his former wanderlust. He disappears for hours on end with his rifle to shoot rabbits. It is while he is on one of his treks that disaster strikes.

I perform the daily task of testing the wine to see how fermentation is progressing. The wine is gaining in alcoholic strength by the day, but I am still not convinced that we have reached the optimum point at which we should stop the fermentation process.

JESSICA'S VINEYARD

I extract a sample from the tap at the base of the first large tank and test it before climbing the ladder to repeat the process at the top.
Maybe I am too pre-occupied with the taste and flavour of the wine and too absorbed in the interior struggle taking place in my head as to whether or not the wine has reached its optimum balance. Or maybe I was overstretching to obtain the most advantageous sample of wine from the centre of the tank rather than from the edge. Or maybe I was careless in the way I placed the ladder against the side of the tank. Or maybe I was simply foolish undertaking the task when I was on my own ... I just don't know. But what I do know is that I suddenly feel the ladder slipping from under my feet. One minute I am leaning over the edge of the tank and the next minute I am catapulted into the vat of fermenting grape juice.
It may sound like a winebibber's idea of paradise: being submerged in a vat of wine. The reality is very different. The whole thing happens so quickly and so unexpectedly that I have no time to take breath before my head plunges below the surface of the liquid. Wine fills my nostrils. The opaque nature of the wine means it's impossible to see. I am plunging to the bottom of the tank like a circus stuntman diving from a tall ladder into a miniscule tank of water at its base.

JESSICA'S VINEYARD

I know I've got to get to the surface. My hands touch the base of the tank and I perform a roll. Then, with my feet on the bottom of the tank, I push my body upwards with all the strength I can muster.

I cannot describe how relieved I am to break the surface and grab a breath. My eyes are stinging from the combination of acid and sugar in the wine. My hair clings to my head like sticky flypaper. I cough and splutter like a consumptive in the last throes of life. But I am alive. At least, I am alive.

I tread water – or, perhaps, I should say, I tread wine. Just wait until Jason hears about this! He'll rag me unmercifully. I can hear him accusing me of being an alcoholic who can't have enough of the stuff and has to dive into a tank to satisfy her addiction. I know I'll be the butt of endless jokes.

Although the experience of swimming in a tank of wine is a novel one, I have no wish to remain there, and so I make for the side. Reaching up, I attempt to grasp the rim of the tank to pull myself up and out. But this is not as easy as it sounds. The level of wine in the tank is three feet below the rim. My arms are not long enough to reach the rim of the tank.

A sudden dread races through my body. I am trapped. I am unable to get out. I have no way of escaping from this tank of fermenting wine.

I continue to tread water as my mind races through all possible scenarios.

JESSICA'S VINEYARD

I attempt to calm my fears by reasoning that it can only be a matter of time before Jason returns from his shooting jaunt. I can surely tread water until then. But what if he doesn't return soon? How long can I keep afloat in this tank?
Panic seizes me and I call out, 'Jason! Jason!'
I've no way of knowing if he's returned or is even in the vicinity, but I know I must let him know where I am. I need him.
I curse myself for my stupidity. Why did I allow myself to get into this predicament? You foolish girl! You steer a successful course through an acrimonious divorce; you purchase your own property in a perfect location; you chance upon a wonderful husband who is everything you have ever wanted in a man; you are on the cusp of a fantastic grape harvest; and now this. You're losing everything for which you've strived. All because of your foolishness!
'Jason! Jason!'
But no answering response do I hear.
I've never thought much about death. It's one of those things in the distant future. I hope that when I die it will be in my own bed, surrounded by loved ones, having attained a great age and with no regrets. I never envisaged drowning at the age of forty in a tank of fermenting grape juice. This has never been part of the plan.

JESSICA'S VINEYARD

'Jason! Jason!'
Why do we live in such an isolated location? There is no one around to hear my cries and come to my rescue. I know I wanted to get away from other people when I moved here, but there is a downside to living in such a remote place. There's no one to turn to for help. We are cut off from the rest of the human race. I almost wish we had nosey neighbours who'd come running at the first sound of my cries.
'Jason! Jason!'
It's then that I hear a most wondrous sound.
'What's going on here?' I hear a disembodied voice ask.
It's the voice of a living person. It's the voice of my saviour. It's not Jason's voice but it has a certain familiar sound to it.
'Help! Help!' I call out. 'I've fallen into this tank and I can't get out.'
'Hold on a minute,' answers the voice. 'I'll get the ladder and come up to you.'
I hear the sound of the metal ladder being dragged across the flagstone floor of the barn and placed against the side of the tank.
Fingers appear on the rim of the tank and then a face.
It is Alan's face.
'What are you doing here?' I cry in terror.

JESSICA'S VINEYARD

'That's a nice way to greet your former husband,' he replies. 'It looks as if I've come at a very opportune moment. I've heard of people spending their afternoons in hot tubs but I've never come across a woman submerging herself in wine before.'
'Get me out of here,' I demand.
'Now, now, remember your p's and q's. There's a little word you need to say before I do anything.'
'Please get me out of here.'
'That's better. A little civility never comes amiss.' Reaching over the rim of the tank he extends his arms until I am able to grasp his hands. It's the first time I've held his hands for more than a year. It's a strange sensation. Not simply because my hands are dripping with sticky fermenting wine but because the man from whom I most wanted to escape has somehow become the person I now most desire to help me. He has rescued me from a premature death by drowning.
Once he has pulled me over the rim of the tank he retreats down the ladder and waits for me to follow him to the ground.
'A fine sight you look,' he says with his customary directness. 'Whatever were you doing to end up in there?'
'I was taking hydrometer readings,' I meekly reply. 'The ladder must have slipped from under me and

sent me plunging into the tank. I've had an extremely lucky escape.'

'You certainly have.' And then he cannot resist adding, 'I've always said you'd never survive without me.'

His old egotism has not deserted him. He's as sure of himself as he ever was. He is always Mr Right whilst I am always The Also Ran.

'I'm grateful for your help,' I honestly reply, 'but you're the last person on earth I expected to come to my assistance.'

'Obviously! You were clearly expecting your business partner to come running to your call.'

I take a deep breath. I know that Alan is not going to like this but he has to know.

'Jason is no longer just my business partner,' I announce with all the assurance I can muster. 'He's now my husband.'

'What!' he explodes in incredulity. 'That lad I saw when I last came here? You mean to say you've married him? You're mad! Any boy who marries a woman of your age is only interested in one thing: getting his hands on her money.'

Maintaining my composure I reply, 'I'm afraid you're wrong. We are very much in love. The difference in our ages is immaterial. Jason loves me and I love him and that's all there is to say about it.'

JESSICA'S VINEYARD

'It's your money he loves,' retorts the man for whom money has always been the most important thing in life. 'He's out to fleece you and you've walked straight into his trap.'
Alan can be so infuriating. He has such a blinkered outlook on life. In his eyes everyone is out to get you.
'If I was a wealthy millionairess there might be some truth in what you say, but I'm not. My entire worldly goods amount to this rural property and a few thousand pounds in the bank. I hardly think a young man, with the world as his oyster, would throw himself away on a woman of such limited means if all he was interested in was getting rich quickly.'
Then, as a final salvo, I add, 'We love each other. I don't expect you to understand that, but we do.'
Then, changing the conversation, I recall my shock at seeing his head appear above the rim of the fermenting tank.
'And what brings you here to Abbeydore?' I demand. 'I thought I made it clear I wanted nothing more to do with you. You have no right interfering in my new life. You're no longer my husband and you have no claim on me.'
'Well that's a fine way to thank the person who has just saved you from drowning. But then, you never were a grateful person. You were never willing to accept that it was me that made you what you are. You thought you were the clever one who was able

JESSICA'S VINEYARD

to make her way through life without my help. But not everyone is as ungrateful as you. There are some who appreciate me. And that's why I'm here today. I've come to inform you that I am shortly to re-marry.'

Although this is completely unexpected I cannot pretend it is unwelcome. Having Alan married to another woman will certainly get him off my back.

'I congratulate you,' I say in a voice that hovers between the genuine and the ironic.

But he hasn't finished.

'She's not an immature dolly bird or a piece of juvenile fluff like your new husband but a woman of taste and discernment.'

It is the most I can do to stifle a laugh. Instead, with a superhuman effort, I say, 'I hope you'll be very happy together. But, if you've come to extend an invitation to attend the nuptials, I very much regret I must decline. I am far too busy here.'

'Swimming in tanks of grape juice it would seem.' Then, before I can answer, he continues, 'Of course I haven't come to invite you to our wedding; I merely wanted to make you *au fait* with my current situation before the realisation dawns that you've made a great mistake coming to this out-of-the-way rural slum and wish you'd remained with me.'

His arrogance is breath-taking! As if I would ever want to go back to him! Even if my business fails and

even if Jason were to walk out on me, there's nothing that would induce me to return to Alan Pope. I don't know what I ever saw in him. But I do know I want nothing more to do with him.
I need to get rid of him before I lose my temper.
'Thank you for the update on your current position, as you so delicately put it, but, as there is as much likelihood of me returning to you as there is of the Pope eloping, I think this should be the final parting of the ways. I am grateful for your help in rescuing me from the wine vat but, I think now is the time for us to go our separate ways with no further contact.'
I have no idea what is going through his mind.
I must look a sorry sight with my hair plastered to my head with sticky grape juice and my clothes clinging to my body like cold compresses, but my spirit is undaunted. Does he really think there's a possibility I might return to him? Or was it just a perverted curiosity to see how I was faring on my own that has brought him back to Abbeydore? There is no way of knowing.
'If that's the way you want it, that's fine by me,' he says. He gives me one final withering stare before turning on his heel and walking out of the barn.
It is only when he has left that I realise how close to death I came. I slide down the stone wall of the barn into a crouching positon on the floor and put my head in my hands. I've had an extremely close brush

JESSICA'S VINEYARD

with death. My stupidity could easily have brought all my hopes and dreams to a very premature end. How could I have been so stupid!

But, as I sit and replay the events that unfolded, doubts begin to creep in.

I have performed the hydrometer testing process at the top of the wine tanks numerous times without the slightest indication that the ladder was unsafe. Ladders don't usually fall to the ground unless they slip on wet surfaces. The flagstones in the barn are perfectly dry. They have never been slippery. The ladder cannot have slipped on a wet floor. The only other way a ladder could have fallen was if sideways pressure was put on it.

My act of stretching over the rim of the tank would have put pressure on the ladder, but it would not have been sideways pressure. I was not leaning to the side. I was leaning forwards towards the centre of the tank.

It is then that a new thought enters my head. A shiver races through my body. Perhaps it was not my stupidity that caused the ladder to slip from under me. Perhaps the ladder was deliberately pushed by someone who knew I would fall into the tank. But who would possibly do such a murderous thing?

My mind instantly focusses on Alan. What really brought him to Abbeydore? His story about wanting to tell me about his re-marriage sounded pathetic at

JESSICA'S VINEYARD

the time. It now seems positively implausible. Why did he not email or phone if he wanted to tell me his news? Did he come here in order to gloat, only to have the tables turned on him when I informed him that I had remarried? He lives more than a hundred miles from Abbeydore. Would anyone travel that distance merely to impart a piece of useless information? The more I think about it the more implausible his story seems.

What really brought him to Abbeydore today? Was it sheer good luck on my part that he was in the barn when I needed rescuing or did his presence in the barn have a more sinister reason? Did he watch me climb the ladder and then, when I was leaning over the rim of the tank, stealthily push the ladder from under me?

But why would he do that? I know that Alan has no sense of humour whatsoever and so it cannot have been a practical joke on his part.

Did he want me to fall into the tank so he could then appear as a knight in shining armour riding to my rescue, thus making me eternally grateful to him for his supreme act of heroism? Did he want me to feel that I owed my life to him so that I would feel under an obligation to him ever after?

The questions ricochet inside my head like bullets fired from the gun of an enraged terrorist.

JESSICA'S VINEYARD

I am so enveloped in my internal struggles that I fail to hear someone entering the barn. It is only when someone asks, 'Are you alright?' that I realise Jason has returned from his hunting trek.
I look up at him from my crouched position on the floor and tears flow down my cheeks.
'Whatever's the matter?' he asks. 'Whatever have you been doing? You look as if you've just emerged from a swimming pool.'
He leans over and pulls me to my feet.
'You're sticky,' he observes. 'Whatever's happened?'
I throw myself onto his chest and allow my tears to stream from my eyes.
'There, there. Don't upset yourself,' he says in his reassuring Australian drawl. He wraps his arms around me and holds me tight against his chest. At last I feel safe.
Fighting back the tears I say, 'I've done a very foolish thing. I was taking a hydrometer reading from the top of the tank when the ladder slipped from under me and I fell into the tank. I could easily have drowned. I called out for you but you were nowhere around. I thought I was going to die. It was the most terrifying experience of my life.'
'My darling,' he purrs. 'You should not undertake hydrometer readings when I am not around.'
'I called out for you and, even though you did not hear my cries, someone else did. You'll never believe

JESSICA'S VINEYARD

this, but Alan, my former husband, appeared and rescued me from the tank.'
'What was he doing here?'
There is a note of hardness in his voice. Perhaps it's natural for a husband to be jealous of his wife's former spouse. There is clearly no love lost between Jason and Alan.
'That's what I'd like to know,' I reply. 'He said he was here to tell me of his forthcoming re-marriage; but, the more I think about it the more implausible it sounds. It may be he just wanted to snoop around to see how I was getting on; but even that sounds improbable if, as he says, he's found another woman and is planning on marrying. Why would he be interested in what his ex-wife is doing? The more I think about it the more suspicious I am.'
Summoning my strength I tentatively ask, 'Could there be a more sinister reason for his appearance? I'm beginning to doubt if that ladder did, in fact, accidentally slip from under my feet.'
'What do you mean?'
'I wonder if it was pushed.'
'What! You think someone deliberately wanted you to fall into the tank?'
I nod my head slowly.
'But whoever would want to do that? And why?'
'That's what I'd like to know. It was either a practical joke or else there's a more sinister motive behind it.

JESSICA'S VINEYARD

Either way, it's unnerved me. Life is no longer bright and carefree. I'm worried.'

JESSICA'S VINEYARD

CHAPTER 14

There is no time to dwell on my close encounter with death. Harvesting the red grapes is upon us and we must swing into action to bring home the harvest and process the wine.
I find it hard to conceal my excitement at the prime condition of the Cabernet Sauvignon grapes. They have swollen and expanded like inflated black balloons thanks to the irrigation system Jason installed and the phenomenally hot summer we have enjoyed. They hang from the wires in the vineyard like purses of black gold medallions awaiting the arrival of a buccaneer to claim them as his own. No wonder previous owners of the vineyard retained the Cabernet Sauvignon vines! They may not fruit abundantly every year but when they do they are magnificent. This is going to be a harvest like no other.
The days are drawing in. Jason and I begin work at dawn and continue in the barn until well into the evening. The autumn sun bathes the vineyard in a warm blanket of contentment. The sun has worked

JESSICA'S VINEYARD

its everlasting magic during the long hot summer months and now smiles benignly upon its handiwork. The early morning dew creeps away imperceptibly as the sun climbs into the sky kissing each leaf and bunch of grapes with a loving touch as it does so. The tiny beads of moisture on each grape glisten and sparkle like diamond dust falling from a jeweller's workbench. The bejewelled grapes hint at the moisture within: sweet, sticky, luscious juice encapsulated in fleshy pulp.

The creative wonder of Nature is beyond the inventiveness of the cleverest scientist. It far outdistances the skill of humans. It is a miracle wrought entirely by Mother Nature. The grapes are her offspring; and I am the midwife who snips the umbilical cords and ushers them into the world.

A deep peace steals over me as I methodically work my way along each row of vines. My progress may be slow; the work may be laborious; but I am incredibly happy. I am partaking in the act of creation. I am at one with the universe. I am undertaking a task that others have performed since time immemorial. I am living life as it should be lived – naturally, in step with Nature.

In all probability, I will never become rich making wine at Abbeydore - but what do I care? All I want is to be happy and content with just enough money to live on.

JESSICA'S VINEYARD

My debut grape harvest shows every sign of exceeding all my expectations. Perhaps I can declare a vintage. A grand cru will certainly get my winemaking business off to a flying start and should put money into our bank account to see us through any subsequent lean years.

I prefer red wine to white wine.

Perhaps that's why I'm happiest harvesting the red grapes. I'm able to imagine the taste of the wine each bunch of grapes will produce: wine with an enticing bouquet, a velvety texture, a subtle flavour, deep tannins and a lingering after-taste.

I smile as I perform my midwifery tasks and observe the trailer filling with the fruits of the harvest.

Jason may not share my rapture as he toils in the barn, but he keeps his nose to the grindstone and manhandles the heavy crates of grapes into the crusher and wine press before transferring the must into the fermenting tanks.

It is strenuous work and I feel sorry for him. He is working in a dark medieval barn that has every appearance of a soulless factory whilst I am enjoying the warmth and beauty of the great outdoors.

Although I feel sorry for him, I am also immeasurably grateful to him. He appeared in my life at just the right moment. I could never have brought home the harvest and processed the grapes without him. Whatever was I thinking when I purchased this

JESSICA'S VINEYARD

vineyard and thought I could manage it singlehandedly?
Midway through the morning I have an unexpected visitor.
He is not only unexpected, he is also unwelcome.
I first catch sight of him as I transfer a crate of harvested grapes onto the trailer. He has seen me and is advancing towards me in a purposeful manner.
He has no right coming into my vineyard. I wish Jason was here.
I straighten my back and prepare for a confrontation. I am determined not to be the one who speaks first and so I hold myself erect and wait for him to speak.
'I thought I saw you here as I drove along the lane,' he begins.
I have no intention of confirming his sighting.
He surveys the overflowing crates of succulent grapes on the trailer; but, rather than comment on my magnificent grape harvest, he has his sights set firmly on my husband.
'Where's that young lad that's been trespassing on my land with his rifle?' he demands.
Oh dear! I know this is going to be an acrimonious encounter.
'Do you mean my husband?' I reply.
This instantly takes the wind out of his sails. The thought that Jason could be my husband has clearly

never entered his head and, at first, he is flummoxed and unsure how to react.

He's not good at thinking on his feet and a long pause ensues before he decides on his way forward. 'Whatever he may be,' he eventually answers. Then, with a rare flash of initiative he says, 'If he's your husband you should exercise some control over him.'

I smile inwardly. I cannot imagine Mrs Spragg exercising any control over her husband. He has every appearance of being a headstrong man who listens to no one and ploughs his own furrow irrespective of what anyone else might say.

'Why? What has my husband being doing to upset you?'

'You know full well what he's been up to. He's been trespassing on my land and shooting pheasants. It's poaching. In the past, he'd be sent to the colonies. That's where I think he belongs.'

I have to smile.

I take great pleasure informing Mr Spragg, 'That would be a great homecoming for him. You see, Mr Spragg, my husband is Australian. He grew up in the penal colonies of the Antipodes. Perhaps it was there that he developed his skill with a rifle.'

He ignores the Australian connection.

'What he does on your land is up to you, but he's no right coming onto my land with his assault rifle and shooting pheasants.'

JESSICA'S VINEYARD

'I didn't know you reared pheasants, Mr Spragg,' I reply with raised eyebrows.
This is a blow below the belt. He doesn't. There is no organised Shoot in this part of the world as far as I know. Any pheasants are survivors from former years. They are fair game for anyone able to shoot them.
My unfriendly neighbour gives me a homicidal look. He clearly doesn't like being outmanoeuvred by a woman.
'What I do and do not do on my land is my business,' he replies with his customary rudeness. 'I just want that lad to keep off my land.'
'Why? What harm has done?'
He snorts. He expresses himself principally through body language rather than words.
'None so far,' he grudgingly replies. 'But I don't like his manner and I don't trust him.'
He waits for a response from me but, when I hold my peace, he adds, 'There's something not right about a boy who goes into a wood and practices shooting a scarf that he's fixed to a tree.'
Is he telling the truth or is this another of his ploys to create apprehension in my mind and unsettle me? I know he would like to get his hands on my property; but, to what lengths is he willing to go?

JESSICA'S VINEYARD

Jason goes shooting for rabbits and pheasants. He's never said anything about honing his target practice skills on his jaunts.
Is Mr Spragg intent on causing difficulties for us? Does he want to unsettle me and make me abandon my vineyard? Is he intent on injecting fear into my mind so I throw in the towel and move away? Then, another thought assails me. If he wants me gone, might he resort to desperate means to remove me? Like creeping into the barn whilst I am taking hydrometer readings and dislodging the ladder on which I am standing?
The man standing before me undergoes a transformation. He is no longer my taciturn, bad-tempered neighbour but a man with murderous intent. He wishes me dead. He wants my property to go to probate so he can get his hands on it. He wants me gone. There's no saying what malign intent lurks beneath those bushy eyebrows. He's been outsmarted by a woman and he carries a deep grudge in his heart. He would like to see me dead. Not only is he willing to play the part of the bad neighbour he's also intent on sowing discord between Jason and me. Might he also want to kill me?
A shudder passes through my body. I momentarily close my eyes.
Once I've regained my composure I ask, 'What's wrong with target practising in a wood? It's the way

to improve his shooting skills and rid our property of the rabbits that attack our young vines.'
'Have it your own way. But I don't trust him. If anyone gets killed around here, I know who the first suspect will be.'
It's a chilling thought – but an entirely unlikely one. Jason is no murderer. He's the kindest, most adorable person I know. Mr Spragg is merely trying to cause discord. The sooner I get rid of him the better.
'Thank you for your warning, Mr Spragg. Unfortunately, I can't remain here talking to you all day. I have grapes to harvest. As you can see, my Cabernet Sauvignon vines have fruited magnificently and I have a bumper crop to harvest.'
He eyes the grapes on the trailer enviously.
I cannot resist asking, 'How have your vines performed, Mr Spragg?'
He inhales deeply and I notice that the bushy hairs protruding from his nostrils quiver as if in silent rage. 'It's not just grapes that make good wine,' he replies, 'It's the skill of the winemaker. Anyone can grow grapes. It's turning grapes into fine wine that's the art.'
'Quite so,' I agree. Then, with a wicked sense of humour, I add, 'Perhaps we could have a wine-tasting session later in the year. We could sample your wine and you could sample ours. It could be very instructive. We could see how two wines, produced

JESSICA'S VINEYARD

within a mile of each other, differed and which was the best.'

He scowls. He's clearly not up for my challenge, but he's unable to decline. Instead, he turns on his heel and, without a further word, retraces his way down the slope towards the gateway of the vineyard.

I reckon I came out of that encounter best.

However, I must warn Jason not to venture onto the Spragg's land. Mr Spragg clearly does not like him and there's no saying what might happen if the two of them met. I don't want Jason sent to prison for murdering our neighbour - much as I dislike the curmudgeonly man.

When I transfer the next trailer of grapes to the barn I tell Jason of my encounter with our unfriendly neighbour.

'Don't go worrying yourself about him,' Jason grins. 'Old men don't frighten me. He's spent so long working on the land he's become as dried up as the outback in summer. We're the trailblazers and he knows it.'

I smile at his youthful assurance. When you're young you're undaunted by anything. The world lies before you and is there for the taking. Jason is used to the wide open spaces of Australia: petty spats in rural England must seem to him totally inconsequential. He thinks big and I love him for it. He broadens my horizons. He gives me courage to do things I would

JESSICA'S VINEYARD

never have dreamt of doing before I met him. My life has been transformed since he entered it. I feel so much younger.

Alan always made me feel older than I actually was. He piled on the angst and the worry. When I looked at myself in the bathroom mirror each morning I saw the ends of my mouth turning downwards as happiness seeped from my life. My once bright eyes misted over with the cataracts of worry. My forehead became a tram driver's interchange. Alan added to my years and propelled me towards old age with increasing rapidity.

But Jason has the opposite effect on me. He makes me laugh. His optimism and energy replenish the wellsprings of optimism and energy within me. I feel I've embarked upon a second adolescence and the effect is exhilarating.

Even when I toil long hours in the vineyard, I do so with joy. I am working in partnership with my wonderful husband. I am pulling my weight. I am contributing to the common cause and this gives me a great sense of fulfilment and contentment.

'I can't say I've ever thought of myself as a trailblazer, 'I answer with a smile. 'But, perhaps you're right. I am the madam of this chateau, who is about to declare a vintage year and launch a grand cru upon the world. I'm going where no woman has gone before'

JESSICA'S VINEYARD

'That's my girl!' he laughs. 'Think big and don't let anything or anyone stand in your way.'

'Even so,' I answer, 'I'd feel happier if you kept away from the Spraggs' land. Mr Spragg clearly dislikes you and I don't want anything to happen to you. My near brush with death is enough drama for me to cope with. I don't want anything else to happen.'

He laughs.

'Don't go worrying about me. I'm a big boy. I'm perfectly capable of looking after myself.'

'That's what I'm afraid of. You don't recognise danger. You've got all the impetuosity of youth and you don't appreciate what could go wrong. Trust me, Jason, just this once. Stay away from the Spraggs.'

'OK, old girl,' he answers. 'Anything to keep you happy.'

I plant a kiss on his gorgeous lips before returning to the task of emptying the trailer and returning to the vineyard to continue the work of harvesting the next load of grapes.

JESSICA'S VINEYARD

CHAPTER 15

Maybe it is because we have so few visitors at Abbeydore that, when we do, they assume a significance out of proportion to their actual interest. Or, maybe it is simply that Jason and I are so happy and content with our own company that we resent others intruding upon our love nest and, when it happens, it affects us disproportionately. Or maybe I am becoming a misanthrope and prefer my own company rather than encountering individuals from the world beyond Abbeydore. But, whatever the reason, I have come to look upon visitors as an intrusion and an inconvenience and sometimes a downright nuisance.

Such is certainly the case with Montague Smythe. He bores me. And yet I know he could be a very useful contact when I come to market my wine; and so I maintain a polite and interested demeanour when he pays us a second visit.

I have no idea he is planning to visit. There is no introductory phone call or email. He simply arrives on our doorstep with his bonhomie undiminished.

JESSICA'S VINEYARD

This time he is prepared for my unorthodox appearance around the corner of the farmhouse. He greets me with an effusive display of congeniality. 'Ah Mrs Pope!' he gushes with all the warmth of a Mediterranean day in high summer. 'How delightful to see you again and looking so well.'
'It's no longer Mrs Pope,' I inform him. 'I am now Mrs Knightly.'
'What!' he exclaims in astonishment. 'You mean to say that, not only have you recently acquired this magnificent vineyard but you have also acquired a new husband? Allow me to congratulate you. Two acquisitions destined to mature and age like a good vintage wine and increase in value as each day passes, I have no doubt.'
I have met men like Mr Smythe many times before. They are so full of themselves and their own perceived eloquence that nothing can dent their egos or stem their flow of verbiage.
'And who is the lucky man to have acquired such a beautiful and personable wife, may I ask?'
I am saved from answering his flattering question because just at that moment Jason appears around the corner of the farmhouse. He has heard us talking and has come to see who our visitor is.
'Allow me to introduce my husband, Jason,' I beam at Mr Smythe.

JESSICA'S VINEYARD

Mr Smythe has the hardest job to prevent his eyebrows disappearing into his hairline or toupee or whatever the thatch of wiry hair is on his head as he beholds my husband. He was clearly not expecting to see such a handsome and athletic young man; but, ever the urbane and sophisticated gentleman, he extends his right hand for a handshake.
'This is Mr Montague Smythe, Master of Wines,' I say by way of introduction.
'I guessed as much as soon as I heard you speak,' Jason replies in his pronounced Australian accent. 'Jessica told me all about you when you called last time.'
Mr Smythe blinks. He is entering unexplored country.
'Jessica tells me you'd like to get your hands on a bottle of Abbeydore Wine. Well, you won't have long to wait. This summer has been exceptional and we're all geared up for a bumper harvest. We'll soon have Abbeydore Wine running in the gutters. There'll be so much of it you won't be able to lap it up.'
He receives a wan smile in return.
'I've no doubt it runs liberally in the gutters of your homeland, but here in Britain we take a little more care of our vintages,' replies the aloof Mr Smythe. 'They need treating with delicacy. Not for us the big boozy Australian wines with alcoholic contents to rival a malt whisky. No, British wines are for the

JESSICA'S VINEYARD

refined palate, offering a sensual temptation to wander down an unexplored path and delight upon the unexpected vistas opening before one's eyes.'
I fear Jason is about to retort with unrestrained Australian directness at Mr Smythe's fanciful imagery and so I quickly intervene.
'What brings you to Abbeydore so soon after your last visit, Mr Smythe?' I enquire with the directness for which I was famed in my former career.
'My dear Mrs Knightly – you see, I've got it right – I was in the vicinity and I felt I couldn't pass without taking another peep at your exquisite vineyard and winery. Some people collect postage stamps. Some people collect cigarette cards. Some people collect holiday memories. Some people collect wives…'
At which point he breaks into nervous laughter unsure how his little joke will be received. He is certainly not a man to collect wives.
' … whereas I collect vineyards. I have visited all the wine producing vineyards in France, most of those in Germany, the majority of those in Italy and a great many in Portugal and Spain. And, in each case, I retain a mental image of the vineyard in question. I have the ability to bring to mind its aspect, its longitude and latitude, its alluvial characteristics, its climatic conditions, its winepresses and its vats. I suppose I am a bit like a train-spotter. I have an irreversible urge to collect more and more mental

JESSICA'S VINEYARD

images to add to my collection. It is, I fear, an obsession that is already hopelessly out of control. There must come a point when I will no longer be able to retain the memory of every vineyard I have visited and still be able to differentiate one from another. But, thankfully, that day has not yet arrived, and so I go on my way merrily adding to my store of mental pictures.'

'So what brings you back to Abbeydore, if you've already got a mental picture of it in your head?' enquires Jason with his customary Australian directness

'Well, that's just it,' replies the avuncular Mr Smythe. 'The image I carry of Abbeydore is so vivid that I cannot expunge it from my memory. And so, as I was passing through Herefordshire, I thought I would relive the memory. It was delightful to meet your wife on my previous occasion, and also to observe your ideally situated vineyard, but I thought that, now that harvest is upon us, it would be good to see the winery in full-scale production.

'You seem to forget, Mr Smythe, that this is a very small winery,' I interject. 'We only have five acres and the total workforce is standing before you. This is not a full-scale facility. We are making wine on a very modest scale.'

'Quite so. But don't be hard on yourselves. Large does not necessarily mean good. Indeed, quite the reverse is often the case. Small is beautiful. The total output of Chateau Simone in Palette is only 30,000 bottles or so each year – but what wine! Its very rarity increases its value unimaginably. Who wants a ship's container of Australian Shiraz when one can have a bottle of Chateau Simone? There is no comparison. Small boutique wineries are where the future lies. You are in the vanguard. I congratulate you.'

Then, before either of us can think of anything to say, he continues, 'I was hoping therefore that you might allow me to have a little peep at your production. I realise this is a great imposition but I cannot tell you how delighted I would be to look inside your medieval barn and observe your winemaking in progress. It will become a memory that I carry with me alongside the wineries of Chateau Laffite Rothschild and Chateau Margaux. Abbeydore Winery will become an indelible impression burned onto the retina of my consciousness and one that I will share with others whenever I mention your wine.'

I am on the cusp of indecision. Part of me wants to keep this nosy inquisitive wine buff out of the barn lest he sees something of our winemaking of which he disapproves. We are newbies. We are not sophisticated vintners. We are feeling our way and hoping things will turn out all right. He, moreover, is an expert. He will instantly notice anything that we are doing wrong. He might well use this against us should he write about our wine. Do we really want to give him privileged access to our winery?

But, conversely, he might be an invaluable help when it comes to marketing. Writers like to have interesting background stories they can incorporate into their articles. An old medieval barn in the foothills of the Black Mountains may be just the sort of image that will lodge in the wine-drinking nation's consciousness and cause them to reach for a bottle of our wine in their masses. This could be our big marketing breakthrough.

I glance at Jason to see if I can read his mind, but all I see is a look of intense boredom. He clearly does not like Mr Smythe anymore than I do. But we are not talking about personal likes and dislikes. This is all about selling our wine. We have toiled long and hard turning grapes into wine, but that will be no use if we can't sell the stuff.

I decide to take the plunge.

'Alright, Mr Smythe. You can have a peep inside our barn providing I can trust your professional integrity not to reveal anything of a sensitive commercial or business nature that might harm Abbeydore Winery.'

'Good heavens, Mrs Knightly! Nothing could be further from my thoughts. I have taken a liking to you and your vineyard and wish to do all I can to assist you.'

JESSICA'S VINEYARD

This is indeed good news, if it is true. I can tell by the look on Jason's face that he is not convinced. Nevertheless, I lead the way to our medieval barn with Jason and Montague Smythe following in my wake.
Mr Smythe attempts to strike up a conversation with Jason.
'So how, may I ask, did you and your wife meet?'
'Our guiding stars sped across the heavens until they collided in a terrific cosmic explosion and two souls became one.'
Mr Smythe is unsure how to react. Is Jason taking the piss or is this just the way Australian boys talk?
I smile to myself as I hear the Master of Wines attempt to adjust to Jason's wavelength.
'So was it a case of Aquarius coming into conjunction with Sagittarius at the Vernal Equinox or have I missed something? If it was, you must be into biometric harvesting here at Abbeydore. Yes, I see you, in my mind's eye, picking your grapes at midnight by the light of the moon, when the air is still and delicate moisture has descended upon each grape imbuing it with a unique nocturnal ambience that will differentiate your wine from all others.'
Before Jason can reply with a dose of Australian reality, I call out, 'Here we are. It will take a minute or two for your eyes to adjust to the low light-level inside the barn.'

JESSICA'S VINEYARD

All three of us step inside the barn.
'Magnificent!' exclaims the Master of Wines. 'It is like stepping into the interior of Chartres Cathedral. There is an otherworldly atmosphere here. I sense it. One only becomes a Master of Wines by having a particularly acute sense of taste and smell. I thank the Good Lord that I have been blessed with both.'
He pauses to take a deep intake of breath.
'The aroma of fermenting wine is like incense ascending into the fan vaulting of Chartres Cathedral. It encapsulates human work and toil being offered to the seat of heaven to receive a blessing before it is returned to us as ambrosia. Who could inhale this heavenly aroma wafting around these ancient wooden beams and not be transported to heaven? This building is imbued with the wonder of the ages. How I envy you! Do you not feel at one with the monks who once worked here? Do you not feel that you are part of a great chain of humanity offering your skills and expertise on the altar of necessity in order to receive heavenly blessings in return? Surely only those who feel this way should work in these hallowed courts.'
I remember that he expressed a wish to own our vineyard and winery on his previous visit. Is he making a second attempt to establish his credentials as the person most suited to own this place? If so, he is wasting his time.

JESSICA'S VINEYARD

He pauses in mid flow. Either he has extinguished his flowery prose or else he is waiting for me to react. But, before I can do so, Jason says,
'You wouldn't wax so lyrical if you had to hump heavy crates of grapes into the crusher and the wine press and then manhandle the must into the fermenting tanks. It's bloody hard work, I can tell you. I've sweated my guts out in here. Rather than being a cathedral it's more like a sweat shop. And as for the smell of the grape juice: let me tell you, it gets up your nose and into your sinuses. It impregnates your clothes. When it spills on the ground it's like a skating rink. Don't give me the lyrical soft soap. This is a heavy duty wine factory and no doubt about it.'
This is clearly not the response Mr Smythe was hoping for, but, seemingly unruffled, he urbanely turns the conversation in another direction.
'Where do you intend storing your wine?' he asks. 'I see you have four large tanks along this side of your barn and about eighteen large barrels along the other side. If all goes well - as I am sure it will - that means you should produce approximately 10,000 bottles of wine. Where do you intend laying down that number of bottles?'
'On the wine racks at the far end of the barn,' I answer.
Even in the subdued light inside the barn I notice his eyebrows perform their rapid ascending trick. He

walks past us to the far end of the barn and examines the extensive racking in the area beneath the mezzanine floor. He then turns and delivers his damning verdict.
'I consider this an entirely inadequate location for storing wine. Wine should be stored at a constant temperature. It is susceptible to the slightest variation in temperature. It needs to be stored in the dark, away from sunlight, undisturbed and where there is no likelihood of temperature fluctuations. That is why all the great chateaux store their wines in underground cellars – away from sunlight, away from the extremes of winter and summer, away from prying eyes and light-fingered thieves. Surely, Mrs Knightly, you have a much better place than this to store your vintage!'
'No,' I reply somewhat dejectedly.
I have not given the storage of our wine any thought. The extensive wine racking at the far end of the barn was clearly intended to accommodate a very large number of bottles. I automatically assumed this was the place that Abbeydore wine had always been stored. Why should I think otherwise? But now, this Master of Wines has sown seeds of doubt in my mind.
Could the poor storage facilities have contributed to the failure of previous vintages? Could this inadequate storage have been the reason the

JESSICA'S VINEYARD

Simpsons failed to make a success of their winemaking business? Are we destined to suffer a similar fate due to the lack of adequate storage facilities?

I see Mr Smythe eying me inquisitively before declaiming, 'I would have thought that a medieval barn constructed by monks would have been equipped with a cellar. The monks certainly knew how to construct a vaulted crypt in their abbey church and so why not here? Surely there must be a cellar, Mrs Knightly, where you can store your wine?'

I shake my head dejectedly.

'There is no cellar: just this racking at the far end of the barn.'

Then, adopting a more positive attitude, I say, 'But, as you can see, it is under the mezzanine floor and is enclosed on three sides. I am sure it is not beyond the wit of man to devise some portable partitioning to close off this end of the barn so the wine is stored in darkness. And the walls of this barn are so thick there is very little variation in temperature during the year. We may not have an underground cellar but we have the next best thing.'

I hope this will assuage his professional ire.

But before he can reply, Jason interjects.

'You surely don't think the monks would leave their wine here, do you? They'd be crazy to do so. They'd transport it back to the abbey where they could keep

JESSICA'S VINEYARD

a close eye on it rather than leave it here where anyone could come and help themselves to it. This was just the workplace. The storeroom would undoubtedly be at the abbey.'

'That's a good point, Jason,' I say, wanting to back him up and counteract the negativity emanating from Mr Smythe.

But our wine expert is not to be deflected so easily. 'The facts would not appear to bear out your theory. There is no evidence of a wine cellar at Dore Abbey. I have made extensive enquires and am convinced that no such facility ever existed.'

'Perhaps that wicked old Henry VIII grabbed all the wine and demolished the cellar to hide his tracks,' smiles Jason.

The look of utter contempt that appears on the face of Mr Smythe is worthy of a Hogarth print.

'I think you will find, sir, that no such wine cellar ever existed at Dore Abbey. But, if you are able to locate one, I would be very interested to hear about it.'

'Come on, mate. I haven't got time to go ferreting around old monasteries. That's a job for the brush and trowel brigade. We live in the present, not the past. And just at present we've got a big job on our hands monitoring our wine and bringing it to its optimum peak. So ... not wishing to be rude... but if you've seen all you want and have an image of

JESSICA'S VINEYARD

Abbeydore Winery burnt onto your retina, it's time for us to get on with our work.'
Mr Smythe sniffs before turning to me and saying, 'I am greatly indebted to you Mrs Knightly for permitting me to see inside this magnificent medieval building. I shall retain the memory with great fondness. And if you would be so good as to let me know when your new vintage is available for sale, I will do all I can to assist its success. You have my card. I shall look forward to hearing from you in due course.'
So saying, he bows and leaves the barn with the air of a man who has contended with demons and triumphed and is able to leave the arena with his head held high.
I look at Jason and burst into laughter.
'Have you ever before encountered such a pompous fool?' I ask him.
He shakes his head.
'He needs to come off his high horse and get his hands dirty. That would knock the corners off him and bring him down to earth.'
'Thank goodness you are not like him,' I say with a rueful smile. 'You keep me grounded. I don't know what I'd do without you. You really are my strength and stay.'
He puts his arms around me and enfolds me in a loving embrace.

JESSICA'S VINEYARD

I am so lucky to be sharing my life with him.

CHAPTER 16

I feel I am on cloud nine now that the magnificent crop of Cabernet Sauvignon grapes has been successfully gathered into the barn, crushed, pressed and transferred into the tanks to macerate.

I perfectly understand why country folk organise Harvest Suppers to celebrate the successful harvesting of their crops.

I experience a great surge of pride at having safely gathered in our grape harvest.

Not that we've had to battle against the elements. The weather has been uncommonly good. It is as though some benevolent spirit has taken me to its heart and bathed my vineyard in endless sunshine making my first harvest a joyful and exhilarating undertaking.

Subsequent years may not be like this, but I am grateful that my first harvest has been such a great success. It has lifted my spirits. It has encouraged me to press onwards. It has strengthened my conviction that I can succeed in my new life.

The actual harvesting process itself has been gruelling, especially for Jason who has worked

JESSICA'S VINEYARD

extremely long hours in the barn processing the seemingly endless procession of crates packed with luscious red grapes. The hard work has taken its toll on both of us. We are too exhausted for love-making. Both of us have operated on short fuses at times. The unremitting round of toil has robbed life of its customary carefree abandonment. The harvest season has exerted a heavy toll on both of us.

But thankfully, all of that is now behind us. All is safely gathered in, as we used to sing in school assemblies at this time of year, and now we can relax. We rest from our labours. We don't have to get up at the crack of dawn and work until late at night. The harvest has been gathered in and we can now feast and relax.

Of course, there is still work to do. We monitor the maceration process daily, racking the red wine from the lees and carefully controlling the fermentation; but the pressure is off and we can amble around the winery with a sense of achievement following all our hard work.

Not that there have been any monetary rewards so far. We have had to invest large sums of money purchasing 10,000 glass bottles, corks, capsules; cardboard packaging and having labels specially designed and printed for us.

Jason has successfully got the bottling machine operational in readiness for the bottling process. But

JESSICA'S VINEYARD

that is still a long way off. The wine must age in barrels for six months at least.
Transferring the wine from the tanks into the barrels is our next task.
We live in our own micro-world, far removed from other people and the trappings of society. We are undisturbed by whatever may be happening in the world. We live for each other and for our wine. Some may think it is a very selfish existence, but I love it; so much so, that I resent intrusions from outside.
So when the sleek Jaguar of Councillor Johnson purrs to a halt outside the farmhouse just as Jason and I are enjoying a cup of coffee and a plate of homemade chocolate cookies, I am not pleased.
'What does that confounded nuisance want now?' I ask through clenched teeth.
'There's only one way to find out,' answers Jason with a grin. 'Invite him into the kitchen and we'll grill him.'
I smile at his youthful playfulness. I hardly think we are a match for a seasoned politician, but it might be fun to see if we can cause him a little discomfort.
As soon as his rat-a-tat-tat is heard on the front door knocker, I leave the kitchen via the back door and walk around the house to confront our unwanted visitor on the doorstep.
'Ah, Mrs Knightly! You must forgive yet another intrusion from me. You must think its election time

JESSICA'S VINEYARD

and I'm on the campaign trail with my frequent visits to your property, but not so. I simply want to have a word with you, if you're able to spare me a few minutes of your time.'

I think of Jason sitting at the kitchen table waiting to get his teeth into the County Councillor.

'By all means', I answer with unfeigned charm. 'My husband and I were just having a cup of coffee. Won't you join us?'

'That would be delightful,' he answers.

I lead the way around the house to the rear entrance and show Councillor Johnson into our farmhouse kitchen.

Jason rises to greet our visitor. Councillor Johnson must be three times Jason's age.

'I don't think we've met before,' states the urbane politician. 'You were not at home when I last called. I'm Cecil Johnson. No doubt your wife has mentioned me. I'm delighted to meet you.'

He conceals any surprise he may have at Jason's youthfulness with the suavity that goes with being a politician of a particular political hue. He extends his right hand for the customary handshake.

'My God, you've got a strong handshake!' he exclaims, as Jason squeezes his hand for all it's worth.

'Everyone's got a strong handshake where I come from,' answers Jason. 'We don't go in for namby-pamby handshakes.'

JESSICA'S VINEYARD

'I see,' responds our somewhat discomfited visitor. 'And, judging by your accent, you come from Australia.'

'That's right, mate: the largest penal colony in the world. All of us are descended from convicts: sheep-stealers, pickpockets, rapists, thugs – you name it and we have it in Australia.'

This is a side of Jason I've never seen before. He has a swagger and a bravado that I never knew existed.

'Well, I hope you fall into none of the aforementioned categories,' replies Councillor Johnson with a nervous laugh. 'Herefordshire is a peace-loving county and we want it to remain that way.'

'Don't you believe it, mate,' retorts Jason. 'We've had vandals and arsonists here at Abbeydore during the short time I've lived here. There may even be a homicidal maniac in the vicinity. Herefordshire is as wild and untamed as the great outback.'

Councillor Johnson is noticeably taken aback.

'I heard about the fire in the barn, of course, but I had no idea it was arson or that you've been subjected to rural vandalism. Have you informed the police?'

'A fat lot of good that would do!' exclaims my husband. 'The police have as much chance of catching a vandal or an arsonist in Herefordshire as catching a dodo in Antarctica.'

JESSICA'S VINEYARD

'I think, if I may say so, you are being a little unfair on the county constabulary. We have one of the lowest crime rates in England and I like to think that is down to the sensible way in which things are managed in this county.'

'Nothing like blowing your own trumpet, mate.'

I am beginning to feel uncomfortable. I am all for a bit of fun but I think Jason may be going a bit too far. There is a fine line between having a bit of fun and being downright rude. The line may be more blurred in Australia than it is in England but I feel I have to intervene.

'And so what brings you to Abbeydore yet again, Councillor Johnson? This must be your third visit this year.'

'Indeed. You must forgive my constant intrusions. You must think me a frightful nuisance.'

He gives Jason a withering look, but before my husband can respond, Councillor Johnson continues. 'The truth of the matter is, I've been thinking long and hard about your business here at Abbeydore. I greatly admire your entrepreneurial spirit. We need more people like you who are willing to work hard to establish new businesses and are prepared to make sacrifices in order to achieve success. I have no doubt Abbeydore Winery will flourish under your tutelage. But have you ever thought what you might be able to achieve if you possessed a greater acreage? Scale is

JESSICA'S VINEYARD

everything. It can't have escaped your notice that Herefordshire farms are getting bigger and bigger every year. Small farms are being amalgamated into larger ones thus reducing the amount of expensive agricultural machinery required and limiting the number of people employed. That makes these larger farms more economic and profitable. So it must be with you. Five acres is a very small parcel of land on which to grow vines. I've no doubt you've been very successful this year, given the exceptional summer we've had. But, just think: if you had double or treble the amount of land at your disposal, your harvest would be double or treble what it is this year. In other words, increased scale would lead to increased profitability.'

'Are you suggesting I undertake double or treble the amount of hard manual labour I've done this year?' asks an incredulous Jason.

But before Councillor Johnson can reply, he continues, 'I've sweated my guts out in that barn turning a five-acre crop of grapes into wine. And now you're suggesting I double or treble my blood, sweat and toil! I'd like to see you undertaking the work I've done this year. You'd soon realise it's no walk in the park.'

'Quite so,' replies the councillor, clearly upset that his sales pitch has been interrupted by someone who is little more than a lad recently out of short trousers.

JESSICA'S VINEYARD

'But not every year will be as good as this one. The Simpsons, who were here before you, failed to turn in a profit for five years. The secret is to make money when the times are good and thus provide security for yourselves when times are bad. It's all a question of scale.'

Taking a deep breath, and having delivered his preamble, he gets down to business. 'I informed you on my last visit that I was very interested in purchasing this property to build a new house for myself. That is still the case. However, I perfectly understand your reluctance to sell so soon after moving here. And so, I've been doing a bit of work on your behalf. I've got some contacts amongst chartered surveyors and I've come to hear of a vineyard, elsewhere in the county, that is shortly coming onto the market. It's a well-established business. It's in a delightful location. It has a good track record and a sales ledger that many would die for. But this is the best bit: it has 20 acres of well-established fruiting vines. Just think of it! Twenty acres! That's four times the size of your present holding. It is capable of producing four times the number of bottles you are currently able to produce. It would generate four times the profit for you.'

'Four times the bloody amount of hard work turning all those grapes into wine,' retorts Jason.

JESSICA'S VINEYARD

Councillor Johnson grimaces at this latest interruption.

'No one makes money from sitting on their hands,' he replies. 'You have to be prepared to work. If, however, you're successful and achieve a handsome return, what's to stop you employing others to do the hard graft whilst you take on a supervisory role? It's how all small enterprises start before they grow into large and successful businesses.'

Then, turning his attention to me in the hope he will make better headway if he deals directly with me, he says, 'Obviously, a vineyard and winery four times the size of Abbeydore is going to sell for four times the price that you paid for your property. But I can pull a few strings. I've been talking with my contact and I'm sure I can acquire the vineyard on your behalf at an affordable price. I, therefore, have a new offer to put on the table. I am willing to purchase this other vineyard and winery before it goes on the market and convey it to you in exchange for this smallholding. You would be getting the best of the deal but I would have a site on which to build a new house to keep Mrs Johnson happy.'

Before I have chance to say I'm not interested, he adds, 'Of course, you would want to see the property before you make a decision. I've no desire to rush you. But, as I say, the property has not yet been put on the market and we have to act promptly if we are to secure it. And so, my suggestion is that the two of you treat yourself to a day out; have a look at the property; perhaps enjoy lunch at *The Masons Arms* which is just across the road; and then, after you've had time to consider the pros and cons, get in touch with me and let me know your thoughts. I can't be fairer than that, can I?'

He gives me a wide smile. He resembles a Cheshire cat who has just devoured an enormous saucer of cream. He has performed his sales pitch and, despite the interruptions from Jason, feels he has done himself proud. He awaits our response to his generous offer.

'Forget it, mate,' declares Jason without a look in my direction. 'I've no intention of slaving over a winepress four times longer than I have this year. If Jessica accepts your offer, I can tell you, I'm leaving.'

I am horrified. The mere thought of Jason contemplating an end to our marriage fills me with unimaginable dismay. But I can tell he's adamant. He dislikes Mr Johnson and has no intention of giving the proposal his slightest consideration. I share his dislike, but I wish he had consulted me before delivering his ultimatum. Marriage is all about sharing. I have always shared my hopes and plans with him. I feel let down by the stand he has so publicly taken without first consulting me.

JESSICA'S VINEYARD

However, I have no intention of allowing Councillor Johnson to come between me and my husband, and so I quickly align myself with Jason.

'I'm very sorry, Mr Johnson, but, as you can see, we have no desire to sell. It may be only a small boutique winery but it supplies our needs and we are very happy here. We have no wish to move. We appreciate the time and trouble to which you've put yourself on our behalf and, although we might seem ungrateful, we thank you for your interest.'

He shrugs his shoulders.

'There aren't many people who would turn down a 400% return on their investment, but if that's how it is with you, so be it. You know how to contact me if you have a change of heart.'

And with that, the somewhat deflated country councillor rises from the kitchen table and with a perfunctory nod of his head leaves via the back door. I wait until the sound of his car recedes down the drive before I turn to Jason and say, 'You were extremely rude to Councillor Johnson.'

'Not rude: just to the point. I can't stand people who give themselves airs and graces and think themselves superior to us. There's something about him I don't like. He doesn't ring true. He's up to no good, mark my words. I can sniff out a rotten apple and he's definitely one.'

JESSICA'S VINEYARD

'You may well be right,' I answer, 'but using our marriage as a bargaining chip in the argument really hurt me. Would you really walk out on me if I decided to sell Abbeydore?'
I look directly into his eyes. I want an honest answer. Is he wedded to me for life or is our marriage an expendable commodity? I await his answer with great apprehension.
But rather than answer he breaks into a great guffaw, springs to his feet and throws his arms around me. 'Who in their right mind would ever want to leave you?' he whispers in my ear as he nuzzles his nose into my hair and enfolds me in a strong embrace. All doubts are banished. I am secure within his enfolding arms. Life goes on.

*

Two days after the unexpected and unwelcome visit of Councillor Johnson, we have yet another visitor to Abbeydore Winery. This time it is not a sleek and expensive Jaguar that pulls up outside the farmhouse but a more modest Toyota.
I watch from the kitchen window as a tall, erect young man emerges from the car, straightens his grey suit jacket and walks purposefully to the front door. I estimate that he is in his early thirties. He has a good head of dark brown hair and a swarthy complexion. Even from a distance I can tell he has very dark brown eyes.

JESSICA'S VINEYARD

I wait for his rat-a-tat-tat on the front door before leaving the kitchen via the back door and walking around the house to confront him sideways on.
He surveys me in a professional manner as if he is used to evaluating those he meets and forming an instant opinion of them. I hope his opinion of me is good. He is certainly good-looking. He smiles and introduces himself.
'Detective Sergeant Rees,' he announces as he produces a warrant card from his breast pocket and extends his arm so I can scrutinise his picture and his credentials.
'I wonder if I can have a word with you.'
'What about?'
'Perhaps it would be best if we went inside.'
I lead the way around the house and into the kitchen. My heart is fluttering. Ever since I was a little girl, I have always been frightened of the police. I foolishly think they know everything about me. They can see into my soul and know everything I have ever done wrong. And, even if I am able to conceal my crimes from them, they have the power and the means to extract the truth and expose my wrongdoings, guilty secrets and past misdeeds.
Although I am no longer a silly little girl, that childhood unease remains. Why is DS Rees here? What possible crime have I committed?

JESSICA'S VINEYARD

The last occasion I came face to face with a policeman was when I applied for a gun licence for Jason.

Oh my god! Don't say Jason's shot someone! Don't say he's had an altercation with Mr Spragg in the woods and murdered him! Don't say DS Rees has come to arrest Jason!

Pull yourself together, Jessica. If he was here to arrest Jason he would be accompanied by other officers and they would almost certainly be in uniform.

Calm yourself Jessica. Think clearly and rationally. There must be a perfectly simple explanation for this unexpected visit from the local constabulary.

'Won't you have a chair?' I ask motioning towards one of our kitchen chairs while seeking to present a calm and assured demeanour in the presence of the detective.

'There's nothing to worry about,' declares DS Rees, probably sensing my unease. 'You've done nothing wrong. I'm here just to see if you can help us in our enquiries.'

I heave a great sigh of relief.

Even if he notices my relief he doesn't show it. Instead he asks, 'Have you received any unexpected visitors recently?'

My mind races back over the past few days.

JESSICA'S VINEYARD

'We don't have many visitors,' I reply tentatively. 'Abbeydore is not exactly Piccadilly Circus.'
He smiles politely.
'But yes, we have had a number of visitors over the past few weeks,' I add.
'Can you tell me who they were?'
DS Rees produces a notebook from his pocket in order to record my words.
'Well, there was my ex-husband, Alan Pope. He appeared quite unexpectedly and fortuitously as it happened. I'd fallen into one of the wine tanks and he came at just the right moment and rescued me.'
'Very fortunate,' mutters the plain clothes officer.
'And then there was Montague Smythe. He's a Master of Wine. He expressed an interest in Abbeydore Wine. He asked to look around our facilities and passed on some useful information regarding the storage of wine.'
'Anyone else?'
'Well, yes: Councillor Johnson. Do you know him?'
'Is that Councillor Cecil Johnson of the County Council?'
'That's the one.'
'May I ask what he wanted?'
'Well, it is very strange. He wants to buy our vineyard and winery; but not to make wine. He says he and his wife would like to have it as the site for a new house.'

JESSICA'S VINEYARD

'Did he make you an offer for your property?' he asks.

'Yes, and a very generous one. At first he offered to pay double what we paid for it at auction; and then, on his last visit, he offered to quadruple the amount we paid for it. It was a very attractive offer, but my husband was not to be moved. We don't wish to sell.'

'I see. And did Councillor Johnson say why he was willing to pay four times the price you paid for this smallholding?'

'He said he wanted to build a house far from the madding crowd. He said that, being in the public eye, he needed somewhere remote where he and his wife could enjoy peace and quiet. He said that our location suited his needs perfectly.'

'May I ask how much you paid for your property?'

'Certainly. It's common knowledge. If I don't tell you, you'll discover it at the Land Registry. I paid £300,000.'

'And so Councillor Johnson offered you £1.2 million for your smallholding. Is that correct?'

'I suppose it must be. He said it would enable us to exchange our vineyard for another one that he knew of that was four times bigger.'

'Did it strike you as strange that someone was willing to pay £1.2 million for your property?'

'Well, not really. As we don't want to sell, his offer was really immaterial.'

JESSICA'S VINEYARD

He nods his head.
'Has anyone else expressed an interest in acquiring your property?'
'Yes. Numerous people.'
His eyebrows rise in surprise.
'Who exactly?'
'Well, our neighbour at the adjoining property, Mr Spragg. I think he would like to get his hands on Abbeydore Winery so he could expand his own vinicultural enterprise.'
'Anyone else?'
'Yes. Mr Smythe, a Master of Wine. He said he was looking for a small boutique vineyard where he could try his hand at wine production. He left me his card.'
'May I see it, please?'
I hand the card to him and he scrutinises it before recording the details in his notebook.
'This is all very mysterious,' I smile. 'Can you tell me what it's all about?'
He snaps his notebook shut.
'I'm sorry Mrs Knightly, but I'm not at liberty to talk about our current investigation. But you have been extremely helpful. You've given me a number of leads to work on'
He rises from the kitchen table and prepares to leave. But before he does so he says, 'If you think of anyone else who has expressed an interest in acquiring your property do let us know. I can be

JESSICA'S VINEYARD

contacted at Hereford Police Station. If I'm not there, you can always leave a message.'
And with that he smiles and leaves.

JESSICA'S VINEYARD

CHAPTER 17

The task of transferring wine from the stainless steel fermenting tanks into the wooden barrels has been a slow and tedious process. We have an electric pump and extensive lengths of piping to convey the new wine into the barrels, but we have to be scrupulously careful to ensure everything is sterile. It only wants one length of piping to be contaminated and we would lose our entire vintage.

Likewise, we have to ensure the inside of each wooden barrel is sterile. We do this using extremely hot water. But with eighteen barrels stacked three high it is no easy task. We work long hours in the barn.

When Jason becomes despondent, I remind him that our hard work will be worth it once we bottle the wine and market the first bottles of Jessica's Vineyard vintage.

It is surprising how long it takes to ensure all eighteen barrels are sterile.

Besides working long hours in the barn, I have to make weekly journeys into Abergavenny to stock up on provisions and supplies.

JESSICA'S VINEYARD

It is just as I am leaving our smallholding in the Land Rover to drive to Abergavenny that my life stops.
I have endured shocks in the past. They have taken my breath away and caused me to freeze. But they have been momentary. For a split second they numb the brain and make rational thought and action impossible.
There was the time when I sliced through my finger cutting apples. For a split second my mind went blank. I knew I had done something terrible but I was unable to register what it was or how to react. I stared in blank abstraction at my finger until crimson blood began to ooze through the gash and run down my hand. It was the sight of the blood that made me spring into action.
But it was no cut to the hand that brought me to a halt as I swung the Land Rover out of the entrance to the Winery. It was the appearance of an alien from another world.
I have read science fiction stories about little green men from other planets invading the earth and have not experienced the slightest fear. Indeed, I laugh at the unbelievable nature of such stories. But this is no alien from another planet. This is my nemesis.
All rational thought disappears. I am no longer in a motor vehicle. I no longer have my hands on a steering wheel and my foot on the accelerator. I am transposed to another universe. Time ceases to exist.

JESSICA'S VINEYARD

I am in limbo. My mental faculties become deranged. I am floundering like a drowning woman in a sea of incomprehension. I have left the tranquillity and peace of Abbeydore far behind and entered an alien world. It is the world of nightmares where strange creatures crawl out of shadows to claw and laugh at their victims with hideous voices. I have entered my version of hell and there is no escape. There is no way out. I am frozen with fear and foreboding. I cease to breathe. I have no need to breathe. I am dead. There is no point in living. All my plans, hopes and desires have turned to ashes. My world has ceased to exist. I am face to face with annihilation. My RE teacher maintained that after death came resurrection. But I don't want resurrection. I want escape. I want annihilation. I want death to swallow me up and plunge me into oblivion. I don't want to confront this evil. I want to run as far as possible from the image before me.

There is no way of knowing how long I remain frozen in time. It may have been minutes. It may have been a split second. It seems
like eternity. But, whatever the timespan my life ceases to exist.

With a supreme act of will, I grip the steering wheel with hands of steel and focus my eyes on the sight before me.

JESSICA'S VINEYARD

There, at the entrance to the winery, completely blocking the narrow lane, is a car. My mind registers it is a blue car. But it is not the car that makes my blood run cold and my heart stop beating. It is the face of the man sitting at the wheel of the car.
I would know that face anywhere: the thin lips, the arched eyebrows, the deep scowl lines from the base of the nose to the chin, and the cold, steel blue eyes. It is a face that is burned onto the retina of my mind for ever.
I thought I had erased it from my memory when I turned my back on the city and came to Abbeydore, but it has followed me. It has sought me out. It has tracked me down. It is merciless. It is the face of a man devoid of warmth and forgiveness. It is my nemesis.
I see a smile spread over the face. It is a cruel smile. It is the smile of a fox that has cornered a chicken and knows its victim has no escape. It is the smile of a perverted sadist about to inflict pain and suffering on its victim. It is the vengeful smile of a man who has waited long for this moment.
I am trapped. His car completely blocks the lane. He has no intention of moving. He is relishing the moment. He has Jessica Knightly (nee Pope) exactly where he wants her: cornered, trapped and helpless.
Act, Jessica, act!

JESSICA'S VINEYARD

I recall a police officer telling me at a cocktail party that the thing that unnerved him most when he pulled a car over was when the driver emerged from the vehicle to confront him head to head, rather than remaining in the driving seat.
I must assume the upper hand and assert my dominance.
I will confront the man blocking my forward progress head to head. But, as I open the door of the Land Rover to advance towards his vehicle, he opens the door of his car and stands leaning against it.
The smile on his face is satanic. I see the cruelty and ruthlessness I knew so well on display. His face mirrors his soul.
He has a companion sitting in the car's passenger seat.
I determine not to be intimidated. I stiffen my sinews and take a deep breath. There is no escaping this confrontation. I have no intention of appearing weak and vacillating as I advance towards him.
'Well, well, well! What a surprise!' he sneers in mock surprise.
It is no surprise. He has deliberately tracked me down and winkled me out. The odds against a chance encounter on a minor lane in deepest Herefordshire are a million to one. This is no fortuitous meeting on his part. This is a deliberately staged confrontation.
'What do you want?' I demand.

JESSICA'S VINEYARD

I know full well what he wants. He wants my head on a platter just like the biblical Salome wanted the head of John the Baptist. He wants me dead. Or, if he is unable to achieve that, he wants to make my life hell. He has discovered my secret hideaway and has every intention of turning the screws so that I suffer both physically and psychologically.

My security has disappeared. The walls of my castle have been breached. My peace of mind has evaporated. I am at the mercy of someone who has me encircled and is intent on victory.

'That's not a very friendly way to greet a former business associate.'

There was never the slightest friendliness between us. He was always utterly mercenary. He was so used to getting what he wanted that, when I outwitted him and successfully secured the seven-figure contract he thought was his, his anger knew no bounds. He saw money slipping through his fingers. He saw his commission evaporating. He saw his bonus atomising. He was not a happy man.

His anger was magnified a hundredfold because he had been pipped to the post by a woman. He accused me of dishonesty, underhand tactics, supplying sexual favours, bribes to secure the contract and anything else he could dredge from his arsenal of dubious practices with which to tar and discredit me. But, of course, he failed. Our company secured the contract and he was left in the wilderness to stew.

Keeping my voice steady and my chin up I ask, 'Can you please remove your vehicle so I can pass?'

He has no intention of moving. He has got me where he wants me and is determined to exploit his advantage to the full.

'Aren't you going to invite me into your winery so I can sample your wine?' he asks with an oily smile.

I have no intention of allowing him to enter my property even if I had wine to offer him.

'I don't know what you're doing here, and I don't really care. But, as far as I'm concerned, you belong to a past chapter of my life and I have no wish to renew the association.'

'Listen to her,' he says to the person inside the car. 'Little Miss Hoity-Toity.'

Then, turning his attention back to me he says, 'The past has an uncomfortable way of catching up with you, Mrs Pope. You may think you've hidden yourself away in a remote corner of the world but the wreckage you left in your wake has not disappeared so easily.'

Just at this moment, the passenger's door of the car opens, and a woman emerges. She is heavily made-up. Her hair is immaculately styled and she wears expensive designer clothes. I feel like a country bumpkin by comparison. Her make-up hides her true

JESSICA'S VINEYARD

face. She could be aged anything between forty and sixty. She stares at me. There is no attempt to disguise the contempt in which she holds me.

'Is this the woman who robbed me of my new home, Henry?'

'The very same,' replies her husband.

'No wonder she's had to adopt a new identity and hide in the depths of the countryside!'

I listen in silence as the two of them berate me. There is no point attempting to reason with two entrenched and bigoted individuals. I was merely doing my job. There are winners and losers in the world of commerce. It's the nature of capitalism. Most of us don't take it personally. We shrug our shoulders when we fail to pull off a deal and move on. But not the Jackson-Jones! They clearly bear a deep grudge towards me.

They see me as a malevolent actor who has upended their financial plans. I am the cause of their financial difficulties. I have become their whipping boy.

'Your vehicle is blocking the lane,' I repeat. 'Can you please move it?'

I know it is a useless request. They have no intention of allowing me to escape.

He leans nonchalantly on the open door of his car and says, 'So this is where you spent your winnings: purchasing a vineyard and winery. I suppose you thought you could escape to the back of beyond and

get blotto on wine; that way, you could erase all memories of your underhand dealings in the City.'
'I never resorted to underhand dealings,' I answer, making a superhuman effort to retain my composure and not allow my anger or my fear to overpower me. 'We were on opposite sides. Only one of us could be the winner. It just so happens that, on that occasion, it was me. It could have been you.'
He emits a chilling laugh.
'Of course it was you,' he sneers. 'You used your feminine wiles and favours to pull off the deal. It was bribery and corruption at its most insidious. You were indifferent to those of us with family responsibilities and dependent on commission to eke out a living.'
'Yes,' chimes his wife. 'I've never agreed with women in the workplace. It's a man's place to earn a living and maintain a family. Career women like you muddy the waters. A woman's place is in the home, providing for her husband.'
I can hardly believe my ears. We are living in the twenty-first century and yet Mrs Jackson-Jones harks back to the nineteen-fifties. She clearly relishes being a kept woman and resents it when her husband is unable to keep her in the manner to which she is accustomed.

JESSICA'S VINEYARD

I have no intention of getting into a political argument about the role of women in the twenty-first century. I want the Jackson-Jones out of my way. 'This is my home and you are blocking the entrance to it.'

'You're lucky to have a home!' exclaims Mrs Jackson-Jones. 'We had to sacrifice our dream home because of you. After all the hard work Henry put in, you came along and ruined everything. I'll never forgive you!'

The man who was once my rival in the business world assumes a different aspect. He is a hen-pecked husband. He is subjugated to a woman who demands material possessions. His domestic life must be hell on earth. He is no longer the assertive businessman with a will of steel but the victim of an oppressive wife. And I have been demonised and made the reason for his inability to provide her with the things she wants.

We stand facing each other. A vast chasm separates us. We inhabit different worlds. I have no desire for material possessions. I am happy living in step with Nature. I have been transported to heaven sharing my life with the adorable Jason. I am perfectly content busying myself around my smallholding and working for the day when Jessica's Wine goes on sale.

JESSICA'S VINEYARD

They, conversely, are consumed by jealousy and anger. Their happiness is dependent on material possessions. I feel sorry for them.

'I am sorry you feel that way about me,' I reply, 'but I assure you I did not profit disproportionately from the business deal that I secured. I received commission, of course, but it was not excessive and it certainly did not enable me to purchase this property. I am here because my marriage ended and I used my alimony to purchase this property.'

I have told them more than I intended, but I have, somehow, to move things on in order to shake them off and get away.

'I'm not surprised your marriage ended!' retorts the painted woman a few feet in front of me. 'Anyone who exchanges the role of a housewife for that of a businessman is bound to come to grief. It's unnatural.'

Jackson-Jones clearly thinks it's time he took control. 'No matter how you came to acquire this bolthole, the fact remains you cheated me of a substantial bonus and plunged me into great financial difficulties. We've had to downsize and curtail our social activities because of you. But I don't see why we should suffer and you shouldn't. I don't forget and I don't forgive. You've inflicted pain on us and now it's your turn to experience pain.'

JESSICA'S VINEYARD

His words send a shiver down my spine. I feel very vulnerable. This is a very isolated spot. I have no way of protecting myself from someone with evil intent. My happiness has been rudely snatched from me. But I am unwilling to show fear.

'I hope you're not making menacing threats against me,' I reply, straightening my back and holding my head high, 'because if you are, I will take legal action. You may have suffered financially from your business dealings in the past but you could lose even more if I take you to law for threatening behaviour and malicious menaces.'

I am bluffing, of course, but I need to move this altercation on.

'Kindly remove your vehicle from the lane and allow me to pass before I summon the police.'

He emits a blood-curdling laugh. It's the most chilling sound I have ever heard. It is the laugh of a psychologically deranged person who delights in inflicting suffering on others. It's a laugh devoid of all warmth or humour. It's a laugh of cruelty and vengeance.

'Summon the police,' he laughs knowing full well I have no means of doing so. There is no mobile phone signal at Abbeydore and the nearest telephone is in the farmhouse. I am trapped. My threat is an empty one and he knows it.

'What is it you want?' I demand.

JESSICA'S VINEYARD

'I want to see you suffer,' he answers. 'I want to see you suffer as I've had to suffer. I want to see you reduced to penury. I want to see you with your face rubbed in the mud. I want to see you regret the day you ever crossed Henry J-J.'

'That sounds incredibly childish,' I reply with a superhuman effort to mask my underlying fear and trepidation. 'Isn't it about time that you grew up and moved on? Life consists of ups and downs. You can't spend your life nursing grievances. You have to pick yourself up, dust yourself down and start all over again.'

'Listen to Little Miss Fred Astaire!' sneers the woman, 'handing out her homespun philosophy. It's all very well for you, darling. You've got yourself a nice little rural retreat. But some of us have to live in the real world. And in the real world you need money if you're to live. You stabbed J-J in the back and ran off with the pickings. You thought you'd got away with it. You thought you could hide here and no one would ever find you. Well, you're wrong! We've found you and now you're going to suffer just as we've suffered.'

I foresee they are intent on harming me and I will have to involve the police. My brain tells me to amass as much evidence as possible to bolster my case for police action.

'And how do you propose making me suffer?' I ask.

JESSICA'S VINEYARD

The same hideous laugh emerges from the lips of the man.

'Wouldn't you like to know!' he exclaims.

I am unsure how to proceed. Should I return to the house and phone the police? Would turning my back on these two individuals blocking my path be seen as a sign of weakness? But what else can I do? I am unable to move forwards and go about my business whilst they block the lane and taunt me. I am in a dilemma.

But salvation comes in my darkest hour.

I don't believe in miracles or divine providence or good luck; but just at that moment a remarkably fortuitous thing occurs. I see, out of the corner of my eye, a movement behind me. Turning my head for a better sighting, I see it is Jason advancing towards me along the drive.

I could not wish for a more opportune appearance. My knight in shining armour is riding to my rescue. Furthermore, he carries this rifle under his arm. A smile spreads over my face.

Whereas, just a few seconds earlier, I was filled with foreboding and inaction, the dayspring from on high has dawned upon me. Fear has been banished. My saviour has appeared to rescue me.

'Anything the matter?' he enquires as he draws near me. 'I saw the Land Rover stuck in the gateway. Anything up?'

JESSICA'S VINEYARD

'Yes,' I reply with renewed confidence and assertion. 'My forward progress is being blocked by this car and the driver is unwilling to move to allow me to pass.'
Jason eyes the two individuals standing either side of the blue car.
'What's the big idea?' he asks in his expansive Australian voice.
They make no attempt to answer. His appearance has caught them off guard. They are unsure who the newcomer is and are unsure how to react.
I supply the information.
'Mr Jackson-Jones is someone I once knew in the city before I moved here. The lady is his wife. They say they have stumbled upon me quite my chance, but that is difficult to believe. They have no good feelings towards me. Mr Jackson-Jones wrongly thinks I cheated him out of a contract we were both bidding for. He says he is intent on making me suffer.'
Jason inhales a deep breath and, as he does so, snaps the bolt on his rifle into action.
I am horrified he is about to shoot the pair blocking the lane.
'No, Jason,' I scream. 'If anyone is on the wrong side of the law it is them. Don't let them off the hook by bringing the weight of the law down on yourself.'
He waves the rifle nonchalantly in the air and then grins.

JESSICA'S VINEYARD

'I wasn't going to top 'em. I just thought I'd spoil their tomorrows.'
'No, Jason,' I reply firmly. 'I think that, now you've arrived, Mr and Mrs Jackson-Jones have changed their minds and are about to leave.'
'Too right they are,' he answers, 'Pronto! while they've still got air in their tyres.'
The pair blocking the lane dither. They know they are no match for a young man with a bolt action rifle and yet they don't want to appear craven cowards running away from a confrontation.
'You heard what the lady said,' he adds. 'Vamoose! Skedaddle! On your way! Get lost!'
Any sense of satisfaction I derive from seeing the two Londoners slinking back into their vehicle is tempered by the knowledge they wish me harm. They may be sent on their way with a flea in their ear today; but, will they be back? How deep is the ill-will they bear me? Have they achieved their objective by frightening me or will they be back to make me suffer in other ways?
As their blue vehicle slowly disappears down the lane, Jason turns to me and asks, 'What was all that about?'
Throughout my altercation with the Jackson-Jones I maintained a stern countenance. I had no intention of letting them see my inner fear. I maintained a resolute exterior appearance. But now they have

gone, my resolve crumbles. I throw my arms around Jason's neck and sob uncontrollably.

'There, there, old girl,' he whispers. 'Don't upset yourself. There's nothing to worry about. I'm here. I'll take care of you. I'm not going to let anyone hurt you.'

He is so reassuring. He appeared at exactly the moment of my greatest need. He is my rock and fortress. What would I ever do without him?

JESSICA'S VINEYARD

CHAPTER 18

Winemaking involves three months of frenetic activity followed by nine months of blissful contemplation. The days spent on sun loungers seemed like a distant memory when the grape harvest was upon us. Our working days were long and arduous.

The weather has been exceptionally good and we've been able to harvest the entire Cabernet Sauvignon crop without interruption. Jason worked like a Trojan in the barn, processing the grapes and transferring the must into the tanks for fermentation. We have now racked the wine, drawing the juice off the must and fining it in order to make it bright and clear. It's very much a case of trial and error. I've read extensively about winemaking but, when push comes to shove, it's all down to personal judgement. I learn as I go along.

Jason is my rock. I don't know what I'd do without him. We work together as a team transferring the wine from tank to tank until it is ready to go into the barrels for aging. The barrels lie on their side and occupy the entire length of the barn. They are

JESSICA'S VINEYARD

stacked three high on wooden racking. They look as if they were put there by the monks of Dore Abbey centuries ago and have remained undisturbed ever since. The circular heads of each barrel are like implacable blank faces peering out of the gloom at mortals beneath. They have seen the generations come and go. They have slept peacefully and undisturbed through each unfolding year. Spiders have spun intricate gossamer webs around them before scurrying into the shadows to see if their traps yield food.

The barrels breathe. The wooden staves, moulded by the coopers of yesteryear, allow moisture to seep through their joints thus providing the angels with their share of the alcoholic feast. The angels dance invisibly over the barrels, light-hearted and fey. If this is what heaven is like, I am all for it.

The stack of wine barrels is my treasure trove. Trapped within each barrel is the fruit of my vineyard and the toil of my hands; my hopes and my dreams; my yesterdays and my tomorrows. These barrels are my treasure chests, worth more to me than the Crown Jewels. This is liquid gold, refined in the heat of the blistering summer sun; purified with the love and passion of my soul; and poised to enrich unknown weary lives with beauty and delight. My red wine will become blood coursing through veins in an intoxicating dance of abandonment; dispelling

JESSICA'S VINEYARD

worries and anxieties and sweeping all before it in a paean of laughter and happiness.

They are my offspring; my act of creation; my enrichment to the world. These barrels represent all that I am and all that I hope to be. They are either the summit of my creativity or else the depths of my despair. All that I long and hope for is encased within these barrels.

They stare at me with their blank faces. They are unmoved by human emotion. They have received and disgorged their contents endlessly. What does it matter to them if the wine is good or bad?

But my vintage must be good! I need to succeed, not simply to earn a living but to prove that I am capable of standing on my own two feet and achieving whatever goal I set myself. This is as much about personal fulfilment as commercial success. I need to know I am strong and capable. I need to know I can exist without the help of others. I need to prove I have inner reserves of strength and determination.

Of course, I'm being unrealistic. I do need the help of others. Without Jason I would not be where I now am. His help has been invaluable. He has worked long hours alongside me to bring home the grape harvest. He has toiled in the barn for long hours, often on his own, and never complained. He has invested as much of his time and energy in Abbeydore wine as I have.

JESSICA'S VINEYARD

But now that the wine is safely stored in barrels he is free to follow his other interests – principally, shooting rabbits.

'There can't be many more rabbits left in Abbeydore,' I remark teasingly as he announces his latest hunting jaunt.

'Don't you believe it,' he answers in his warm Australian accent. 'Rabbits breed like ... well, rabbits. No sooner have I eliminated one family than another springs up to take its place. Abbeydore must be the rabbit capital of the world.'

I smile at his youthful humour. I don't begrudge him his sport. He deserves to have time to himself and I know he enjoys being on his own in the great outdoors.

'Just keep away from the Spragg's land,' I warn him as he slings the rifle over his shoulder and plants a kiss on my forehead.

'While you're away I'll tidy up the far end of the barn so we're ready for bottling, whenever that may be.'

I wave a fond farewell as he disappears down the lane in search of rabbits.

Whilst he's away, I move to the barn and begin the task of clearing the area under the mezzanine. This end of the barn has an extensive wine rack extending from the floor to the ceiling of the mezzanine. This is where, in the past, reserve vintages have been laid down to mature in the bottle.

JESSICA'S VINEYARD

Today the rack resembles an abandoned dovecote draped in cobwebs and memories of long departed vintages. Hessian sacks, packing crates, and general winery detritus litter the area.

When Jason constructed his makeshift toilet at this far end of the barn he clearly did not trouble to clean or clear it of its junk. Perhaps that is the genetic difference between men and women. Men ignore disorder whereas women must have things tidy and shipshape. Or, maybe, it's more to do with age. Young people can happily live amongst chaos whereas older people need order and cleanliness in order to be happy. I prefer the first suggestion. I don't like to think that age affects our outlook on life. I may be twenty years older than Jason but I like to think I'm young at heart. Yes, it must be a gender thing rather than an age thing.

As I ponder these thoughts I embark upon the tidying and cleaning process. The level of light at this far end of the barn is not good. I guess the previous owners of the winery wanted subdued light here to prevent the wine deteriorating. The low light-level may well be the reason why so much rubbish has been consigned to this end of the barn: out of sight, out of mind. I've clearly got my work cut out. Removing old sacks, broken crates and discarded cardboard packaging is straightforward if somewhat

JESSICA'S VINEYARD

tedious. What is not so easy to deal with is the large amount of broken glass on the floor.

Shards of green broken bottle glass glint mysteriously in the gloom evidencing butterfingers, mishaps and curses.

Were these bottles empty when they smashed or did they spill their royal contents over the flagstone floor? Were they the final remnants of the Simpsons' tenure or do they date from much earlier times? Did the monks of Dore Abbey bottle their wine here or did they keep it in wooden casks? I'm sure Mr Smythe would know and be only too pleased to deliver a lecture on medieval winemaking. But, perhaps I would prefer to remain in ignorance rather than endure another of his didactic monologues.

Whether the broken shards of glass are ancient or modern they need removing.

I carefully sink to my knees and, working with a small dustpan and brush, sweep the broken glass into the pan before transferring it into a waste bin.

I kneel before the extensive empty wine rack like a suppliant kneeling in homage before an all-powerful deity. I see rows and rows of bottles lying supine and wondrously maturing. I worship the unseen vision before my eyes.

'Stock is as good as money,' I hear Alan whisper infuriatingly in my ear.

JESSICA'S VINEYARD

But I am not worshipping money. I behold a vision of heaven, where all impurity has been purged and the pure goodness of life is encapsulated in the dark recesses of a medieval barn. I am worshipping at my altar. These visionary bottles are my offering to the world: Jessica's gift to the human race. The sacrifice of the first forty years of my life is now redeemed and transformed into a rich bounty to flow into the lives of countless others.

I am so immersed in my otherworldly rapture that I am oblivious of all else. It is only when a distant sound intrudes upon my transcendental meditation that I am jolted back to reality. It takes a second or two for my brain to identify the sound. It is a deep, rumbling sound. It is like the pedal notes of a church organ. The vibrations are low. They are felt rather than heard.

Whatever the cause may be, my brain warns me to be alert. This is no comforting sound. It is the sound of a bear's growl. It is the sound that precedes an earthquake. It is a sound that inspires fear.

I am unable to locate the direction from which the sound is coming from my kneeling position on the flagstones. I twist my head to the left and look down the length of barn. The stainless steel tanks stand silent and motionless. No sound do they utter.

JESSICA'S VINEYARD

The centre aisle of the barn is empty. There is no one to be seen. And yet, the sound is growing in intensity every second

How I wish I possessed the head of an owl that was able to swivel yet further and observe the entire interior of the barn. But, alas, I am only human; and so I instantly swing my head in a 180 degree arc to observe the right-hand side of the barn.

I am instantly seized with panic. I freeze. I am unable to move. My reason deserts me. My brain turns to cotton wool. I cannot comprehend what my eyes see. Is this some scene from a horror movie? Am I really here in my barn in Abbeydore, in the depths of the Herefordshire countryside, or am I inhabiting a fantastic world created by a film director intent on making his audience quake in their boots?

Act, Jessica, act, my brain screams. This is no time to be paralysed by fear. This is a time to act.

Dropping my dustpan and brush and springing from my knees faster than an athlete leaving the starting blocks on a world-record-breaking attempt on a 100 metre sprint, I spring to my feet with milliseconds to spare.

The rumbling, grumbling, angry monsters are almost upon me. They are out to kill me. They want my blood. They want my mangled corpse. They want to crush me. They want to destroy me. They have murderous intent. I am a sacrificial victim.

JESSICA'S VINEYARD

I throw myself headlong into the central aisle of barn and hold my breath.
It is only when the sound of the deep death throes subside and an eerie silence descends upon the barn that I am able to haul myself into a sitting position to see what has happened.
Two large barrels have fallen from the framework that holds them and have crashed to the ground. They have broken loose from the top two rows of barrels – just behind where I was working. The barrels have not shattered but rolled on their sides towards the wooden bottle-rack. They must have gained momentum from their fall and this propelled them towards me with increasing velocity. If they had knocked me to the ground they would have killed me. Each barrel weighs 600lbs. I would not have stood a chance.
I thank my lucky stars I was able to escape from their path just milliseconds before it was too late. I've had an exceedingly lucky escape.
I take a deep breath and close my eyes. I suppose I should utter a prayer of thanks for a merciful delivery but I don't. Instead, I demand an explanation.
What caused those barrels to fall from the stack? They've occupied their place along the north wall of the barn for years. The timber that supports them is as strong today as it was when it was first erected. I should know. I and Jason have only recently

JESSICA'S VINEYARD

transferred wine into each of those barrels. They were perfectly stable and secure. There was never the slightest hint that they were dangerous or liable to collapse. Quite the contrary, in fact. They were built to last and showed every sign of doing so.

So what caused the racking to collapse and send two barrels crashing to the ground? Has woodworm infected the timbers and weakened the structure? Or is there some other explanation?

The questions race through my mind at a speed of knots.

I want answers. It's no good sitting in a heap on the cold floor and thanking my lucky stars for my deliverance. I need to know what caused my near brush with death.

I haul myself upright and make my way to where the lethal barrels previously resided - but it is too dark to see very much. I need a lamp.

I go to the farmhouse and collect our powerful handheld lamp before returning to the barn.

Directing the beam of the lamp along the back wall, I see the cables that Jason laid when he added lights and power to his mezzanine room earlier in the year. But it is not this that interests me. I direct the beam of light onto the racking supporting the heavy barrels of wine. The diagonal struts, that were supporting the end two barrels on the second and third rows, have

JESSICA'S VINEYARD

failed. Rather than stand rigid and firm, they have collapsed and lie lifeless and ineffectual.

I squeeze into the space along the wall behind the barrels and shine the lamp intently on the failed wooden struts. I then examine the framework that is still doing its job as it should. The struts are held in place by wooden pegs. I examine the joint holding the two struts that have failed. The wood has not split or fractured. So where are the wooden pegs that held the two end barrels in place? I sweep the floor with the lamp but no pegs can I find. This is very strange.

There is usually an explanation for everything that happens in this world. I pride myself on being an intelligent woman. I'm capable of sifting evidence and arriving at a plausible explanation for the things I encounter. I do not have to resort to the supernatural or poltergeists or evil spirits to explain the seemingly inexplicable. There is always a logical explanation for everything that happens in this world.

So what has happened here?

I knit my brows and lean back against the stone wall. This barn must have seen many strange and unaccountable things during its lifetime: produce stolen, maybe; angry disputations over tithes, maybe; disappointment and tears over perished goods, maybe; but murder?

JESSICA'S VINEYARD

Could this be an act of premeditated murder? Has someone deliberately removed the pegs from the racking so that the barrels intentionally crashed down upon me whilst I was working? It seems unbelievable.

But then I remember my near brush with death in the wine tank. That seemed like an accident at first, but the more I've thought about it the more inexplicable it has become.

This, however, is no accident. Wooden pegs don't accidentally remove themselves from interlocking pieces of timber. The pegs have been deliberately removed.

I shudder. Someone wants me dead. Someone is prepared to go to inordinate lengths to remove me from Abbeydore. I am a marked woman. This is the second unsuccessful attempt on my life. A third may not be unsuccessful. I shiver again. I am in real danger.

I used to think that the business world I previously inhabited was a jungle. I was careful to watch my step. I was circumspect in sharing confidences. I kept my north eye open at all times in case I was stabbed in the back by one of our business rivals. It was very much a case of dog eats dog and devil take the weakest. But when I came to Abbeydore I thought I had left all that behind. I thought that, by burying

JESSICA'S VINEYARD

myself deep in the countryside, I was escaping the urban jungle and the wild beasts that inhabit it. But, instead, I find myself trapped in a situation I don't understand and from which I see no escape. In the city it was commercial murder that was practised, but here in the country it's more like actual murder that's afoot.

Why would anyone want to murder me? I may have ruffled a few feathers and bruised a few egos when I was working in the city. I clearly upset the Jackson-Jones, but, surely, even they would not want to kill me?

I may have pipped the Spraggs to the post when I purchased this property; but surely their disappointment would not turn them into murderers. Who, then, is intent on eliminating me? And why? Alan mysteriously appeared when I nearly drowned in the wine vat. Could he be behind this attempt on my life?

I know he nurses a deep grudge over the way I walked out on him. He thinks I made a fool of him and demeaned him in the eyes of his colleagues. He bears me no goodwill. But would he resort to murdering me? If abandoned husbands acted like that, the world would be littered with corpses. No! He may not be enamoured with me but I can't see him resorting to murder, especially, as he says, he's found another woman to share his life.

JESSICA'S VINEYARD

So, who else might want me dead?
I think of Councillor Johnson. The police are clearly interested in him. Could he be responsible for other unexplained deaths in Herefordshire? Does he earmark the owners of out-of-the-way properties so he can eliminate them and seize their land? Does his urbane exterior mask a psychotic disorder? Does he have me firmly in his sights? Was he angered by Jason's rudeness at our last encounter and is he intent on revenge?
He might think that, if he removes me from the scene, Jason will no longer want to remain here on his own and he will get his chance to acquire my property. My death could be part of a clever plan on his part to get what he wants without having to spend a fortune acquiring it. The more I think about it, the more likely it seems that Councillor Johnson has something to do with my near brush with death. Although all possible suspects race through my mind, I know I am unlikely to arrive at the truth on my own. I need help.
An image of the confident DS Rees comes into my mind. He impressed me with his professionalism. He said that if I thought of anything else I was to contact him. He gave me his details.
I will contact him.

JESSICA'S VINEYARD

But, before I do so, I need to examine the damage that has been caused to the bottle rack at the far end of the barn by the cascading barrels of death.
Extracting myself from the narrow space behind the barrels and the wall, I shine my lamp on the scene at the far end of the barn.
The two displaced barrels hit the wooden bottle racks with incredible force. I shudder to think what they would have done if they had struck me. The barrels themselves appear to be intact. I guess they were made to withstand rough handling. The bottle rack, however, has not come off so well. A large section has been smashed to smithereens by the weight and force of the two barrels.
Oh dear! We could do without this! Our outstanding grape harvest means we need the full capacity of the bottle rack if we are to store our precious wine.
Instead, I see splintered wood and shattered dreams. Some Nordic god has swung his hammer and reduced our dreams to matchsticks. The shelving lies shattered and demolished.
I now know how victims of war must feel when they see their homes destroyed by bombs leaving just a curtain flapping in the wind or a picture askew on a partially surviving wall. All the memories of the past contained within that house are shattered. Home comforts cruelly snatched away. Security dissipated in a flash of carbine.

JESSICA'S VINEYARD

I could easily sit down and cry, but an inner voice tells me otherwise. Pull yourself together Jessica and see what can be salvaged from the ravages of the battlefield.

I pick my way gingerly through the splintered wood. The shelving that was at right angles to the end wall has taken the brunt of the impact. I begin dragging the shattered debris to one side so I can estimate how many storage spaces have been lost.

The mangled and splintered wood separates from the remaining intact racking quite easily.

As I pull the smashed and fragmented wood to one side, my eye alights upon a strange object. It glints in the shadows. I stare intently at it in an attempt to understand what it is. I wish there was better lighting at this end of the barn. I need the hand lamp once again if I am to examine the strange object.

Once I have the lamp in my hands, I pull away more of the splintered wooden racking to reveal a metal ring set into the flagstone floor. If it were set into the walls of the barn I would assume it was for securing something with a rope or a chain, perhaps. But why would anyone want to affix a metal ring into a stone floor?

It is then I know how Archimedes felt when he shouted 'Eureka!' and jumped out of his bath. He had discovered an important scientific principle: that which had been hidden from human knowledge for

JESSICA'S VINEYARD

centuries had become perfectly plain and all who came after would benefit from his discovery. He had shone a light on a hitherto unrecognised scientific fact: water is displaced in exact measure to the object placed in it.

I am fully clothed and kneeling in a dark and dingy barn and yet I have exactly the same sensation. I have discovered something of great importance. This metal ring, set into the flagstones, can only mean one thing. There must be a cellar beneath the barn and this must be the entrance to it.

My excitement knows no bounds. If there is a cellar here could there just possibly be a stash of stored wine here as well? I claw with my fingers to lift the metal ring and pull on it; but, alas, I lack the necessary strength.

All thoughts of my near brush with death are swept aside by the excitement of what may lie hidden beneath my feet.

JESSICA'S VINEYARD

CHAPTER 19

I remember the excitement I experienced when I was a small child in the weeks leading up to Christmas. My anticipation and longing for Christmas Day made me tingle with excitement. Would I receive the things I most wanted? Would Santa Claus be sure to visit me whilst I was asleep? Would the big day never come?

I must have driven my mother mad with my persistent pestering. Christmas was like no other time in the year. I only received presents at Christmas. It was special. It was exciting. My childhood excitement was uncontainable.

Waiting for Jason to return from his hunting trip is like waiting for Christmas all over again. My excitement knows no bounds. I must tell him my discovery. The knowledge of it is burning a hole in my brain. I need to share my newfound secret.

I pace up and down the barn with increasing frustration. Where is Jason? Why has he not returned? What can be keeping him? Why doesn't he sense I've made a tremendous discovery? Surely the telepathy that exists between a husband and wife should alert him that something momentous has occurred at Abbeydore Vineyard. I want him here. I want to share my new and exciting discovery with him.

Time often stood still when I was a child. I would beg my mother to tell me how much longer I had to wait for Christmas Day to arrive. Her answer always specified some distant length of time that never seemed to shorten. I would hang my head and purse my lips in barely concealed anger, but it made no difference. The feeling of impotence never disappeared. I was unable to shorten the period of waiting.

Even as an adult I am still unable to accelerate the passage of time. I may wish for Jason to return with all due speed and urgency, but my wish has no practical effect.

The minutes lengthen into hours. Time has never dragged so cruelly. I repeatedly look at my wristwatch to ensure it is still functioning.

Jason does not return until midway through the afternoon.

I see him approaching and rush out of the farmhouse to meet him on the drive.

'Jason!' I cry with undisguised excitement. 'You can't imagine what I've discovered.'

He looks at me with a blank expression on his face and shakes his head.

JESSICA'S VINEYARD

'I've discovered a cellar! There's a cellar beneath the barn and there's no saying what it might contain.'
I wait for him to react, but he remains strangely mute; and so I rush onwards.
'We know that some of our vines are a hundred years old, so what's to say there aren't bottles of hundred-year-old wine down there.'
My excitement is not mirrored on his face. Indeed, he frowns.
'What's the matter?' I ask. 'Aren't you excited?'
Perhaps women are more easily excited than men. Or perhaps we are just unable to hide our emotions as skilfully as men. Or perhaps men are more questioning than women and want absolute proof before they accept what someone else tells them. Or perhaps the thrill of discovery can never be adequately conveyed to another person: it is unique to the person who made the discovery; anything else is second-hand. Or perhaps men tease out the implications of new discoveries before owning them. O perhaps ... Well, who knows? All I know is that I feel disappointment that Jason doesn't share my overwhelming excitement at the discovery I have made and the untold possibilities it might open up.
'Where is this cellar?' he asks in a prosaic manner.
It is then that I recall the event that led to my discovery and a shiver runs down my spine.

JESSICA'S VINEYARD

'It was concealed beneath the wooden wine racks at the far end of the barn.'

I frown. My initial excitement begins to wane. I recall the event that brought the metal ring in the flagstones to my attention.

'I had a close brush with death,' I continue in a more subdued manner. 'Whilst I was on my hands and knees brushing shards of glass into the dustpan, a section of the timber framing that supports the wine barrels collapsed and sent two barrels crashing into the bottle racks. I was lucky to avoid being seriously injured.'

'Holy Carmichael!' he exclaims. 'How on earth did that happen?'

'I don't know. But you know what they say: good often comes out of evil. Luckily neither of the barrels ruptured when they hit the floor but the racking took a pounding. As I was clearing the splintered wood I noticed a bright metal object recessed into the flagstones. When I shone the lamp on it, I saw it was a metal ring. That can only mean one thing. It must lead to a cellar beneath the barn.'

I pause as a new thought suddenly invades my mind. 'Do you remember that strange young man on a bicycle who came here some while ago? He asked if we had a cellar. I seem to remember he spent most of his time on his hands and knees, ostensibly taking photographs and making measurements. But perhaps he was really searching for the entrance to our cellar. The more I think about it, the more exciting it becomes.'

'Come on,' he says. 'Let's have a look.'

We make our way to the barn. The bright florescent lights over the stainless steel tanks cast ghostly shadows down the length of the barn. They extend their tentacles to the dingy far end beneath the mezzanine ceiling.

I angle the beam of the lamp I am holding towards the two wayward barrels and the shattered wine rack. The light of the lamp glistens on the metal ring in the floor.

We advance upon it on our hands and knees.

'It looks as if it could be there to raise the flagstone,' he reluctantly agrees.

He grasps the ring with both hands and tugs on it but it refuses to move.

'I tried to lift it,' I inform him, before realising this is a stupid remark. If he, with his athletic prowess is unable to lift the flagstone, there's no way I could ever do so.

He gives me a sideways glance but refrains from comment. Instead, he says, 'We need a length of rope. If we attach it to the ring and then use our combined strength we might be able to lift the flagstone. It looks heavy. And it looks as if it hasn't been moved for years.'

JESSICA'S VINEYARD

He goes to the entrance of the barn and takes down a length of thick multi-stranded rope from a peg on the wall and returns to where I'm standing. He carefully threads the rope through the metal ring and pays out a good length. Handing one end of the rope to me, he takes the other. We move a distance back from the ring and brace ourselves for the task ahead.
'On the count of three, pull,' he commands.
I stiffen my sinews and take a deep breath.
'One, two, three, pull.'
We both exert our full strength - but to no avail. The flagstone refuses to budge.
'I know,' he says. 'We'll try holding the rope over our shoulders and pulling. The added height may be just what's needed to lift the blighter.'
And so, turning around, we each place our length of rope over our shoulders. On the count of three we exert our full strength and pull towards the barn doors.
Having failed on our previous attempt, I am resigned to failing again; but, to my great surprise, a grating and groaning sound is heard behind us and we both stumble forwards as the tension on the rope slackens. I cannot help laughing as we stagger like a couple of inebriated drunkards in an attempt to remain upright. Then, glancing over my shoulder I see that the large flagstone is upended.
'We've done it!' I exclaim.

JESSICA'S VINEYARD

Taking care not to allow the flagstone to fall back into place, we maintain the tension on the rope and retrace out steps to the gaping cavity in the floor. I feel like Allan Quartermaine standing at the entrance to King Solomon's Mines. What treasures lie at our feet? What untold mysteries are about to be revealed? What riches await us?

I direct the beam of the lamp into the void. A wooden set of steps leads into the darkness. My initial reaction is to push ahead and venture into the unknown chamber. But a warning voice in my head makes me hesitate.

There have been two recent attempts on my life. Is it wise to venture into a dark, unknown void? I recall Allan Quartermaine becoming trapped inside King Solomon's Mines with dwindling food supplies and no way of escape. I have no desire to share his fate. Abbeydore cellar may not possess the fortuitous secret exit that acted as Quartemaine's salvation. I have no intention of being trapped and perishing in an underground dudgeon.

For once in my new life I have no desire to be a trailblazer.

I turn to Jason and ask, 'Are you feeling brave enough to venture into the unknown?'

'Sure,' he answers nonchalantly. 'But first, we'll fasten this flagstone securely with the rope to ensure our entrance and exit remains open.'

JESSICA'S VINEYARD

Only when this has been done does he descend into the abyss, shining the beam of the lamp ahead of him as he goes. I follow in his wake, glad that I'm not attempting this on my own.

The beam of light dances on the roof and walls. It reveals a forest of stone pillars supporting the floor above.

We are grave robbers entering a crypt. We are here to despoil this underground repository of whatever treasures it conceals. We are intruders. We do not belong here. We have invaded a world of shadows and darkness.

An eerie silence hangs over this mausoleum. Ghosts of the past inhabit this underground cavern. The monks of Dore Abbey glide silently between the pillars appearing from nowhere and disappearing into obscurity. Their cowls are pulled over their heads masking their faces if, indeed, they have faces.

The moving finger of time has failed to touch this subterranean world. It lies beyond the confines of time and space. There is neither day nor night. This is a place of perpetual darkness.

I hear disembodied voices needling my brain. Why are you here? Why have you disturbed our peace? What right have you to enter our place of sanctuary and rest? The voices are accusative and hostile. They growl. They throb with barely concealed malice. I am unwelcome. This is an alien world that I have no right to enter.

Away! Away! Remove your warm breath from the chill humidity of our dwelling. Take your beating heart and coursing blood from this place where neither sun nor snow disturbs the even temperature. Remove the pulsating life of the world above and leave us to rest in peace in our world of undisturbed darkness.

My nostrils detect a faint odour. It is not the intoxicating perfume of the angels' share seeping from the wooden barrels that fills the barn above our heads but a fusty, damp, airless smell that causes the microscopic hairs in my nose to quiver with fear. This is not the air that humans breathe. This is the air of a sepulchre. The pallor of death hangs in the air like a suffocating shroud wanting to enfold those foolish enough to venture into this long-forgotten country.

A shiver runs down my back. It is not caused by a sudden drop in temperature. Indeed, the temperature in the cellar is remarkably temperate. I shiver because I feel I am an intruder. I have no right to be here. I am trespassing on the past inhabitants of this place. I am disturbing their shadows. I am trampling on the dead. The darkness says 'You should not be here. Return to the land of the living from whence you came. Return to daylight. Return to the warmth of

the sun and the light of the day. Leave our place of sanctuary. Be gone!'
But of course I do not go. This may once have been the preserve of those from bygone years but I am now the owner of Abbeydore Vineyard. This is my property. This vast expansive cathedral is mine.
Jason sweeps the beam of the lamp around the interior revealing a vaulted roof supported by the forest of stone pillars. I have been walking above this vaulted roof in blissful ignorance of what lay beneath ever since I took possession of Abbeydore Winery. In the blink of an eye, the square footage of the barn has doubled in size.
But, impressive as this vast subterranean space is, it is not the architecture that rivets my attention but the walls on either side. They are not flat. They consist of an unending river of arches stretching far into the shadows at the far end of the cellar.
My heart rate quickens. The arches are not empty but filled with wooden racking supporting endless rows of bottles reclining on their side.
'Wow!' exclaims Jason as his brain and mine synchronise and come to an identical conclusion. 'We've been sitting on a goldmine!'
'That remains to be seen,' I say, adding a note of caution to temper his enthusiasm. 'It all depends on whether this cache of wine is any good.'

JESSICA'S VINEYARD

We move towards the first bin and stare at the dusty bottles. They look as if they have lain undisturbed for a hundred years. I feel like the Prince stumbling upon Aurora's castle after her hundred year slumber. Cobwebs mark the passing of time. Fine particles of dust coat each bottle in a film of mortality. Not a fingerprint is to be seen on a bottle. They've remained undisturbed, sleeping just like the Sleeping Beauty, waiting for the day a handsome prince would arrive and raise them from their slumbers.

I cannot resist sharing my whimsy with Jason.
'Don't you feel like the handsome prince in The Sleeping Beauty stumbling upon a castle in which everyone is sleeping?'

I see him shake his head in disbelief. Perhaps men are not as susceptible to whimsy as women.

'I don't feel like a prince just at present. I feel more like a millionaire; or a gold prospector in the Wild West who has just discovered a rich seam of gold.'

How like a man to see everything in material terms! But I'm not to be deterred.

'Well to me, you are the handsome prince who is just about to give the kiss of life to this underground storehouse and bring it back to life. I am Aurora and the two of us will now live happily ever after.'

But Jason is not listening. He has taken a bottle out of the bin and is carefully examining the label in the light of the lamp.

JESSICA'S VINEYARD

'It's from here alright,' he declares as he brushes away the film of dust masking the label. 'Abbeydore Cabernet Sauvignon. Mis en bouteille au domaine.' Then, with another brush of his hand over the label, he says, '1933. Wow! This bottle is almost one hundred years old. This could be worth a fortune.' He is correct. I have read that 1934 vintage bottles of Chateau Laffite Rothschild fetch £1,600 at auction. We can't expect English red wine to match that but our 1933 Cabernet Sauvignon must be rare and, providing it hasn't gone off, its rarity value alone could make it worth £1,000 a bottle.

'Are all the bottles from the same vintage?' I enquire.

'Let's find out,' he answers instantly.

So saying, we systematically work our way along the length of the cellar, examining each bin in turn. The necks of the bottles point accusative fingers at us daring us to disturb their rest. They resemble multiple rocket launchers about to discharge their contents on an unsuspecting world. They point to the future. They are aimed at wine gourmets: those who appreciate and savour the distinctive taste and aroma of a fine wine. They seek the discerning palate and the sensitive nose. They yearn to accompany a gourmet meal or linger in the glass over a romantic dinner for two. They are poised for action.

The corks, that have held the contents of each bottle captive for nearly a hundred years, are about to pop

JESSICA'S VINEYARD

and discharge their precious contents. A veritable arsenal of fine wine is about to find appreciation and stimulate sublime ecstasy. Only I stand between them and a waiting world.

Every bin in the cellar contains the 1933 vintage. It must have been an exceptional year for so many bottles to be produced and laid down.

Jason carries out a quick calculation based upon the number of bins and the number of bottles in each bin.

'There must be 10,000 bottles here,' he declares in an awestruck voice.

The human calculator then commutes the number of bottles and the possible worth of each bottle.

'That's £10,000,000!'

I nod my head.

Not only is this a tremendous sum of money but, if it proves to be a fine wine, it will act as a superb advertisement for Abbeydore Winery.

'Let's take a bottle to sample,' I suggest. 'The only way to know if the wine has aged well is to sample it. Let's prepare a casserole with those rabbits you caught today and see how the wine goes with game.'

Clutching a bottle of our very own Abbeydore wine, we emerge from the depths of the cellar and carefully replace the flagstone over the entrance.

It is then that I recall the events leading up to the discovery of our underground treasure trove.

JESSICA'S VINEYARD

'Perhaps we ought to roll one of those barrels over the cellar's entrance in case any unwanted visitor returns. The fewer people who know about the 1933 store in our cellar the better.'

The two of us manoeuvre the cumbersome barrels until they completely hide the metal ring and flagstone entrance to the cellar.

The excitement of discovering the underground cellar banished all thoughts of the frightening occurrence that led to its discovery. That memory now returns with a frightening urgency.

'Jason: these barrels didn't fall from their place in the stack on their own. They were deliberately designed to injure or kill me.'

'What on earth do you mean?' he asks.

'Well, after I recovered from the initial shock of my near brush with death, I fetched the lamp from the house and examined the barrel stack. The timber cross-members are secured by wooden pegs. The pegs supporting the end two barrels are missing. Someone has removed them so that the slightest movement would cause the end two barrels to come crashing to the ground where I was working.'

'Who on earth would do a thing like that?' he asks with a pained look on his face.

'I don't know,' I reply slowly. 'But someone clearly wants us out of here. First it was the vandalism in the vineyard. Then it was the barn fire. Then it was me falling into the tank of fermenting wine and nearly drowning. And now it's this. Someone wants to get their hands on this place and is prepared to go to any lengths to achieve their end.'

I suddenly feel very vulnerable.

'Jason: I'm afraid. I don't like it. I've had two near brushes with death: what's to say that the next won't prove fatal. Jason, I'm scared.'

'Don't worry your head,' he answers as he puts a consoling arm around my shoulders. 'You've got me looking after you. You've got nothing to fear. If I catch anyone up to no good they'll find the barrel of my rifle up their nostrils. Just enjoy your secret treasure trove.'

He places a warm kiss on my forehead. I am so fortunate to have him as my husband. He exudes confidence and safety.

'Let's go back to the house,' he says, 'and crack open this bottle of Chateau Abbeydore. I want to see if it's as good as it's made out to be.'

And with that we leave the barn and return, hand in hand, to the farmhouse clutching our precious bottle of 1933 Chateau Abbeydore.

JESSICA'S VINEYARD

CHAPTER 20

I imagine that those who drink a hundred-year-old bottle of Chateau Laffite Rothschild do so to the accompaniment of *foie gras* or caviar or Kobe beef steaks or Piedmont white truffles. After all, if you're able to afford £1,600 for a bottle of wine you may as well have equally expensive food to accompany it. There cannot be many who crack open a hundred-year-old bottle of wine to accompany rabbit stew, but that's what Jason and I do.

Our sense of excitement is palpable. I have never before tasted a really old vintage wine. My overwhelming sense of anticipation vies with childhood memories of Christmas Eve. Something great is in store. I don't know what it is, but I know it is new; opening a door into a new chapter in my life; leading me to places I have never been before; enriching my life with wonder and excitement; affording untold smiles and laughter. I tingle on the brink of discovery.

The 1933 bottle of Abbeydore wine does not look very prepossessing. The label is discoloured. Pinpoints of earth-coloured mould pepper the paper

JESSICA'S VINEYARD

on which it is printed. The passing years have sought
to inflict their worst on the bottle, but the dark-green
glass has withstood their ravages. The label may look
dishevelled and careworn, but the bottle is intact.
The dark red capsule that encloses the cork has lost
its pristine gloss with the passing years but my hope
is that it has served its purpose in preserving the cork
beneath.

I fondle the bottle in my hands as a mother might
hold her new-born child. There is so much promise
enclosed in my hands; so much potential. Has my
offspring grown in stature and strength? Has this
babe in arms become the grand old man of wisdom
and maturity? Does this bottle offer new creation?
I am at the tipping point of my life. Either this bottle
will propel me into a bright new future, with untold
business opportunities, new circles of friends, new
social milieus, new fame and fortune or it will plunge
me into the depths of despondency.

I hold my future in my hands.

I rotate the bottle slowly, heedless of the dirt and
dust that adheres to it. What do I care about outward
appearances? It is the contents of this bottle that
concerns me.

I read the label for the umpteenth time.

Mis en bouteille au domaine. This wine was bottled here
at Abbeydore. By whom? I need to examine the title
deeds of my property and discover who owned this

vineyard in 1933. Was it a local man who lived all his life in this quiet backwater of Herefordshire? I somehow doubt it. There was no market for English wine in the 1930s. Local men grew hops, apples and produce for the local market. And so, who planted five acres of vines in order to make wine?

He must have been an enterprising individual. I imagine him to be a well-travelled man, who had toured the chateaux of France, sampling the vintages, refining his palate, discovering the wines he liked, learning from the winemakers, observing the art of viniculture and, all the while, nursing a dream to own his own vineyard and produce his very own wine. Yes, he must have been a person with a vision, very much like me.

Was 1933 his best year? Why are there no other vintages stored in the cellar beneath the barn? Did previous years result in failure? Even the best winemakers declare only occasional grand cru vintages.

The maître of Abbeydore must have been a brave man. He pitted his wits against the hostile English climate and the British public's lack of interest in wine. He could, possibly, have made a great deal more money growing apples for the cider industry like others in the neighbourhood. But no: he was a wine aficionado. He needed to prove to himself and

JESSICA'S VINEYARD

to others that good wine could be made in England. He was on a mission.

How I would like to greet him and shake his hand! He was a trailblazer. I owe my involvement in the wine industry to him. He planted and cared for the vines that I now tend. I stand on his shoulders and build on his vision.

He must have known that his 1933 vintage was good – why else would he have laid down 10,000 bottles? He must have felt like Moses viewing the Promised Land but knowing he would never enter it himself. It would be for those who came afterwards to inherit his legacy. He looked to a bright future when the work of his hands would be lauded and praised. I must discover his name so I can honour him in the way he deserves.

I rotate the bottle once more in my hands.

Fourteen per cent alcoholic content it reads on the label: a strong red wine. Good. The strength of the alcohol will have acted as a preservative. My sense of anticipation increases. The portents are good. The vintage must have been exceptional for such a large number of bottles to be laid down in the cellar and then left to age. The wine has a good alcoholic content. All that remains is to discover the condition of the cork.

So many wines are ruined by the deterioration of the cork in the neck of the bottle. If the cork dries out and air enters the bottle, the wine oxidates. I have experienced numerous corked wines.

'Would you like to taste the wine before I pour it, madam?' is the unctuous mantra of innumerable sommeliers.

Of course I want to taste it to ensure it's not corked! I smile as I remember people in restaurants pretentiously swilling their wine around their glass and rolling it on their tongue as if they are judges at the International Wine Competition about to decide whether to award it a Bronze Medallion or merely place it in the Commended category. There is a great deal of pretension and snobbishness when it comes to wine tasting.

The only thing one needs to do when a sommelier asks if one wishes to taste a wine before it is served is to test if it is corked. If it is, the resultant taste is instantly recognisable: musty, fusty or even sheer vinegar.

What is the quality of the cork in the bottle I hold in my hands? Did my 1930s predecessor invest in good quality corks from Portugal or did he skimp to save money and, in so doing, risk losing his entire vintage? Surely not the latter! He was a man of discernment. He was ahead of his time. He was no cowboy out to make a few quick bucks. He was a man intent on forging a legacy. I tell myself that only the best was good enough for him.

JESSICA'S VINEYARD

Taking my sommelier's knife, I carefully remove the lacklustre red capsule that hides the cork. The cork looks sound. It shows no signs of deterioration or disintegration. This is as it should be. The bottle has lain on its side for nearly a hundred years keeping the cork moist. Furthermore, the temperature in the cavernous cellar will have remained constant thus protecting the cork from the extremes of contraction and expansion. Everything looks good.
Now comes the moment of testing.
'Are you ready, Jason?' I ask with an ear-to-ear smile on my face.
'As ready as I'll ever be,' he returns. 'This had better be good or we've got an awful lot of stuff to pour down the drain.'
'Don't even think about it,' I reply, with some exasperation that Jason should even harbour such negative thoughts. 'This is a grand cru that will make Abbeydore Winery a leading producer of high-quality boutique wines. We are poised on the launch-pad for a great future. We are venturing where no one has gone before. We are about to sample a revelation.'
He shakes his head in disbelief at my inherent enthusiasm.
'Pull the cork and let's make up our own mind about the wine.'
I carefully twist the corkscrew until its Archimedes screw disappears from view. Then, with the skill of a

JESSICA'S VINEYARD

dentist extracting a troublesome tooth, I gently
remove the cork.

It gives a reassuring plonk as it leaves the home it has
occupied for the past one hundred years. I am
pleased to see that the base of the cork is thoroughly
moist and has a most pleasant patina.

I pass my nose over the neck of the open bottle. A
most delicious smell of dried fruit, leather and
tobacco assails my nostrils. I have never before smelt
anything like it. It is a revelation. It is unique. I close
my eyes and inhale a lungful of sheer ecstasy. This is
the nectar of the gods. This is an otherworldly
experience. This is sheer pleasure and delight. I am
transported to other realms.

I have always been very sceptical of the writings of
mystics who claim they are transported to heaven
and see visions that are beyond the power of human
words to describe; but this is heavenly. I am lost in an
aura of delight.

'What's it smell like?' interjects Jason. His words act
as a rude intrusion on my otherworldly experience,
but they serve to bring me down to earth.

'It's like nothing else I've ever experienced,' I reply.

'Does that mean it's good or bad?'

'Oh good!' I answer, 'A hundred times good! Better
than anything I've ever experienced in my life. If the
wine is as good as its bouquet, we'll be joining the
gods in drinking ambrosia this evening.'

JESSICA'S VINEYARD

He shakes his head in disbelief at my rapture and pushes two wine glasses towards me.
I know I must be very careful pouring my liquid riches. A hundred-year-old wine is bound to have thrown sediment and I don't want to contaminate the liquid with the debris at the bottom of the bottle.
'I suppose we should really decant the bottle before we sample it,' I say, 'but I can't wait for that. Let's take our chances and taste it.'
I gently pour a small amount from the bottle into our two glasses.
It is the rush of crimson blood, bright and alive. It dances in the light of the farmhouse kitchen. It is carefree. It is filled with gay abandonment. It laps each glass as it trickles into it. It is like a brook in springtime babbling over stones and flowing inexorably towards the ocean where all cares and worries are subsumed in oblivion. It is blood coursing through the veins. It is alive. It breathes. It gurgles like a baby making its first sounds in the nursery. It is full of promise and expectation.
When I've poured a small amount into each glass, we hold it to the light and examine its luminosity.
It is as clear as the day it was made. No shadow despoils its beauty. No cloud obscures the sun's bright beams that ripened the grapes and miraculously transformed them into this prized

possession. We hold our very own act of
transubstantiation in our hands and I know it's good.
'What do you think of the nose?' I ask, knowing full
well Jason will never have experienced anything like it
before.
'It's certainly got a big conk,' he replies in his very
own Australian vernacular.
'Can you detect the same delicious smell of dried
fruit, leather and tobacco that I can?'
'Now you come to mention it, I think I can. It's a
strange combination; but it's not unpleasant. At least,
the wine's not outlived its usefulness and gone off.'
'The portents look good,' I say, as I eye the glass of
liquid ambrosia in my hand. 'Now for the moment of
truth: what does it taste like?'
We both sip from our glasses at exactly the same
moment. We are like a pair of synchronised divers
taking the plunge from the top board of an Olympic
Swimming Pool. Will we score maximum points or
will our foray into fine wines end with us being
disqualified and banished from the contest for ever?
I allow the liquid to linger in my mouth. I savour its
mellow tones. It is like a warm caress from a doting
lover. It is as smooth as silk and as exotic as a ride on
an Arabian magic carpet to paradise.
I allow the wine to leave my mouth and embark upon
its journey to my bloodstream where wine and blood
become mingled in an intoxicating river of delight. It

JESSICA'S VINEYARD

has cleansed my palate like pure spring water whilst leaving behind a wonderful fruity aftertaste.

The wine is a perfectly dry red wine, with no acidity or bitterness. The big fruit flavours of a young wine have become secondary, tertiary and other flavours have come forward – earthy, savoury flavours.

It is a joyful, complex tasting experience, rich with cassis, red berries, tobacco, truffle, lead pencil, spicy and earthy notes. I have no doubt this is fine wine par excellence.

'What do you make of it?' I ask Jason.

'It's certainly very different from the big Shiraz's we have in Australia. It's not a glugging wine, that's for sure. But it has character and a distinctive flavour. I'm no expert on vintage wines, but I think the bigwigs of the wine industry would go nuts over something as unusual as this.'

'They will,' I answer confidently. 'This is a vintage wine to rival those of the great French chateaux. And the fact that there is only a limited supply should inflate its value tremendously.'

I take another sip from my glass.

'I feel I'm on a voyage of discovery,' I add. 'Each sip opens up new vistas. It's a layered wine offering fresh delights with each sip. This is a wine for the sophisticated wine connoisseur – and sophisticated wine connoisseurs usually have deep pockets. Our cellar of vintage wine will keep us solvent even if this

JESSICA'S VINEYARD

year's vintage fails to fulfil our hopes and
expectations. It will also bring us to the notice of the
wider wine-purchasing public. A great deal of wine is
down to marketing – and that's where Mr Smythe,
our Master of Wine, might prove very useful.'
'I don't like that man,' declares Jason. 'He's too full
of himself. He needs bringing down a peg or two.'
I smile as I recollect their last encounter.
'Well, I think you made a pretty good job of doing
that at your last encounter. But sometimes it's best to
bite your tongue and hold your peace – especially if
the person can prove useful.'
Then, reverting to the glasses of wine we are holding
in our hands I ask, 'What do you make of the
aftertaste? I think it has a lingering and elegant
finish.'
'It certainly leaves a nice taste in my mouth. I think
we've hit the sweet spot. Leave the wine another ten
years and it'll probably be past its best. I reckon
we've found the optimum drinking window.'
I agree wholeheartedly. Our 1933 Cabernet
Sauvignon vintage is a winner and we have an entire
cellar full of it. The future suddenly looks very rosy.
We consume the remainder of the bottle with our
rabbit stew. It may be an unorthodox way to sample
a high quality fine wine but the meat and vegetables
perfectly complement the wine. I could savour this
combination endlessly. But I won't. At £1,000 a

JESSICA'S VINEYARD

bottle, my Chateau Abbeydore is destined for the fine wine market. We will have to make do with more modest fare.

*

The euphoria surrounding the discovery of the cellar filled with unimaginable treasures has gradually subsided as the demands of everyday life intrude. I have come down from cloud nine to concentrate on more mundane matters. But as I do so, my mind annoyingly reverts to the event that led to the discovery of our secret cellar: the collapse of the timber framework supporting the barrels and my near brush with serious injury or death. I am unable to banish this thought from my mind.

Jason has been largely dismissive. He is firmly of the opinion that the timber framework was so old it was inevitable it would fail one day. He says that when we filled each barrel with the equivalent of six-hundred bottles of wine we were putting a tremendous strain on the structure. It was unfortunate that the timbers gave way just when I was working in the vicinity. He said it could have happened at any time. I was just unlucky to be in the vicinity at the time.

He may be correct, but I am not wholly convinced. The absence of the wooden pegs in the framework worries me.

If this was just an isolated incident I could, perhaps, shrug it off; but coupled with the cutting of the wires

JESSICA'S VINEYARD

in the vineyard, the barn blaze and my near-drowning in the wine tank, I am not so sure.

I am standing on the brink of an exciting new chapter in my life. The future offers infinite possibilities. The last thing I want is for this to be cruelly snatched away from me by a fatal accident. If three attempts have been made to remove me from Abbeydore, might there be a fourth? And, whereas the previous three failed, might the fourth succeed? It's a worrying thought. It dogs me constantly.

I am unsure how to act.

Jason, for all his love and care, does not see it as a problem.

He says that as long as he is around I have nothing to fear. He will protect me from harm. This is true. He is a tower of strength and his athletic strength and youthful stamina make him an ideal personal minder. But he is not always around. He likes to go off on his own with his gun for long periods of time.

I don't begrudge him time on his own. I can't expect him to spend all his time with me. But I can't forget that my near brushes with death, in both the tank of wine and the crashing barrels, were when he was away and I was on my own. It feels as if someone has the vineyard under surveillance and waits until Jason is away before they act. It is a disturbing thought. I do not like to think that someone is constantly

JESSICA'S VINEYARD

watching me and waiting for an opportunity to pounce.

After much soul-searching and perplexity, I decide to take matters into my own hands.

I have always involved Jason in all decision-making. We work as a team and I have no wish to do anything behind his back; but, on this occasion, I resolve to take the initiative and not tell him what I am doing. I don't want him to think I don't trust his ability to protect me.

When he disappears on his next rabbit hunting jaunt, I pick up the phone and speak to Hereford Police Station. The only person I know at the police station is Detective Sergeant Rees and so I ask for him. After a considerable wait, I eventually hear his voice at the other end of the line.

'Mrs Knightly,' he announces, 'How may I help you?'
'Ah!' I stammer, trying to think how best to begin a conversation with a detective. 'I hope you don't mind me phoning you …'

I wait for a reassuring reply but am met with silence.
' … I know that you're a very busy man …'

But still no response. Oh dear! This is proving more difficult than I thought. I have no alternative: I must put my fears into words and risk the consequences.

'… You may remember when you visited Abbeydore, that I mentioned my near brush with death when I fell into one of our large tanks of wine. It was only

the unexpected appearance of my ex-husband that saved me from possibly drowning. Well, another event has occurred that could have proved equally fatal. Whilst I was on my hands and knees in the barn sweeping shards of broken bottle glass into a dustpan, two of the extremely large barrels, containing six-hundred bottles of wine each, fell from the racking and narrowly missed me. At first, I thought it was merely an accident but, on closer examination, I discovered that the pegs securing the racking were missing. I now think it may not have been an accident but a second attempt on my life.'
I await a response. When it comes it is calm and measured.
'This is certainly a cause for concern,' says the disembodied voice at the other end of the phone line. Then, after a pause, he says, 'Are you able to come to the police station here in Hereford and provide a full statement of everything that has happened? It may be that you have just been unlucky in having two accidents in close proximity or it may be that things are not all that they seem. A full statement from you will enable us to open an investigation.'
A great feeling of relief flows through me. I am not being written off as a neurotic woman. DS Rees is willing to investigate on my behalf. I no longer feel isolated. I have the Herefordshire Constabulary

behind me. My faith in DS Rees increases by the minute.

'Of course,' I reply. Then, remembering my business motto of seizing opportunities whenever they occur before someone else has a chance to get his nose in, I say, 'Would tomorrow morning be a convenient time for me to call and see you?'

'That would be excellent,' he answers. I can almost see a smile on his face as his words register in my brain.

The die is cast. I will visit Hereford Police Station tomorrow morning and make a full statement to DS Rees.

CHAPTER 21

It is said that a problem shared is a problem halved. That is certainly how I feel now that I have shared my concerns with DS Rees. Someone else is dealing with the things that have happened to me. I am not alone.

I have Jason, of course, and I feel very secure when he is around, but he does not want to shadow me all the time. He's a young man. He wants to be out and about. He likes the great outdoors and it would be suffocating for him to spend all his time watching over me. Although we are very close, we both need our own space. And so, when I inform him I am going into Hereford the following day he raises no objections. But then, neither does he offer to accompany me.

'I reckon I saw a muntjac deer yesterday when I was in Fuller's Wood and I've got my sights firmly set on him,' he says. 'I've not tasted a good venison casserole since I came to Abbeydore. It would make an ideal accompaniment for another of those bottles of wine from the cellar.'

JESSICA'S VINEYARD

I don't doubt this is true; but, I've no intention of cracking open bottles of our 1933 vintage every time we want a wine to accompany a meal. It's much too valuable.

'Why don't we try Abbeydore Nouveau instead?' I suggest.

'What!' he exclaims in surprise, 'You want to try the stuff we've just put into the barrels?'

'Why not? The winegrowers of Beaujolais do it every year. No sooner have they harvested their crop than they race to get a bottle of the new vintage onto the tables of the best restaurants in the world for the first Thursday of November.'

'But isn't the wine incredibly acidic if it hasn't had time to mature in a barrel?'

'The wine has a light, young and fruity character,' I inform him. 'That's part of its appeal. It's like no other wine on the market. And you've got to take your hats off to the Beaujolais growers. They've carved out a niche market for themselves – and they don't have to go to all the trouble of storing wine for years before they sell it.'

Jason is not convinced.

'But, surely, they can't sell new wine for the same price as vintage wine that has been laid down and allowed to mature in barrels for years?'

'They don't sell it for huge prices. A bottle will normally set you back £15 to £25. There are no

JESSICA'S VINEYARD

premier crus or grands crus at lofty prices and scarce availability. They price their nouveau wine considerably lower than village-level burgundy, which is the rough equivalent in the wine hierarchy.'
'Well, if our Abbeydore Nouveau tastes OK, why don't we sell it straightaway? £15 to £25 a bottle sounds good to me.'
I laugh.
'You don't think we'd get £15 to £25 do you? Get real! Restaurants and bars have around a 70% profit margin on the wine they sell, while retailers typically take between 30% to 50%. Then, there's distribution costs. We'd be lucky if we got £7 a bottle.'
'There's a bit of a difference between that and the £1,000 we hope to get for the stuff in the cellar.'
'There certainly is. And then there's another problem.'
'What's that?'
'We grow the wrong sort of grapes. The Beaujolais growers use Gamay grapes. Gamay grapes have the ability to be crushed and fermented using the carbonic maceration process which makes it quite distinctive from other grape varieties. Sorry, Jason, but we're in this for the long haul. Our Cabernet Sauvignon grapes are designed for aging wine. But that doesn't stop us drawing off a little of our new vintage to accompany the venison. It'll be interesting

JESSICA'S VINEYARD

to compare and contrast it with the wonderful wine we sampled yesterday.'

*

The following morning, Jason slings his rifle over his shoulder, gives me a fond kiss on the cheek and disappears in search of muntjac deer. As soon as he has left I prepare to travel to Hereford for my interview with the handsome DS Rees.
Since moving to Abbeydore I've become very much a country girl. I wear jeans and open-necked shirts around the vineyard and am not overly concerned about my appearance. There's no one here to impress in this isolated location. But, today, I decide to wear a skirt and blouse. I take a little more trouble than usual with my hair and even apply a discreet amount of makeup.
As I look at myself in the mirror I see the lines that advancing age have etched on my face. The frown lines at the top of my nose are becoming particularly noticeable. Could these be caused by the worrying events of recent months? I raise my eyebrows to chase them away. But, when I do so, I see tramlines appearing on my forehead. Age is stamping its mark on me. I will soon become a shop-soiled, returned reject, languishing in obscurity. Jason will cease to find me attractive. I will become a yesterday's woman isolated in the middle of nowhere and left to vegetate.

JESSICA'S VINEYARD

I apply more foundation cream to my face and stare more intently at the image in the mirror.
'Mirror, mirror, on the wall, who's the fairest of them all?'
The mirror makes no response. But neither does it crack from side to side. I laugh at my vanity. There's no denying I'm a middle-aged woman. The miracle is that Jason has bound his life to mine and is willing to share in my inexorable decline. I smile again. Life is not so bad after all.
I leave the house with a spring in my step.
Perhaps it's the fact that I am dressed like a woman who is taking pride in her appearance; or perhaps it's the thought of meeting the dishy DS Rees; or perhaps it's the fine autumn weather; but, whatever the reason, I am in good spirits.
I climb into the old Land Rover and bring her to life. My decidedly feminine attire and the old Land Rover don't go naturally together. Perhaps I should have given the old girl a good clean before venturing into the county town to see the dishy police sergeant. But it's too late to think of that now. Time is marching on and I have an appointment to keep.
As I pull out of the entrance of the winery and set off in the direction of Hereford, my thoughts are very much on what I am going to say in my statement to DS Rees. I try to remember the sequence of events that have unfolded and the dates of each incident.

JESSICA'S VINEYARD

Perhaps my mind is too intent on framing the words I will share with the police sergeant to realise that everything is not as it should be with the Land Rover. It is only when I came to Fordham Hill that reality dawns. I depress the brake pedal to regulate the speed of the vehicle as it begins its descent only to find this has no effect. The Land Rover's brakes refuse to engage.

I pump the brake pedal furiously, cursing my high heeled shoes as I do so. Why am I not wearing sensible flat-soled shoes? I stamp on the pedal like a madman battering a helpless victim to death, but to no effect.

All the while the speed of the Land Rover is increasing. I yank at the handbrake in a desperate attempt to slow down the forward movement of the vehicle. At first, this seems to help; but then, without warning, the tension in the handbrake cable snaps and I am left holding a metal lever in my left hand that is as useless as a silver teaspoon.

I try to force the gear-lever into a lower gear so as to use the engine to slow down the vehicle, but the engine is racing too fast. There is a grinding of cogs that sounds worse than a dentist's drill on full power in the hands of a demented Frankenstein monster. The road ahead is perfectly clear.

Should I steer the Land Rover into the ditch? To do so will almost certainly cause it to flip over. Will the

JESSICA'S VINEYARD

hedge on the other side of the ditch break the forward movement of my out-of-control death machine or will the vehicle plough straight through the hedge and pitch and roll down the hillside? Questions, questions, questions and no easy answers. I don't bother to look at the speedometer. The Land Rover is hurtling down Fordham Hill faster than it has ever done before. The exact speed is immaterial. Saving my life is my sole concern. I must do something to stop this deathly rollercoaster before it is too late.

My mind is in turmoil. I am normally very good at examining problems, considering various approaches and possible outcomes and then deciding on the best way forward. But I have no time for such deliberations. I am hurtling downhill at an ever-increasing speed.

The time to throw open the driver's door and bail out has long since passed. I am encased in a metal box on wheels, hurtling down a precipice at a speed of knots. Just like the Gadarene swine, who found themselves in a similar predicament, I'll soon perish, if not in the sea, then in a Herefordshire farmer's field.

I have heard it said that the whole of one's life flashes before one's eyes the moment one dies. If that is so, I can only thank my lucky stars that I don't have such an experience.

JESSICA'S VINEYARD

I am not going to die. I will somehow survive. I will not let this death-trap rob me of the new life that has opened before me.

But my ability to devise a survival strategy is vanishing by the second. My life's stopwatch is racing onwards and my options are dissipating by the millisecond. I am in the hands of fate. I am impotent. The forces of Nature are greater than me. Speed equals velocity over time. I am pitched against physics: an insignificant human battling against the immutable laws of science.

As the Land Rover reaches the bend at the bottom of Fordham Hill it careers madly across the road, mounts the verge, plunges into the ditch and performs a graceful gymnastic somersault before ploughing into the hedge and coming to rest on its roof. That is what I am told must have happened. All I know is that I saw the world as never before. Trees stood on end. The blue sky became an azure carpet beneath my feet. Trees developed an amazing ability to grow horizontally. Grass blinded me with its greenery. Blades of grass were thrust into my face forcing me to examine each blade in minute detail. And then there is nothing. All goes black. Life ceases to exist. My nightmare is over. I slip into unconsciousness. My troubles are behind me. The motherly arms of oblivion reach out and enfold me in a loving embrace.

JESSICA'S VINEYARD

'Hello, hello. Are you alright in there?'
A strange voice seems to float in the air. Why is it seeking to disturb me? Can't I be left in peace in the land where pain and suffering are no more and an eternal peace reigns?
'Hello, hello. Can you hear me?'
Do I want to hear you? Can't you see I'm sleeping? I am exceedingly tired. I need to rest. Please don't disturb me. Let me sleep untroubled.
'Don't worry. There's help on the way.'
What is this sound that intrudes on my sleep and refuses to go away? It sounds strangely familiar. Perhaps all voices sound familiar when one leaves this world and drift into infinity.
'Just keep still until they get here.'
Who gets here? Where is here? Where am I? With an inner sigh and a supreme act of will, I prise open my eyelids and view the scene.
I see something from *Alice in Wonderland*. Everything is upside down. Nothing is as it should be. Why am I staring at an upturned hedge? Why am I suspended in space? Why is this steering wheel pushing hard into my chest?
'Help is on the way,' repeats the disembodied voice. I know that voice. Where have I heard it before? It is a cavernous voice. Have I descended to the world of the dead and is this the voice of the creatures that inhabit the underworld? It is speaking in my left ear.

JESSICA'S VINEYARD

With a superhuman effort, I inch my eyes a few millimetres to the left to see where it is coming from. Peering through the broken window of the Land Rover is a face I've seen before. I struggle to put a name to it. It's certainly not the face of a friend. I would never be attracted to such a craggy, earthbound face. And yet, I feel I know the person. I close my eyes and take a deep breath.
Perhaps it is the flow of oxygen to my brain that causes me to blurt out, 'Mr Spragg'.
It is indeed my Abbeydore neighbour, Wilfred Spragg. What is he doing here? I did not ask him to accompany me on my journey to the police station in Hereford. Why has he appeared to taunt me in my hour of need?
'Ah! You're not dead, at least,' the cavernous voice exclaims. He almost wishes I was; then he could get his hands on my land. But I have no intention of dying simply to please him. I try to speak, but no words come out. I feel tired. I want to sleep but I know that to do so could prove fatal. The craggy face of my hostile neighbour, peering at me just millimetres from where I am suspended, makes me determined to stay awake.
'It's a good job I was on my way back to Abbeydore or else no one might have seen you until it was too late.'

JESSICA'S VINEYARD

Even in my hour of greatest need, his thoughts are on himself and his fortuitous intervention. He will crow like a cockerel in a farmyard at his heroic exploits in rescuing me and bringing me back from the dead. How I wish it had been anyone other than him to come to my assistance!

'I've phoned the Emergency Services and they'll be here before long.'

Then, with a rare show of interest in my predicament, he asks, 'Have you broken anything?' How the hell should I know? I'm strapped into a car seat in an upside down position, unable to move and with blood running to my head and he asks for an orthopaedic assessment of my bone structure.

I focus on the different parts of my body. My legs are trapped beneath the steering wheel and I am unable to move them.

Am I paralysed?

A shiver of dread passes through my body. Please don't say I'm paralysed! I can cope with broken bones, lacerations and sprains, but please, don't say I'm paralysed! I'm too young to spend the remainder of my life in a wheelchair. I've got a vineyard to run. I've got a young husband. He's got virile masculine needs. I can't be paralysed! It would ruin everything. I've got so much living to do! I've got a treasure trove of unbelievably fine wine to launch on the world. I've got a golden future awaiting me. Surely I can't have all of this snatched away from me by a stupid road accident! Oh why is life so unfair! I was on top of the world when I left home this morning. I even made a special effort with my appearance. Everything was hunky-dory less than an hour ago. And now this! In just sixty-minutes my whole life has been turned upside down. I may never be able to walk again.

'Well, have you broken anything?'

I mutter incoherently. As I do so, the distant sound of a siren is heard. I have no idea if it belongs to a fire engine, an ambulance or a police car but it certainly gives advance warning of its approach.

The repulsive, craggy face just millimetres from mine, has also heard it.

'That'll be the emergency services,' he says unnecessarily. 'I told them where to find you.'

The sound gets louder and louder until it resembles two notes of a punk band's first foray into pop music amplified to such a level that no one can tell how lacking in musical ability the band really is. I feel my head throbbing. I can do without this assault on my hearing. I have been physically assaulted. Isn't that enough?

I hear scuffling in the world outside my upside-down prison cell. The offensive face of Mr Spragg withdraws and is replaced by Fireman Sam wearing a helmet that is twice the size of his head. All firemen are Fireman Sams as far as I am concerned.

'Don't worry ma'am. We'll soon have you out of there,' says the voice in the helmet. 'Just remain still and leave the rest to us.'

As if movement was an option!

I see navy blue trousers and black boots moving backwards and forwards across my line of inverted vision. Men are issuing orders. The sound of a power-tool replaces the punk band's decibel-shattering debut single. A hand reaches through the shattered window of the Land Rover holding a pair of earphones.

'I'm just going to place these around your head to deaden the noise of the angle-cutter as we peel you out of this old tin can. There's nothing to worry about. Just remain perfectly still until we're able to get to you.'

The sound of ripping metal shatters the peace of the Herefordshire countryside. It sets my teeth on edge. Give me the soothing sound of a crosscut saw nibbling through wood any day to that of an angry hacksaw screeching through metal! My teeth jangle and quiver as the angle-cutter does its work.

'There, that's it,' smiles Fireman Sam as the entire side of the Land Rover is pulled away and the barrier separating me from the outside world is removed.

JESSICA'S VINEYARD

I feel a complete idiot strapped to the roof whilst my rescuer has his feet firmly on the ground. It's a most unladylike encounter.

I suddenly become aware that my skirt has performed an about-turn and is no longer concealing my legs but is covering my chest and leaving my legs exposed to the full view of the emergency services. Oh the indignity!

But Fireman Sam does not appear to notice my state of undress, or, if he does, he is too much of a gentleman to comment on it. Instead he says, 'We're going to cut through your seatbelt and then the paramedics will lift you gently onto a stretcher. You don't have to do anything except keep perfectly still.' He's a man of his word and, in next to no time, I find myself lying on my back on a stretcher en route to Hereford County Hospital.

The paramedics ask me numerous questions. They get me to move my toes and lift my legs, wiggle my fingers and lift my arms – all of which I am able to do to my great relief. I am not paralysed. I may be concussed, battered and bruised but I am not defeated. I am a survivor. I live to fight another day.

JESSICA'S VINEYARD

CHAPTER 22

Time ceases to exist. I am unaware of the day or the time. It is irrelevant. I am not going anywhere. The cares and concerns of mundane life are far from me. I have risen above mundane concerns and float in a dreamlike state between waking and sleeping. Life is going on around me, with hospital staff scurrying in all directions intent on doing whatever it is they are doing. I am merely an observer. I exist in a different realm. I have discovered nirvana in a hospital bed in Hereford.

White-coated doctors and blue-uniformed nurses glide in and out of my vision but do not impinge upon me. How can they? They belong to a different realm. They have not attained the blessed state I inhabit.

I close my eyes and remember my vineyard at harvest time, basking in the late autumn sun, laden with succulent grapes waiting for my secateurs to transfer them to the barn where a miracle will turn them into delectable wine. A smile passes over my face. I am so lucky to have found my metier. I was destined to be the successful chatelaine of an English vineyard. Providence has smiled on me and I am blessed. Doubly blessed! I also have a wonderful husband – someone who accepts me for who I am. He is unconcerned with our age difference. He is perceptive and sees beyond my aging exterior and lined face to the real me beneath. He appreciates my maturity and I relish his youth.

When I left Alan I never thought I would find a new soulmate in the depths of the Herefordshire countryside; but Jason stepped into my life and answered my deepest needs. The Fates have indeed smiled on me.

I smile in return as I inhabit my very own version of heaven.

But then my smile fades. There is a serpent lurking in the grass. Someone wants to kill me. Someone nearly achieved their objective when the brakes on the old Land Rover failed.

My smile is replaced by a frown. Why would anyone want to kill me? I have never done anyone harm. The brake failure might be an accident if it was an isolated occurrence, but not following on so soon after my near-drowning in the tank of wine and my narrow escape from the crashing barrels in the barn. Fate may well deal an occasional unexpected thunderbolt: it does not deliver three in quick succession aimed at the same target.

JESSICA'S VINEYARD

Dreams of marital bliss and nightmares of death are horribly intertwined. I am hideously confused. I clutch at the hospital sheets and grind my teeth. Life should not be like this. I am losing my grip on reality.
'Are you alright darling?'
I know that voice so well. It is my knight in shining armour riding to my rescue.
I open my eyes and see Jason sitting in the chair by my bedside.
'Oh, Jason!' I cry before losing control of myself and breaking into uncontrollable tears. My restraint has crumbled. The dam holding back my distraught and confused thoughts has finally broken. I can no longer maintain the allusion that I am in control. My trapped emotions well up and burst the dam I have struggled so hard to maintain. My eyes release pent-up waters cascading down a wall of concrete. There is no need to hold back. Jason is here beside me and all is well.
'There, there, old girl. Don't upset yourself. You're safe here. The doctors say you'll make a complete recovery. You've had a very lucky escape.'
'Oh, Jason,' I stammer between my tears. 'Everything was going so well and now this has happened.'
'It's one of those things,' he replies. 'I should have realised that old Land Rover was liable to let us down; but I never, for one minute, thought it would malfunction so badly and with such serious

consequences. I can't bear the thought of losing you. It's a miracle you came out of this alive.'

'I know,' I sigh as I recall the events on Fordham Hill. 'I thought I was going to die. The brakes refused to work. I tried everything to bring the vehicle to a halt but it was no use. It just got faster and faster and then it overturned.'

I feel tears welling up again in my eyes as I recount my near brush with death.

'I know, I know,' he says as he reassuringly strokes my hand. 'It must have been a nightmare. But, whatever you did, you prevented a worse tragedy. It could have been a lot worse.'

I nod my head in a resigned manner. It could indeed have been worse. It could have resulted in my death.

'I guess the old Land Rover is a write-off,' he says. 'Do you know what's happened to it?'

I shake my head. Quite honestly, the Land Rover is the least of my concerns. I want to know how long I have to stay in hospital. I want to know when I can return to Abbeydore and convalesce.

'How did you get here?' I ask.

'In a police car,' he answers with a wry smile. 'The bobbies came to tell me what had happened and kindly offered me a lift with them back to Hereford so I could visit you in hospital.'

'That was kind of them.'

JESSICA'S VINEYARD

'I guess I'd better hire a car whilst I'm here in the city so we have some way of getting to and from our place.'

I nod in agreement.

'Is there anything I can get you?' he asks.

Of course there is nothing. My every need is attended to by the hospital staff.

'No. All I want is to return to Abbeydore as soon as possible.'

'Well, I think they're going to keep you in overnight. They want to monitor your condition. You've been badly concussed, they say, and they want to ensure everything is OK before they discharge you. I'll return tomorrow with a new car and drive you back to The Abbeydore Convalescent Rest Home.'

'I can't wait.'

'And I'll ensure you have the personal attentions of the Manager at all times to facilitate a speedy recovery.'

I smile at his attempt at humour.

'That will work wonders if past experience is anything to go by.'

He gives me a big grin before he rises from his chair and places a warm kiss on my forehead.

'Until tomorrow, then …' and with a farewell wave of his arm he is gone

JESSICA'S VINEYARD

A smile spreads over my face as I thank my lucky stars for having such a wonderful husband. I close my eyes and bask in matrimonial euphoria.
Time passes.
'Mrs Knightly,' a voice whispers in my right ear.
I come out of my reverie and open my eyes.
The chair previously occupied by my husband is now occupied by another handsome young man.
I cannot prevent a smile reappearing on my face.
'Detective Sergeant Rees,' I say.
'Correct,' is his no-nonsense response. 'I'm pleased to see that the accident hasn't affected your memory recall.'
But before I can respond, he continues, 'I've no wish to tire you so soon after what must have been a horrendous experience, but I would like to ask you a few questions if you feel strong enough to answer.'
'Indeed I do. I was on my way to see you in any case. We may as well have our meeting here as at the police station.'
He nods as he pulls a notebook from his pocket and prepares to record the information he is seeking. He embarks upon his questions.
'When was your Land Rover last serviced?'
Oh dear! This is not going to sound good.
'Not since I acquired it in the spring,' I answer truthfully. 'It came with a twelve month MOT

certificate and so I assumed it was in full working order.'

'Has anyone carried out any work on the vehicle over the intervening months?'

'Not that I know of. Jason tends to look after our agricultural machinery. He has never mentioned anything about the Land Rover. It always appeared to perform well and has never seemed to need attention. Why do you ask?'

A frown passes over the handsome face of the detective sergeant.

'Your brakes failed on Fordham Hill because there was no hydraulic fluid in the brake reservoir. That could only be caused by a fracture somewhere in the brake lines; but there is no evidence of this. Have you any idea why the brake fluid was deficient?'

I shake my head in bewilderment. Jason might have an answer but I know nothing about the inner workings of an internal combustion engine.

'In the light of what you told me on previous occasions,' continues the policeman, 'there could be a more sinister reason for what has happened. You mentioned, when I visited you at Abbeydore, that you had a near-death experience when you fell into a large tank of wine.'

'Yes,' I sigh. 'At first, I thought it was caused by my own stupidity and I failed to place the ladder correctly when I climbed to the top of the tank to take a hydrometer reading. But, the more I think about it, the more I'm convinced there must be some other explanation. I was pitched forwards into the tank rather than sliding to the side as I would expect if the ladder had slipped.'

He does not comment but continues, 'And then you mentioned to me on the phone that you experienced a second worrying brush with death when two large barrels fell and narrowly missed you.'

'Yes. At first I thought it was just an unfortunate accident. The barrels sit on very old timber framing and I thought that age must have weakened the structure and caused them to plunge to the ground and narrowly miss me. But, upon closer inspection, I was unable to find the pegs securing the collapsed timber framing.'

He makes no comment, but continues, 'And now you've had a third close encounter with death when the brakes of your Land Rover failed.'

This is not so much a question as a statement of fact. Spoken in the detective sergeant's cool detached manner he makes the event sound even more chilling. I am a marked woman. Someone wants to kill me.

After a pregnant pause, DS Rees says, 'I've been conducting a number of enquiries following my visit to your vineyard at Abbeydore. You provided a comprehensive list of those who had recently visited your premises. We've carried out some background checks on them and this has revealed some interesting facts. I think the time has come for us to pull our information together and get to the bottom of what is going on. There have been three unsuccessful attempts on your life: a fourth may prove fatal. We need to act and act quickly.'

I close my eyes and shiver. But this is no time for self-pity. There is something else the detective sergeant should know.

'I think I should tell you of another worrying encounter I've had at Abbeydore,' I say. 'Shortly after your visit, I came face to face with a man I had not seen since I worked in the city. He was lying in wait for me in the lane by the entrance to our property. His name is Henry Jackson-Jones. He had his wife with him, also. He refused to let me pass. He regaled me with a catalogue of grudges he held against me. They all related to commercial business transactions. To me, they were part of the cut and thrust of commerce. But he clearly did not view them in the same way. He thought it was personal. He thought I had deliberately sought to inflict harm on him and his wife. Nothing could be further from the truth. But he was not convinced. He vowed to take vengeance on me.'

JESSICA'S VINEYARD

I pause and shudder as I recall the hateful encounter before asking, 'Do you think he might have a hand in what has happened?'

'It's hard to say, but it clearly makes him a suspect. I'll get to work on it and see what we can find out about him.'

'Everything was going so well before all of this,' I sigh. 'Our vineyard has yielded a terrific harvest thanks to the exceptional weather. All seemed set for the brilliant launch to our first vintage. We've also discovered a cache of old vintage wine in our cellar that could take the wine world by storm. We estimate it might have a market value of up to £10 million. All seemed to be going so well and now this.'

'Perhaps your very success has filled someone with greed or jealousy.'

'Maybe. But do people murder from jealousy?'

'They do if they think they will prosper as a result.'

'Oh dear! I wish I knew what to do.'

'Might I make a suggestion?'

The handsome man sitting by my bedside can make as many suggestions as he wants. I trust him implicitly. He has a calm assurance. I sense he also has a good brain. At the moment, he is my only bulwark between life and death. I need his assistance if I am to survive and come through this nightmare alive.

'Please do,' I answer with genuine gratitude.

JESSICA'S VINEYARD

'Can I suggest a wine tasting?'

I look at him in puzzlement. This is not the help I was expecting. Why indulge in wine tasting when it is my life that is on the line? Surely there are more practical options that could be pursued.

Perhaps my face reveals my inner thoughts too clearly because he immediately seeks to clarify his suggestion.

'Everyone likes wine, especially if it is expensive and is being offered free of charge. I think that an invitation to a free wine tasting of the recently discovered Abbeydore vintage should illicit a good response. Of course, we will be very selective whom we invite. I suggest we start with Mr Montague Smythe. He's a wine buff and is sure to come. Then there is Councillor Johnson. I'm sure he's no stranger to a good glass of burgundy and, given his interest in your property, would almost certainly attend. Then there's that strange young man, Mr Quinten Stretcher, who seemed more interested in the flagstones in your medieval barn than in any of the building's other features. Perhaps he has a nose for cellared wines. Then, as an act of good neighbourliness, why not invite Mr and Mrs Spragg? It was, after all, Mr Spragg who was the first on the scene when you had your motor accident. I'm sure he must be very concerned about your wellbeing and would certainly wish to come. He might even raise a glass to toast your good health.'

I somehow doubt it, but I refrain from saying so. 'That's quite an assorted guest list,' I reply.

He smiles, before adding, 'But I haven't finished yet. You said that this Henry Jackson-Jones and his wife bear you ill will. Well, what could be better than an exemplary glass of very expensive wine to heal old wounds and extend the olive branch of forgiveness? It is extremely difficult to nurse grudges against someone who extends the hand of hospitality. A glass of your excellent vintage wine might smooth over past differences and place Mr and Mrs Jackson-Jones in a more amiable frame of mind.'

'I cannot say I share your optimism,' I reply, 'but I'm willing to give it a try if you think it might work.'

'And, while we're on the topic of reconciliation and forgiveness, why not invite your ex-husband Alan and his new fiancée as well? He clearly takes an interest in you to have visited Abbeydore on two separate occasions already.'

I sigh. Something tells me this is not going to be a particularly enjoyable wine tasting.

'That makes eight guests,' concludes the police officer, 'which, with you, your husband, me and a couple of plain clothes police officers will make a total of thirteen people in all. How does that sound to you?'

JESSICA'S VINEYARD

'It sounds a bit like assembling all the suspects in the library in an Agatha Christie novel for a final denouement,' I say with a hollow laugh.
He smiles.
'Perhaps that's where I got the idea,' he replies. 'Now I'll supply you with the names and addresses of each of the guests so you can send out invitations. We need to move fairly rapidly before anyone has another opportunity to take a pot-shot at you. Do you think you will feel fit and well in a fortnight's time?'
'Until I get out of this hospital bed I won't know whether or not I can walk, let alone run a wine tasting at Abbeydore,' I answer, 'but, providing all goes well, I'm happy with a date in a fortnight's time.'
'Excellent. We'll liaise over the exact details. I'll leave it to you to lead the tasting as my knowledge of wine is woefully inadequate.'
'In that case I will have to give you lessons.'
And on that harmonious note we part: he to furnish the addresses of the proposed guests and me to ruminate on personal one-to-one lessons on wine appreciation with the handsome DS Rees.

CHAPTER 23

Jason is not happy with the planned wine-tasting. 'We need to launch the 1933 vintage Cabernet Sauvignon at a proper wine event,' he declares angrily, 'and not with a bunch of weirdos who can do nothing to advance our wine and ensure it hits the market with a bang.'

There is truth in what he says; but I promised DS Rees I would go along with his plan and, as my life is more important to me than marketing our vintage wine, I am not about to backtrack.

'And why should we sacrifice a bottle of wine worth £1,000 simply to please a policeman?' he argues. 'He probably thinks he'll get a free tipple and then be able to boast to his colleagues that he's tasted a £1,000 wine. Let him stick to cups of tea in the police canteen.'

Jason clearly does not like the police.

I think he's being unreasonable. I have no qualms about sacrificing a bottle of our wine if it means I can live in peace and safety thereafter, and so I overrule Jason.

JESSICA'S VINEYARD

'I'm sorry you don't approve, but I've given my agreement to the wine tasting and the invitations have been sent out. There is no going back.'
I still feel delicate after my accident, but I have not lost my resolve. I am committed to DS Rees's course of action and I am determined to see it through.
A frosty atmosphere exists between us for the next twenty-four hours.
My enforced convalescence means I have plenty of spare time on my hands. It occurs to me that I've never told Celia Braithwaite of my marriage to her fellow countryman and so I dash off an extended email to her.
I also undertake research on the title deeds of Abbeydore Winery to discover who owned my vineyard in 1933. The results are revelatory!
My vineyard was owned by a certain Oliver Gotobed. I have never before come across this surname. It makes me smile. But it also proves invaluable. The number of people with the surname Gotobed is decidedly limited. This makes searching historical documents that much easier. If it had been a Mr Jones or a Mr Smith, I might have struggled. But Oliver Gotobed is such a distinctive and unusual name that I have no trouble researching him on the internet.
I discover he was conscripted into the RAF in 1939 and joined Bomber Command. Alas, his wartime

JESSICA'S VINEYARD

service lasted only three years. He was shot down over Germany in 1942 and killed. His grave is in the Berlin Commonwealth War Grave Cemetery.

How sad that he should have left the peaceful Golden Valley in Herefordshire to end his life amidst the gunfire and carnage of Nazi Germany! He was summoned to a bed in a foreign land with earth as his blanket.

And how cruel that he should never taste or profit from his superb 1933 vintage wine! He laid down the bottles thinking that once the war was over he would return here and continue his brave wine-making adventure.

But Fate had other ideas. His treasure trove of fine wine was cruelly snatched from his grasp and has lain undiscovered for nearly a hundred years. It has fallen to me to enter into the inheritance of this brave pioneer in English winemaking. I profit at his expense.

This thought brings me to an abrupt halt.

If he was robbed of his treasure could I be about to share the same fate?

There have been three attempts on my life. Any one of them could have been successful. Might I suffer the same fate as Oliver Gotobed? Is Abbeydore Winery cursed? Is there some malign presence brooding over this place intent on snatching success from the grasp of those who try and prosper here?

JESSICA'S VINEYARD

Am I destined to suffer the same fate as him? I instantly seek to banish this chilling thought.
I turn my attention instead to learning more about the year my treasure trove of fine wine was made. It would seem that 1933 was an exceptionally hot year – the fifth hottest of the century. The hot weather extended from June through to September. No wonder the Cabernet Sauvignon grapes prospered and produced such an outstanding harvest! Oliver must have rubbed his hands with glee as he gathered in his harvest. He proved that Cabernet Sauvignon grapes could be grown in this country and yield a great harvest. I know exactly how he must have felt. Our grape harvest this year has been exemplary. I share his sense of rapture and elation. I reach out across the decades to the grave he occupies in the Berlin cemetery and shake his hand. We are partners in viniculture. We were both prepared to confront the dismissive noises of others and triumph over adversity in order to produce fine wine. Oliver and I are fellow compatriots. Our vision soars above the mean-spirited tunnel-vision of lesser mortals. We are the trailblazers. We are the innovators. We seek to make Abbeydore the centre of excellence and renown. Oliver and I are destined to occupy a place in vinicultural history. Soon his foresight and skill will be lauded by others. They will hail his 1933 vintage as a gift from the gods.

JESSICA'S VINEYARD

I hope he is smiling and savouring his success from the Elysian Fields.

*

Two weeks elapse between sending out the invitations to our wine tasting and the great day itself. I derive a certain satisfaction from the fact that all the recipients reply to say they are coming. DS Rees was correct. No one turns down an invitation to taste a rare and expensive wine when it's offered free of charge.

When the afternoon of the wine tasting arrives, I experience a fluttering of butterflies in my stomach at the thought of what lies ahead. But my faith in DS Rees is unshakable. I'm sure he knows what he's doing. I am determined to play my part exactly as he has requested.

The first to arrive is Mr Montague Smythe. He is an hour early.

DS Rees and his fellow officers have not yet arrived; but fortunately Jason is on hand to provide support. 'What time d'you call this?' demands Jason in his direct manner. 'The invitation said three o'clock.' Montague Smythe looks down his nose at my husband. He would like to give him the rough edge of his tongue but he knows it would be counter-productive and so he merely smiles and says, 'I'm sorry if I've inconvenienced you by my early arrival but, really, the excitement of this event has proved

JESSICA'S VINEYARD

more than I can resist. I hardly slept a wink last night dreaming about the stupendous discovery you have made. If I am correct – and I think I am - you have unearthed a hoard of the greatest wine this country has ever produced. It will set the wine world alight! I have known about the 1933 vintage for years. It has become part of the folklore of the wine trade. But never have I experienced the sensation of tasting it. I cannot tell you how excited I am! I cannot thank you enough, Mrs Knightly, for inviting me to this tasting. I feel I am on the brink of a new world. I see the Promised Land stretching before me: a land of milk and honey; a golden land waiting to be explored and conquered. You can rely on me, Mrs Knightly, to give you an entirely unbiased opinion of your vintage. I will bring my knowledge of the world's finest wines to bear so that my opinion will be firmly anchored in reality. Have no fear, Mrs Knightly, Montague Smythe is at your service and is ready to share the fruits of his knowledge and experience with you.'
'That's good to know, mate,' answers Jason. 'But it still doesn't get around the fact you're an hour early. Why don't you go and have a walk around the vineyard and return at 3.00.pm? We won't crack open a bottle until then. OK mate?'
Mr Smythe frowns before realising that nothing is to be gained by arguing with Jason and so he leaves the

JESSICA'S VINEYARD

barn to while away an hour walking around the vineyard.

During the intervening hour, Jason and I roll some small wooden casks into the centre of the medieval barn and stand them on end. They will serve as tables. We carry wine glasses from the house and place them on the upturned casks. I provide jugs of water and small savoury biscuits to accompany the tasting. All is set.

DS Rees and a plain clothes colleague arrive in an unmarked car and then another colleague arrives in a separate car. Introductions are carried out before DS Rees draws me to one side and gives me whispered instructions as to how I am to proceed.

Other cars arrive as three o'clock approaches. Councillor Johnson glides to a halt outside the barn in his gleaming Jaguar and emerges with a vote-winning smile on his face.

'Well, this is a great surprise,' he beams. 'I never thought you would be marketing wine so soon after moving here. You must be trying to outclass Beaujolais Nouveau. I just hope the results are as good. But, if they're not, and your vintage proves disappointing, I am still willing to help out. Just remember, my offer still stands.'

He glides into the barn just as Montague Smythe returns from his perambulation of the vineyard. The two gravitate towards each other. Maybe they attended the same public school or maybe it is simply a case of like attracts like.

The next guests to arrive are Wilfred and Myrtle Spragg in their battered Astra car. Mr Spragg has made an effort to spruce himself up for the occasion but there is no disguising the fact he is like a fish out of water. He shifts uncomfortably from foot to foot while his wife hides in his shadow.

I make a beeline towards them.

'Mr Spragg,' I smile, 'I've not had an opportunity to thank you for coming to my assistance when I had my accident on Fordham Hill. I was fortunate that you were travelling along the road at exactly that time. I am so grateful you phoned the emergency services and enabled my rescue.'

He nods but makes no other reply.

'And this must be your wife,' I beam as I gaze at the diminutive woman standing in the shadow of her gnarled husband. 'What a pleasure it is to meet you.' The fact that we have been near neighbours for nearly nine months and not encountered one another does not exactly bode well for any future good neighbourly relations.

I wait for her to respond, but she appears to share her husband's dislike of words and merely nods her head. She is one of those people I know I shall instantly forget as soon as she leaves the barn.

JESSICA'S VINEYARD

But, just as I search in my mind for something else to say to my two taciturn neighbours, I see, over their shoulder, two new arrivals entering the barn.

'Please excuse me,' I say, 'but I've just seen some new arrivals and I must attend to them.'

The new arrivals are not ones I particularly want to see but at least they provide an escape route from the sepulchral atmosphere engulfing the Spraggs.

I advance upon the couple who have just entered the barn. I know the man only too well but the woman accompanying him is new to me. I focus my attention upon her. She is middle-aged but clearly wishes to appear much younger judging by the adolescent clothes she is wearing. Her hair is dyed blonde and she displays a jeweller's cornucopia of sparkling gem stones suspended from her earlobes. She is clearly a woman who likes the good things of life. I hope Alan is able to afford her.

As I get near to the pair, I get a better view of her face. She has cold grey eyes. They stare unblinkingly at me. No doubt she is trying to get the measure of me. Any signs of aging on her face have been removed, either by the generous application of makeup or Botox treatment.

Alan claimed his fiancée was no dolly bird or piece of fluff. She is certainly not a bright young thing. She appears to me to be a rather cold and calculating person, if first impressions are anything to go by.

JESSICA'S VINEYARD

I smile at her but receive no smile in return.
She probably thinks I'm a country bumpkin wasting my life in the depths of the countryside. Not that I care. She is welcome to her fashionable clothes and cosmetics. She is also welcome to Alan.
My smile encompasses the thought that Alan will have his work cut out managing the expectations of his new woman. I don't think she'll be as forgiving and compliant as I was. I sense he has a fight on his hands. I metaphorically rub my hands together in glee.
'Allow me to introduce my fiancée, Deirdre,' states Alan. Turning to his recent acquisition, he says, 'This is Jessica, my ex.'
The two of us shake hands in a meaningless fashion.
'I'm so glad both of you have been able to come today,' I say. 'I know it's a long journey from London to this remote neck of the woods, but I hope you'll think it was worthwhile.'
'I somehow doubt it,' replies my infuriating ex-husband. 'I expect we're about to have our teeth set on edge by your foray into winemaking. I told you before, it's a skilled trade and you know absolutely nothing about it. I reckon you're heading for a fall. You're going to make a complete fool of yourself in front of all these people. Well, don't say, I didn't warn you.'

JESSICA'S VINEYARD

In any other circumstances I would be enraged by his pompous egotism, but, today, I know I am on a winner and am quite content to let him have his say, knowing he will soon have to eat humble pie.
Before he can embark upon another lecture designed to impress Deirdre with his eloquence and self-assurance, I spot a new face appearing around the barn doors.
'Please excuse me,' I smile, 'I've just seen someone else arriving and I must go and greet them.'
The new face is a young face. It belongs to the PhD Student with an inordinate fascination for medieval barns – especially those built by the Herefordshire School of Masons.
'Ah, Mr Stretcher,' I beam at the rather gawky individual standing blinking in the doorway as his eyes adjust to the subdued lighting inside the barn.
'Oh yes,' he replies as if reminding himself that really is his name. Then, in a supreme effort of self-assertion he says, 'It's awfully kind of you to invite me to your wine-tasting. I do enjoy good wines; but I never thought, when I embarked upon my jaunt around the Herefordshire countryside, that I would be invited to a wine tasting. It really is jolly kind of you. I don't know what I've done to deserve such a favour.'
You'll soon find out, I think to myself.

JESSICA'S VINEYARD

'Let me introduce you to Mr Smythe,' I respond.
'He's a Master of Wines and should be able to
provide you with some valuable assistance when it
comes to the tastings.'
'That's awfully kind of you,' he stammers as I lead
him across the barn to where Messrs Smythe and
Johnson are deep in conversation – or, maybe, I
should say, where Montague Smythe is lecturing
Councillor Johnson on grape varietals and the
influence terroir has upon a resultant wine.
The last of the invited guests to appear is Henry
Jackson Jones and his wife. I catch my breath. I have
no desire to cross swords with either of them again.
They are only here because DS Rees insisted they
attend. They are like an elephant in the barn. Their
presence overshadows all else and yet they cannot be
ignored.
I turn in desperation to find Jason.
'Jason: can you deal with the Jackson-Jones. I really
don't feel up to another altercation with them. Give
them some of your masterful Australian small talk –
and keep them as far from me as possible.'
'Leave them to me, old girl,' he states with
undisguised relish.
I watch as he crosses the barn to the new arrivals and
launches into a no-nonsense, verbal assault on the
couple he last encountered at the end of his rifle

JESSICA'S VINEYARD

barrel. Thank goodness he's dealing with them and not me!

As I turn to re-join the assembled guests, I find DS Rees at my elbow.

'I think everyone's here,' he whispers. 'Let's make a start.'

I know what I have to do.

Taking a deep breath, I pick up a wine glass and a metal knife and produce a ting-a-ling-a-ling sound on the side of the glass. It has an immediate effect. The babble of conversation ceases and all attention is fixed on me.

'Ladies and gentleman,' I begin, 'It gives me great pleasure to welcome you to Abbeydore Winery for our first ever wine tasting. I know that some of you have travelled a considerable distance to be here today. I hope you'll consider the time and effort well-spent.

'As many of you will know, my husband and I only acquired Abbeydore Winery this year. We could not have asked for a better first year to commence our exciting journey into wine production. The weather has been superb and we have had an exceptional grape harvest. We have great hopes that our first vintage will be an outstanding success. But, of course, this year's wine is too immature to taste at present, let alone launch on the market. And so, it is not this year's vintage that we have invited you to sample but

JESSICA'S VINEYARD

one that this vineyard produced in 1933 when a certain Oliver Gotobed was its owner and winemaker. He was very much a pioneer. There was no market for English wines in 1933; and even the handful of people that did grow grapes at that time did not grow the Cabernet Sauvignon variety. It was thought they could only flourish in hot Mediterranean countries. But Mr Gotobed thought otherwise. He was a man of vision. He planted five acres of Cabernet Sauvignon vines and waited for results. His faith and vision were rewarded in 1933. 'An exceptionally hot summer resulted in the vines yielding a superb harvest. He bottled the wine and laid it down knowing it would only improve with age. Alas, he never lived to taste the fruits of his labours. He was conscripted into the RAF at the start of the Second World War and was shot down over Germany in 1943. He is buried in the Commonwealth War Graves Cemetery in Berlin. 'His store of wine remained hidden and forgotten until recently when my husband and I discovered a cellar beneath this barn.'

I notice Montague Smythe nodding his head vigorously.

'You, ladies and gentlemen, will be the first to taste a wine that has lain undisturbed for nearly a hundred years. This is a momentous occasion. I hope I've filled you with a sense of anticipation and excitement.

JESSICA'S VINEYARD

But, before we sample the wine, someone else would like to say a few words.'

I make a gesture with my arm in the direction of DS Rees.

'Thank you, Mrs Knightly,' replies the urbane policeman as he steps forward and surveys the thirteen people assembled before him.

'I am not a wine expert. I am a police officer. I am not here today to taste wine but apprehend a potential murderer.'

A gasp issues from the people clustered around the upturned casks in the centre of the barn and a look of consternation appears on the faces of those unaccustomed to maintaining poker faces to conceal their true feelings.

'As Mrs Knightly has informed you, she is newly-arrived in Abbeydore. She only came here in the spring; and yet, during the past nine months, there have been three attempts on her life. Somebody clearly wants to see her dead.'

His eyes sweep around the assembled suspects. There is an uncomfortable shuffling of feet as each person falls under the piercing glance of the detective sergeant. His eyes come to rest on Mr and Mrs Spragg.

'Mr and Mrs Spragg clearly have an interest in seeing Mrs Knightly dead. They both want her land. They wanted to get their hands on it when it came up for auction but they were out-bid by Mrs Knightly. They were clearly not happy. And yet what could they do?' Without waiting for an answer he continues, 'They could seek to make her life as difficult as possible so that she eventually packed her bags and moved away. They had a motive for removing her. They also had numerous opportunities. They live very close at hand. Mr Spragg always timed his visits to this property for when Mrs Knightly was alone. There was a motive and plenty of opportunities. But would Mr and Mrs Spragg resort to murder? I think not. Even if they killed Mrs Knightly, her husband would enter into possession of the property. They would have to kill him as well if they were to get their hands on Abbeydore Winery. Somehow I don't think Mr and Mrs Spragg are serial killers. I think, therefore, we can eliminate them from our enquiries.'

A noticeable wave of relief spreads over the craggy face of Mr Spragg and the anonymous face of his wife. It is as if the sea has just washed over a sandy beach and removed all trace of detritus. They are cleared. They can breathe again.

The policeman's eyes roam around the group once more until they rest upon Henry Jackson-Jones and his wife.

'Mr Jackson-Jones and his wife clearly bear ill will towards Mrs Knightly,' he continues. 'They purposely went out of their way to discover Mrs Knightly's whereabouts and then travelled a hundred-and-fifty miles to confront her with menaces. They blame her for their lack of business success. Jealousy and envy are two very potent motives for murder. They have a motive and their unaccountable appearance in the area means they also had opportunity. They would clearly shed no tears if Mrs Knightly came to a sticky end; but, are they murderers? They had nothing to gain from her death except the perverted satisfaction that she had achieved her comeuppance. Furthermore, because they made their dislike of Mrs Knightly so obvious, they would naturally be the prime suspects in the event of her death. Was their dislike and resentment so intense that they would willingly risk a lifetime prison sentence? I think not. They had too much to lose if they acted so foolishly. I think, therefore, we can eliminate the Jackson-Jones from our investigation.'

Henry Jackson-Jones cannot contain his outrage. 'To even think I might be a potential murderer is preposterous! I have never heard anything so outrageous in all my life!' he bursts forth. 'I'll not have my good name tarnished by you, police officer, or anyone else for that matter. You should be ashamed of yourself!'

'My husband's right!" screams his wife. 'We don't indulge in dirty tricks and operate on the edge of

JESSICA'S VINEYARD

criminality like Mrs Knightly. We're good law-abiding citizens.'

'Furthermore,' interjects her husband, 'we pay our taxes that pay your salary, young man. You need to be careful what you're saying or you'll find yourself dismissed from the force for tarnishing the names of good law-abiding citizens.'

DS Rees remains silent and unmoved by the tirade that flows from the Jackson-Jones's.

It is only when they have exhausted their vitriol that he calmly replies, 'Both Mr and Mrs Knightly witnessed the criminal threats you made when you encountered them at the entrance to this property. Might I suggest that, if you don't want us to pursue the criminal nature of those threats, you remain silent and allow me to continue with my conclusions?'

The two of them scowl but are silent.

DS Rees's eyes glance around the group once more before resting upon my ex-husband and his fiancée. 'Mr Pope,' he states. 'You were married to Mrs Knightly for nearly twenty years, I understand. Your initial attraction must have been motivated by feelings of love, I presume. Unfortunately, it would seem, the love disappeared from your marriage and your wife decided to leave you. This was contrary to your wishes. Might your anger wish her harm? There have been numerous instances of angry men killing their wives. One thinks of Dr Crippen and his unfortunate wife. Might you wish to vent your anger by killing her? You certainly made that possibility more credible when you appeared in this barn at the very moment she was drowning in one of the wine vats. You were the obvious suspect. You could easily have been the person who removed the ladder on which she was standing and catapulted her into the vat. But, once again, what would you gain by her death? You had found yourself a new prospective wife. Would you want to risk losing her and everything else that you owned in exchange for a full life jail sentence? I somehow think not. I think, therefore, we can eliminate you from our list of potential suspects.'

'As if I'd murder my ex-wife!' exclaims Alan. 'I've often felt the urge to strangle her when she behaved so unreasonably; but I would never do so. I am no murderer.'

'I'm glad to hear it,' states the detective sergeant with a wry grimace on his face. 'I must warn you that strangulation is an extremely serious crime against the person. I strongly urge you to combat any such feelings you might harbour in the future.'

He then turns his attention to Montague Smythe.

'Mr Smythe,' he announces in his cool and professional voice.

'Please don't tarnish me with the brush of criminality, police officer,' declares the wine expert. 'I have done nothing wrong whatsoever. I have a perfectly clean driving licence. Not a single point on it. I have always kept on the right side of the law. I've no desire to dabble in underhand or dubious undertakings. I derive my pleasure from wine. And, as His Majesty's Prisons do not serve wine, as far as I am aware, I have no desire to be incarcerated in a teetotal wilderness. Give me the wide open terraces of the Rhone Valley or the undulating delights of Burgundy. I am a free spirit, police officer. Nothing would induce me to do anything that might rob me of my freedom and consign me to a future without wine.'

He is in full flow and, no doubt, will occupy the remainder of the afternoon if DS Rees does not intervene and stop him.

'Quite so, Mr Smythe. I am willing to believe that your principal interest in life is wine and that is why you are here this afternoon. But your actions may not be as pure as you would like us to believe.'

'Whatever do you mean, police officer?'

'On your own admission, you said you knew of the existence of a 1933 vintage Abbeydore Wine. You said you had striven determinedly to locate that wine. You knew of its quality and were desirous to sample it. It represented the pinnacle of your lifelong passion with wine. It was the equivalent of the Crown Jewels to you. You must find it. You must experience for yourself this elusive Holy Grail. It was this that

JESSICA'S VINEYARD

brought you to Abbeydore. You were prepared to go to any lengths to get your hands on a bottle of the 1933 vintage. You were even prepared to purchase this entire smallholding from Mrs Knightly in order to satisfy your quest. But you were frustrated at every turn. You might well have been tempted to take matters into your own hands. If Mrs Knightly were to quit Abbeydore you would be able to get your hands on the property and discover its secret hoard of vintage wine. That might have led you to vandalise the vineyard and even cause a fire in this barn in an attempt to drive Mrs Knightly from this place.'

'My dear sir: that is quite preposterous!' exclaims the outraged Mr Smythe. 'I would never resort to criminal activity, no matter how desperate I was to get my hands on a bottle of the 1933 vintage.'

'Maybe not to the extent of vandalising a vineyard or resorting to arson,' agrees the detective sergeant. 'But you were not above other clandestine activities.'

He pauses as if waiting for Mr Smythe to remonstrate with him; but the Master of Wines remains strangely mute.

'We've been making a few enquiries,' continues the detective sergeant, 'and we've discovered that you employ a personal assistant.'

He casts his eyes around the assembled guests until they rest on one of them.

JESSICA'S VINEYARD

'Mr Quinten Stretcher is no post-graduate student pursuing a doctorate in medieval stone barns. He is none other than your PA.'

The young man with the mass of unruly hair shuffles nervously, but DS Rees has no need for him to respond. He continues, 'Upon making further enquiries we discover that Mr Stretcher has a keen interest in amateur dramatics. On 4th August he hired a costume from Fox's Theatrical Costumers. It was a strange request. He hired a Cistercian monk's habit.'

'So you were the Charlie we saw in the moonlight at the corner of our barn!' I blurt out.

'Quite right, Mrs Knightly,' affirms DS Rees. 'And do you know what he was up to?'

'I think I do,' I reply. 'He was searching for the entrance to the cellar beneath our barn.'

'Quite right. He failed to find anything when he examined the interior of the barn and so assumed there must be an external entrance to the cellar. You caught him removing earth from around the outside walls of the barn in his attempt to discover that entrance. Of course, he was unsuccessful; and your husband's rifle shot scared him off.'

There is a pause before DS Rees confronts the tassel-headed youth head on.

'Am I right?'

JESSICA'S VINEYARD

After just a moment's indecision he nods his head. But, before he can say anything more, Montague Smythe launches into full flow.

'Police officer: my PA has done nothing wrong. He was merely searching for the entrance to an underground cellar. Had he found it he would instantly have informed Mr and Mrs Knightly. He was performing an act of pure charity. He was seeking to bring to light that which has been hidden for the ages. He, like me, was moved only by an altruistic desire to unleash upon the world a treasure trove of vinicultural delight that would enrich mankind's enjoyment and add another chapter to the great chronicle of vinicultural history. He was acting from the highest motives. There was never any suggestion of criminality.'

'I'm inclined to agree with you, Mr Smythe," replies DS Rees. 'But I must warn Mr Stretcher that trespassing on other people's property and undertaking unauthorised excavations is against the law; and if the intention was to steal whatever was discovered, that makes the crime even more serious. You had a very lucky escape, Mr Stretcher, when Mr Knightly discharged his rifle at you. I hope it will act as a warning not to venture onto other people's property in future – even if you are disguised as a monk and think your costume will somehow offer you protection.'

JESSICA'S VINEYARD

The detective sergeant's warning appears to have the desired effect.
Both Mr Smythe and his PA remain strangely mute. DS Rees then scans the assembled guests once more before alighting upon Councillor Johnson.
'Councillor Johnson,' he declares. 'You have shown an unusual interest in Abbeydore Winery. According to Mrs Knightly you have made three visits to this remote spot in the past nine months. I realise that politicians are keen to gain votes from constituents, but there must be more populous areas of the county for you show your face if you wish to garner support. Your constant visits here are therefore suspicious.'
'There is nothing suspicious whatsoever about my visits,' interjects the affronted councillor. 'I explained to Mrs Knightly that I was looking for somewhere to build a new house. I've scoured the county and this is my preferred location. It is quiet and out-of-the-way. It offers seclusion and peace from the demands of acting as a county councillor. My wife has taken a liking to the location and we would like to acquire this property if at all possible. I don't see anything untoward or suspicious about that.'
DS Rees smiles. 'Some would find it very suspicious to offer £700,000 for an agricultural smallholding that, less than a year ago, was sold for £350,000 at auction. It would not be a very wise use of one's money.'

JESSICA'S VINEYARD

He looks intently at the county councillor but when he fails to respond, the detective sergeant proceeds.
'It was the unusually large amount of money you were prepared to pay in order to acquire Abbeydore Winery that brought me here in the first place. Leaving aside your unlikely story about wanting to build a house in this out-of-the-way location, what other reason might you have for wanting to acquire this property?'
'Really, officer, you are behaving in an absurd manner. I am not used to having my word questioned. I happen to be on very close terms with the Crime Commissioner and I suggest you take care what you say if you don't want me to refer you to her for rudeness and discourtesy.'
DS Rees smiles.
'I think you'll find that the Crime Commissioner shares my interest in your financial dealings, Councillor Johnson. Indeed, we have conducted exhaustive enquiries into your activities in recent months and made some very interesting discoveries. We have found that you were privy to a government scheme for a new, experimental solar power storage facility in the county. According to the government brief, the location has to be away from centres of habitation. It has to be within 10 miles of Madley Communications and Earth Tracking Station and it has to have a southerly aspect in order to capture the

JESSICA'S VINEYARD

full strength of the sun. Abbeydore Winery fits the bill perfectly! I suggest, Councillor Johnson, that you wished to purchase this property so you could then offer it to the government and make a substantial financial killing as a result.'

But before the county councillor can protest his innocence, DS Rees continues, 'We have been looking at your other recent business dealings and a common pattern seems to emerge. You use your insider knowledge as a county councillor to secure financial advantages for yourself. This, as you must surely know, is illegal. So there was a clear motive for wanting to acquire Abbeydore Winery. But, the question we have to ask is: were you prepared to murder in order to line your own pocket? You might be prepared to scare Mrs Knightly into quitting her property and thus enabling you to purchase it, but would you be prepared to murder her? You might be willing to prowl around at night with a pair of wire cutters and wreak havoc in her vineyard; you might even resort to arson to render this barn unusable and thus ruin Mrs Knightly's chances of making a living here. But would you be willing to murder her? The jury is out on that.'

'I'll see you're stripped of your stripes, sergeant, for making such outrageous accusations against me. Your behaviour is outrageous!'

JESSICA'S VINEYARD

DS Rees maintains a granite demeanour. Whatever thoughts may be going through his mind, he maintains a cool and professional exterior.
'Which brings us to the only other person who might wish to see Mrs Knightly dead,' he declares.
A tense silence descends upon the barn. It is the silence that precedes a deadly avalanche in the Swiss Alps. It is the silence before the fall of the guillotine in the French Revolution. It is a tangible silence. It is cold. It breathes ice. It freezes into inaction. Time ceases to exist. Yesterday and tomorrows are poised in a split second of indecision. It is a silence destined soon to be shattered. But when it is, what will be the aftermath? I hold my breath. I know what's coming.
'There is someone here who puts material gain above human kindness and compassion. There is someone standing among us who is willing to play on the feelings of emotionally damaged individuals in order to line their own pocket. There is someone here with no moral scruples but a single-minded obsession with their own enrichment. There is someone here who is willing to stoop so low he will cruelly play on a woman's heartstrings in order to enrich himself. There is only one person in this barn who is willing to act in this despicable way and that is Jason Knightly.'
All eyes swing around to where Jason is standing. I see a look of terror fill his eyes. He resembles a caged

animal. His nostrils dilate and panic distorts his face. He is trapped. His bravado has left him. His youthful assurance has deserted him. He is no longer the confident young Australian. He is a failed murderer. With the speed of a panther springing to seize its prey, he hurls himself towards the doors of the barn, intent on making a lightning escape.

But he has failed to take account of the two plain-clothes police officers stationed either side of the doors. They instantly grab him and quickly subdue him before handcuffing his hands behind his back and leading him out to the waiting police car.

A tense silence descends upon the barn. Everyone is looking at me. Most do so with compassion in their eyes. My husband has been arrested and taken away in handcuffs. Everyone knows that the person with whom I have shared nine wonderful months was, all the time, seeking to murder me. The natural bond between a husband and wife has been cruelly abused. I am alone once more.

'I'm terribly sorry, Mrs Knightly,' whispers the detective sergeant. 'I wish things had turned out differently. Please accept my sincerest sympathies.'

I give him a wan smile and take a deep breath.

I have suspected for some time that the love Jason and I once shared had come to an end. The detective sergeant's revelations have not, therefore, come as a complete shock. I was prepared for it.

JESSICA'S VINEYARD

I knew it was coming. Women have an innate ability to sense when things are not as they should be. When Jason and I first made love it was exactly as I remembered first love to be. We were both consumed with unbelievable passion. There was no satisfying our carnal lusts. We made love continually. There was no end to our sexual desires. But, as the months went by, I sensed that Jason no longer regarded me as his soulmate. Our lovemaking became less frequent. It was invariably me who initiated the lovemaking. Nothing was ever said, but I knew deep down that Jason did not really love me. He enjoyed satisfying his masculine sexual drive with me but it was not an expression of love. It was an animal thing.

The passionate kisses we initially shared became a mere peck on the cheek or the forehead. I could tell he no longer loved me. And yet I was afraid to broach the subject with him. He was all I had. I did not want to lose him.

It was only when I had my near-fatal brush with death in the old Land Rover that I knew I had to face reality. I had either to live in the real world, and accept whatever pain and heartache that involved, or not live at all. Self-preservation overrode all other considerations and that is why I went to the police.

JESSICA'S VINEYARD

But this is no time to wallow in self-pity. The people in the barn are here to witness the launch of my great viniculture discovery – the bottle of 1933 Cabernet Sauvignon.

Taking a deep breath and addressing the others in the barn I say, 'Ladies and gentleman: now that we have cleared the air and dispelled misunderstandings we can embark upon a new and exciting chapter in the life of Abbeydore Winery. Let me remind you why we are here. We are here to taste the 1933 vintage Cabernet Sauvignon that has lain dormant and undiscovered until now.'

So saying, I take the decanted bottle of 1933 vintage wine in my hands. But, just as I am about to dispense a tasting, I have a sudden idea.

'Mr Smythe: you are the wine expert. Would you be so good as to act as our sommelier and release this wine on an expectant world?'

'My dear Mrs Knightly, nothing would give me greater pleasure.'

I do not think I have ever seen such a look of rapture on the face of an old man as that which appears on the face of Montague Smythe. It is the face of a child on Christmas morning that has just been given the new bicycle he has yearned for all year. It is the face of a person about to be reunited with a lover after years of enforced absence. It is the face of a saint

JESSICA'S VINEYARD

who has beheld a beatific vision. It is the face of a man transported to heaven.

All eyes are upon him as he slowly takes the decanter from my hands with the reverence of a worshipper receiving the Holy Grail.

The bouquet of the wine greets his nostrils like gossamer silk gently brushing against the skin. He inhales and a look of ecstasy spreads over his face. 'Sheer bliss!' he exclaims more to himself than to anyone else. 'Absolutely divine! I am transported to heaven! I am in the presence of the angels! What a bouquet! I detect dried fruit and leather and tobacco. What a combination! This rivals the great wines of Bordeaux. This is the English equivalent of a Chateau Laffite! This will give the French a run for their money! Sheer ecstasy! I could linger over this carafe for eternity simply inhaling the flavours that assail my nostrils!'

'Well, some of us haven't got all day to hang around here while you waffle on,' intrudes Henry Jackson-Jones.

He has lost none of his aggressive directness that was always his defining characteristic. 'Just get on with it and pour some into the glasses so we can make up our own minds about the stuff.'

Mr Smythe is brought back to earth. He looks visibly affronted that anyone should intrude upon his act of worship. He was communing with another world and

JESSICA'S VINEYARD

now this plebeian individual has intruded upon his most sacred moment. He sniffs in disgust.

'This precious wine must be handled with extreme care,' he announces. 'It is not just a case of pouring it into glasses. A wine that is a hundred years old will have deposited sediment. It must be nursed and gently coaxed from this carafe. We, ladies and gentlemen, are midwives ushering new life into the world. I hold in my hands a unique act of creation. It is a moment to treasure. It is a moment to engrave upon the retina of our consciousness for eternity. We will never experience anything like this again. I cannot impress too strongly how blessed we small band of aficionados are to witness this momentous event.'

I would hardly describe those clustered around the upturned casks in the barn as wine aficionados. I detect a slight uneasiness amongst those for whom this flowery language is proving tedious and so I urge him on.

'Please pour small amounts into each glass, Mr Smythe, so we can conduct a wine tasting.'

'Don't rush me, Mrs Knightly. These occasions are not to be rushed. Nevertheless, I will do as you say; but I must impress upon everyone that they are not to drink this wine as if it was a pint of beer at the local pub. This wine must be clasped in the hands. You must wrap your hands around the glass. You must inhale the boutique and identify the flavours. You must then sip gently from the glass. Note, I said sip and not glug. If you are to savour the full riches of this wine you must treat it with respect. This is no smash and grab wine. This is a regal lady, dressed in her most costly apparel, affording you a gracious audience. Treat her with respect. '

I do not think I have ever seen wine poured so slowly into wine glasses. The sight of the dark red liquid trickling into each glass is like a blood transfusion slowly dripping into a recumbent patient. Having carefully filled ten wine glasses with the hundred-year-old wine he gracefully hands a glass to each of those assembled around the upturned casks. Then, in a slow-motion display of synchronised imbibing, each person raises their glass to their lips, inhales the aromas and takes a tentative sip.

Who will be the first to speak? Who will be the first to deliver a verdict on my hundred-year-old wine? There was never really any doubt.

Montague Smythe launches himself upon the company like a ballroom dancer whisking his partner to the centre of the dance floor.

'What an experience!' he exclaims. 'Words fail me!' This is manifestly untrue, but it gives him a moment or two to gather his thoughts and embark upon his verdict.

JESSICA'S VINEYARD

'This is a perfectly dry wine with no acidity or bitterness. The big fruit flavours of a young wine have become secondary and other flavours have come forward – earthy, savoury flavours. Such flavours! It is a joyful, complex tasting experience, rich with cassis, tobacco and truffle. There are both spicy and earthy notes. This is a wine to rival all other exclusive vintage wines. And to think, it began its life here in rural Herefordshire in 1933.'

'So how much is it worth?' intrudes Jackson-Jones.

'A bottle of Chateau Laffite of this age can command a price of £1,600,' replies the Master of Wines. 'This wine may not have the name of a great chateau behind it, but it has provenance. Mrs Knightly's account of the heroic exploits of the man who laid down this wine will add greatly to its value. Not only will people want to enjoy this superlative example of the English winemaker's art in the early years of the twentieth century but they will also want to align themselves with the wartime hero who sacrificed his life in the cause of justice and freedom. He died so that we might live. We enter upon his inheritance.'

'And so how much is a bottle of this stuff likely to fetch?' repeats the infuriating Jackson-Jones.

'If a hundred-year-old bottle of Chateau Laffite can command a price of £1,600 why not this also?'

Turning to me, the mercenary Jackson-Jones asks, 'How many bottles of the stuff have you got stashed

JESSICA'S VINEYARD

away?'

I have no intention of telling him

'Not a limitless number,' I reply with a smile. 'If you would like to buy a bottle you'd better act quickly and stump up £1,600 before it's all gone.'

'I'd never pay that sort of money for a bottle of wine!' he replies in disgust.

'My dear sir,' interjects Mr Smythe, 'We all derive our pleasure in different ways. You may not appreciate a fine vintage wine; but, for those of us who do, money is immaterial. It is the experience we treasure. It is worth much more than filthy lucre.'

Before things become more confrontational, I ask the others in the barn for their opinion of my vintage wine.

Councillor Johnson feels called upon to venture his opinion.

'Of course I am not as qualified as Mr Smythe to pronounce judgment on this wine; but I do appreciate a good Burgundy and I think this is on a par with some of the best I've tasted.'

'Not just on a par!' exclaims the Master of Wines in feigned horror. 'This is in a class of its own.'

Councillor Johnson shrugs his shoulders and says, 'I bow to your superior judgement.'

'What about you, Mr and Mrs Spragg,' I ask.

There is a shuffling of feet and downcast eyes but I am not to be deflected. I am familiar with the length of time it takes my neighbours to form sentences and am prepared to wait for them to speak in their own good time.

'I don't think you can take credit for this wine,' eventually replies the dour Mr Spragg. 'This is the work of someone who lived and worked here long before you arrived. I'm waiting to see what you can do yourself.' Then, rather mixing his metaphors, he adds, 'The proof of the pudding lies in the wine you make yourself. And none of us have had a chance to sample that yet. I withhold my judgement until then.'

I notice that his mousey wife nods her head in mute agreement.

Some people are so ungracious!

'And what about you, Detective Sergeant Rees? Is this your little tipple?'

He smiles revealing his perfectly white teeth.

'I can't claim to be a wine expert but I know what I like. I certainly like this. Whether I would be prepared to pay £1,600 for it is questionable, on my police officer's salary, but I appreciate its layers of distinctive flavour.'

'Exactly, young man!' explodes Mr Smythe. 'There are constantly unfolding layers to be discovered with every sip. You have the makings of a wine connoisseur, if I am not mistaken.'

JESSICA'S VINEYARD

The remainder of the afternoon evaporates in a haze of wine tasting and small talk before the various guests drift away.

My former husband cannot resist a final barb before he leaves.

'I said that young gigolo was only interested in your money but you wouldn't listen to me. You thought you knew best. That was always your trouble. You never listened to me. Perhaps you'll realise now that men are much better judges of character than women. I saw straight through him the moment I saw him.'

'Thank you for rubbing salt into my wounds,' I reply sardonically. 'I trust your new wife will enjoy your personal brand of saline treatment in the weeks ahead. Now, if you'll excuse me, I have other things to do.'

And so saying, I break away and fall straight into the ambit of the Jackson-Jones.

My natural reaction is to turn and escape, but before I can do so, Henry Jackson-Jones delivers his valedictory salvo: 'I came here his afternoon determined to make you suffer in the same way Deidre and I suffered due to your underhand tactics; but I see I don't have to bother. Someone else has done the job for me. Your new husband has been arrested and is likely to be incarcerated at His Majesty's pleasure for a considerable time; and then, being a foreign national, will almost certainly be deported. I consider that a very suitable punishment for you. I trust you'll enjoy your isolation in this godforsaken neck of the woods. At least it will allow you time to reflect on your underhand and despicable conduct in the past.'

With that, he turns and heads towards the barn doors. But his wife can't resist a final barb aimed at me, 'I agree with everything my husband says.'

I smile and shake my head. They leave Abbeydore having accomplished their mission. Hopefully I will never see them again.

The Spraggs cannot resist a final turn of the knife before they leave.

'I shed no tears at the arrest of that young man,' declares my gnarled neighbour. 'He was a menace to the neighbourhood roaming around with that rifle of his. I reckon the next attempt on your life would have been with his rifle. Why else would he go into the woods and do target practice with one of your headscarves? We can do without the likes of him around here.'

With that, he nods his head and leaves. His wife follows dutifully behind him.

Once they have left, Mr Smythe draws me to one side and says, 'Mrs Knightly, I would deem it a great honour if you would allow me to advise you on the sale and marketing of your exemplary wine. I will give it a glowing recommendation in the broadsheets; but there are a lot of sharks in the business world and I would hate to see you swindled out of your treasure trove by unscrupulous individuals. I am very happy for DS Rees to conduct a police check on my character and background to prove I am a thoroughly trustworthy man. But I do urge you to secure your wine immediately and navigate the auction process with stealth. I would be delighted to assist you. I ask nothing in return except, perhaps, one or two bottles of your vintage to savour when the cares of this world become too much for me.'

I see DS Rees nodding sagely.

I thank the Master of Wines for his offer of help and arrange to meet him tomorrow to finalise details. Once he has gone I am left alone in the barn with DS Rees.

'Well, what a day!' I declare. 'A day of extremes! I've been catapulted into a new career as a fine wine producer and I've seen my husband led away in handcuffs to prison.'

'Congratulations on the first and sincerest sympathies on the second.'

I look into his eyes and say, 'This has come as no surprise.'

Then, with a deep sigh followed by a pause, I say, 'You are not the only one who's been making enquiries. I've conducted my own. I contacted my

JESSICA'S VINEYARD

Australian friend, Celia Braithwaite, and asked her to undertake some investigations on my behalf. She discovered that Jason was not a gap-year student at all. Rather, he was a junior clerk in the probate department of a firm of solicitors in Sydney. They informed her that he appeared well-settled and was making good progress when, suddenly and without warning, he handed in his notice and left.'

The policeman standing by my side nods his head. I am clearly telling him things he already knows. But having begun, I am determined to finish.

'Celia informed the law firm that Jason had turned up in England and was now married to me, her childhood friend, Jessica Pollack. This immediately alerted the firm to what was afoot. The law firm was tasked with administering the will of my late father, Garfield Pollack. He had died the previous year leaving an extremely large estate to his only daughter, Jessica. The solicitors had been unable to locate me, probably because I had married and changed my name to Pope. Jason saw this as a golden opportunity to track me down and wheedle himself into my confidence in order to share in the unexpected wealth that was coming my way.'

'That certainly provided a clear motive for his actions,' adds DS Rees. 'All he had to do was to find you and gain your affections.'

I nod my head resignedly.

JESSICA'S VINEYARD

'I was a fool,' I tell him. 'I should have known that no virile and handsome young man would want to sacrifice his life for a woman like me! But I was so alone. I had taken on this vineyard singlehandedly and discovered I couldn't manage it on my own. Jason appeared at just the right moment to provide the help I needed.'

'Yes,' agrees the detective sergeant. 'As soon as he had his feet under the table he set about making you even more dependent upon him. He was the person who cut the wires in the vineyard. He wanted you to turn to him for help and security. He was the one who staged the fire in the barn so he could appear the brave rescuer who saved your business from ruin. He probably couldn't believe his luck when you agreed to marry him. That was the realisation of all his dreams! Should anything happen to you, your father's fortune would naturally pass to him.'

'Exactly!' I concur. 'All he had to do was to get rid of me. I was the thing that stood between him and a life of riches and glamour. I was the middle-aged woman who was an unwanted encumbrance. I had to be removed.'

'Don't be too hard on yourself,' smiles the policeman. 'And don't write yourself off as a middle-aged woman. You're very young at heart. I think you have a great future ahead of you. Your cache of

expensive wine will launch you into the wine world in spectacular fashion. You have a lot going for you.'
I smile and thank him. He has been a great help to me and a tremendous tower of strength.
Before he leaves, he says, 'This is an isolated spot. I wouldn't want to see any further harm come to you. I'll keep an eye on you.'
Then, almost as an afterthought, he says, 'Would you like me to call in from time to time to see how you're getting on?'
I would like that. I would like that very much.

JESSICA'S VINEYARD

JESSICA'S VINEYARD

By the same author

THE WAGES OF LOVE

A talented music teacher's love of music leads to a prison cell where music, love and religion produce a bewildering cocktail of hope and despair.
In his debut novel, the author explores the power of music, love and religion to sustain and transform life.

ISBN: 9798367230284

THE GIFT

When gifted music teacher Simon Copeland is released from prison on licence, he not only has to survive but also confront the psychological demons within him.
Will music be his salvation or does he need to delve deeper to discover lasting personal fulfilment?
In the sequel to *The Wages of Love*, the author explores creativity in both the life of Simon and the English composer Sir Edward Elgar.

ISBN: 9798395998767

JESSICA'S VINEYARD

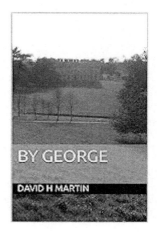

BY GEORGE

George, 6th Earl of Coventry (1722-1809), is one of the wealthiest landowners in England. He is used to having his own way. But when he meets the bewitching redhead Lena, he discovers there are some things his money cannot buy.
Set against the backdrop of the building of Croome Court, Worcestershire, the author explores the hinterland between the deadly sin of lust and the cardinal virtue of love.

ISBN: 9798373247894

JESSICA'S VINEYARD

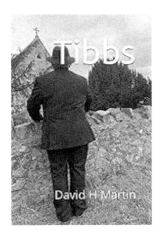

TIBBS

When the unassuming Rev Tibbs is sent to a rural parish in a backwater of the Diocese of Dunchester, he has no idea of the turbulent times that lie ahead. His good intentions are frustrated at every turn.
He has to battle with a belligerent lord of the manor, a dysfunctional parochial church council and the caustic comments of the regulars in *The Thistleton Arms*.
But, despite all his difficulties, he has one advantage over his adversaries.
ISBN: 9798856516844

JESSICA'S VINEYARD

Printed in Great Britain
by Amazon